Bolan tossed the device into the backseat

"Damn, that thing is handy," James said. "Stony Man ought to license it to the cops to stop speeders."

"Yeah," Bolan said, "and it also fried the *vatos'* cells so that they can't call for help. Who knew EMP could be so helpful?"

"Uh, how are we gonna catch all these guys?"

"We'll have to round them up the old-fashioned way...." Bolan trailed off as he felt a warm circle of metal press into the back of his neck hard, pushing his head forward. He froze.

"All right, *putas.* Move just an inch and I'll splatter your brains all over the car."

Other titles available in this series:

Sworn Enemies
Dark Truth
Breakaway
Blood and Sand
Caged
Sleepers
Strike and Retrieve
Age of War
Line of Control
Breached
Retaliation
Pressure Point
Silent Running
Stolen Arrows
Zero Option
Predator Paradise
Circle of Deception
Devil's Bargain
False Front
Lethal Tribute
Season of Slaughter
Point of Betrayal
Ballistic Force
Renegade
Survival Reflex
Path to War
Blood Dynasty
Ultimate Stakes
State of Evil
Force Lines
Contagion Option
Hellfire Code
War Drums
Ripple Effect
Devil's Playground
The Killing Rule
Patriot Play
Appointment in Baghdad
Havana Five
The Judas Project
Plains of Fire
Colony of Evil
Hard Passage
Interception
Cold War Reprise
Mission: Apocalypse
Altered State
Killing Game
Diplomacy Directive
Betrayed
Sabotage
Conflict Zone
Blood Play
Desert Fallout
Extraordinary Rendition
Devil's Mark
Savage Rule
Infiltration
Resurgence
Kill Shot
Stealth Sweep
Grave Mercy
Treason Play
Assassin's Code
Shadow Strike
Decision Point
Road of Bones
Radical Edge
Fireburst
Oblivion Pact

Enemy Arsenal

A GOLD EAGLE BOOK FROM
WORLDWIDE

TORONTO • NEW YORK • LONDON
AMSTERDAM • PARIS • SYDNEY • HAMBURG
STOCKHOLM • ATHENS • TOKYO • MILAN
MADRID • WARSAW • BUDAPEST • AUCKLAND

First edition October 2012

ISBN-13: 978-0-373-61556-8

Special thanks and acknowledgment to
Travis Morgan for his contribution to this work.

ENEMY ARSENAL

Printed in U.S.A.

Weapons are an important factor in war, but not the decisive one; it is man and not materials that counts.

—Mao Tse-Tung

A weapon is not evil in and of itself—it is merely a tool, one that can be used by evil men against the innocent, or by good men to protect the innocent. When I take up arms against evil, it is with the sole notion to protect the innocent and punish the guilty.

—Mack Bolan

PROLOGUE

A glass of chilled champagne dangling between his fingers, James Barrett leaned on the luxury yacht's polished teakwood railing and watched the golden-red sun sink into the deep blue waters of the glass-smooth South China Sea.

Sure is a far cry from Nebraska, he thought. Indeed, he'd never imagined seeing this much water in his life, not counting a family vacation to the Great Lakes when he was ten years old. Barrett glanced back at the receding Philippine Islands, where he'd just spent three intoxicating days. He was living the life he'd always dreamed of, but every moment, every second of pleasure he tried to enjoy was colored by the faint, niggling feeling that he didn't deserve any of it, that he was, quite simply—a fraud.

But he knew that was just his father talking again. Barrett had worked harder than anyone he knew to achieve what he had, beginning with working two jobs to scrape up the money to attend the state university; suffering the ribbing of his redneck coworkers for studying during his lunch break at the slaughterhouse; going home after a full shift just four hours before class started and standing in the shower for thirty minutes, trying to wash the blood and dead meat stink out of his skin and hair; fighting to stay awake in his classes, knowing he had to work another twelve-hour shift that night, and somehow bull through a full class load of homework and papers, as well, week after week, month after month.

It had taken him five years, but at the end, he had graduated not only with a diploma, but also with a partial scholarship to Yale, thanks to an endowment from one of Lincoln's founding families. The scholarship had the unusual stipulation that the winner had to attend a school outside the state, and Barrett wondered if whoever had set it up had hated the endless, flat plains as much as he did.

Compared to getting through college, law school was easier, at least on his body. His mind was taxed to the limit, but Barrett relished the purely intellectual challenge after years of backbreaking labor. He excelled there, interning at the *Yale Law Journal* and matching wits and legal expertise with some of the finest minds in the nation.

"A peso for your thoughts."

As always, the sound of that sultry voice behind him made a frisson of delight course through his body. He turned to see a goddess-made-flesh walking toward him, dressed in a bikini that barely covered her slender body. Her bronze skin glowed in the fading rays of the tropical sun, under a long, silky mane of honey-blond hair that cascaded down her back and shoulders. Over the tiny swimsuit she almost didn't have on was a sheer, silky white hip-length peignoir that fluttered in the gentle ocean breeze, revealing tantalizing glimpses of long leg and the delightful swell of her breasts. Barrett shifted his stance, letting his loose cargo shorts hide the sudden tightness in his groin.

"Just had to come out and watch the sunset again."

She smiled, revealing even white teeth. "I figured as much. Dad and my brothers can get to be a bit much after a few drinks."

"Hey, it wasn't them. I like your father, really. He accepts me for who I am, just like his daughter."

"Mmm, I like the sound of that." She stepped close to him, the scent of jasmine and coconut body lotion almost overpowering him. Slipping her slim arms around his neck, she leaned up and kissed him, her lush lips tasting like a combination of sweet guava, rum and mint. Her tongue teased his, drawing it out, then darting back and forth. James wrapped his arms around her waist and pulled her close, his love-fogged brain barely remembering not to crush her to him, the way he wanted to do every time she came near.

He'd first met Rachel Kirkall during his junior year, at a frat party he had wrangled an invitation to for no good reason he could think of at the time. Later, he had wondered more than once if it was fate. Spying a blond-haired vision across the raucous living room awash in loud music, body shots and pot, he had homed in on her as if in a trance. Upon arrival, however, he had interrupted a drunken fraternity brother's clumsy advances by "accidentally" spilling his beer on the guy, then ducking his clumsy swing and burying a fist that had seen its share of fights into the blue-blood's stomach, leaving him retching on the floor.

He'd expected the blond beauty to be shocked, but instead she'd said, "Thanks, now let's get out of here." Grabbing his hand, she had pulled him into the rainy night. They had found a nearby Starbucks, and spent the next four hours deep in conversation.

He'd learned she was a local from Connecticut, and was attending architect school, but he hadn't found out that she was part of *the* Kirkall family until he had idly searched her name after their second date. After a brief, terrifying few minutes scrolling through the family's public business holdings, including a sizable stake in a major league baseball team, he'd wondered if he'd ever see her again, or if he was just a passing fancy she was amusing herself with for a few weeks or months before moving on to someone more in her stratum. But that thought was immediately replaced by an even scarier one—that he might already be falling in love with her.

The two opposing thoughts had consumed him until their next date, but he'd managed to contain his fear and desire while stretching his scant budget to the limit to take her out to dinner at Ibiza.

Toward the end of their meal, some of her friends had stopped at their table, and although they were perfectly polite, James sensed the way they were looking at him. Rachel had ignored the pointed looks and narrowed brows, and it was only afterward, when they were sharing a glass of ten-year-old port she'd insisted on buying, that he'd worked up the nerve to ask her the question he knew had been on her girlfriends' minds.

"Why am I with you?" She had smiled when she heard it, and James felt himself standing at the edge of an unfamiliar precipice, teetering, either about to fall over or step back, depending on her next words.

"First, you know who I am, and you haven't asked about my father, except once, when you wanted to know what he did for a living. Second, this is our third date, and you still haven't tried to get into my pants yet—"

That hadn't been for a lack of desire on James's part,

but he hadn't dared to even attempt a move like that, not wanting to destroy the romantic illusion he'd been enjoying so far.

"But most importantly, when I look at you, I see a man who hasn't sold his soul to anyone yet. *That's* why I'm with you."

Soundlessly, James toppled over the edge, falling head-over-heels in love with her in that very moment.

They had been inseparable for the remainder of the school year, with James even winning over a few of her friends, and surviving a nerve-racking holiday weekend at her parents' palatial mansion upstate, where he'd only gotten lost twice. Her three older brothers had been protective of her and skeptical of him, but James hadn't given them a single reason to doubt his sincerity toward Rachel. And he'd spoken the truth about her father—he did like the man, whom, he hoped, saw a kindred spirit in James. The elder Kirkall had also built himself up from practically nothing, striking it rich in shrewd foreign investments, then bringing his hundreds of millions back home to reinvest in America's infrastructure. Barrett had made it clear he wasn't expecting a handout, that he was just happy to be with Rachel, and fully expected both of them to make their own way, whatever that might be and wherever it might take them. He didn't know if it had been his directness or his honesty that had made the difference, but when Rachel's family had invited him along on their Southeast Asia cruise at the end of the term, he'd jumped at it.

But at that precise moment, thoughts of her father, his last year at Yale or anything else for that matter were the furthest thing from his mind. Keeping one hand around her waist, he let his other one creep up toward her breast, cupping it gently, his touch making her tremble and mold her lithe form even closer to him. While they enjoyed each other's lips again, her hands roamed, as well, slipping underneath his shirt to caress his broad chest, making James even more thankful he'd made the effort to stay in shape over the school year. He managed to set the champagne flute on the railing and curved his arm back around her, moving his fingers down to her finely sculpted rear and squeezing gently.

Rachel broke their kiss with a soft gasp. "Hey now, what do you think my family would say if they came out here and saw you taking liberties like that?"

James didn't relinquish his hold on her for a moment. "They'd see a man who is head-over-heels in love with you—which just might get my ass kicked, depending on who saw who first."

"Fortunately for you, the masters of the universe are still backslapping each other belowdecks, leaving us with a few more minutes…." Rachel tilted her head up again, sending an invitation James didn't hesitate to accept. He leaned down again, his lips about to hungrily devour hers when something on the ocean caught his eye.

"Mmm, what was that?" Despite the glorious distraction right in front of him, Barrett raised his head to try to get a better view of what he'd spotted.

"With me warm and willing in your arms, you pick now to find a dolphin?" Rachel mock-teased him, turning in his arms to look off the starboard bow.

"It wasn't a dolphin. It looked more like a bunch of driftwood, but with something on top. Hang on a sec."

James disentangled himself from Rachel's embrace and walked to the other railing, grabbing a handheld battery-powered searchlight as he approached the rail. Flicking on the million-candlepower light, he swept the incandescent beam back and forth across the water.

"There!" Rachel grabbed his hand and redirected the light. "Is that it?"

"Yeah. Jesus, someone's out there!" James played the beam over the small mass, which looked like a crude raft cobbled together out of scrapwood and two oil barrels lashed together. What might have been a small pile of rags on top was actually a child's body, lying motionless on the small platform's surface. The makeshift float drifted toward them in the calm water, about thirty yards ahead off the right side.

"Holy shit! Call the bridge, have them turn to starboard. I'll see if I can snag it." Rachel grabbed an intercom handset from the wall while Barrett snatched a long boat hook from the wall rack and ran to the back of the vessel. Feeling the deck shift slightly underneath him, he realized the captain had turned toward the raft.

As he passed by a door, it opened and a crew member stepped out, followed by Stuart, one of Rachel's brothers. "Can I be of assistance, sir?"

"Yeah, there's a kid on a raft to starboard. I'm gonna try to snag him as we pass." Barrett led the two men to the rear of the boat, where he stepped onto the flat deck used for launching smaller boats or personal watercrafts.

"Would you rather that I take care of this, sir?" The mate was as insistent as he could be under the circumstances, even gently reaching out for the pole with one hand.

James shook his head. "No, I've got it, but I'd appreciate some backup just in case it's heavier than it looks."

"Careful. You don't want to take a dip out here, James. Sharks, you know." Nattily attired in khaki shorts and a pressed tropical shirt, Stuart lounged against the wall, drink in hand, content to let the other two men take the lead.

"Just make sure I don't go in with it."

"I've got you, sir." The mate was polite, with a subtle British accent. Barrett tried not to think too much about how he was being supported, with the man's arm around his waist, but his eyes focused on the raft, now just a few yards away. He reached out with the pole and caught a board, only to have it tear free when he tried to draw the rickety vessel closer, making it rock back and forth.

"Careful, James!" Rachel, her robe wrapped around herself, watched from the walkway.

"I'm trying, dear. Almost…got him…" Barrett stretched out again and wedged his hook into a gap between two boards, hearing the scrape of metal on metal. He pulled the pole in, watching the platform move closer. "Get ready to grab him."

"Right." The raft bumped the corner of the luxury yacht, and the steward reached down and plucked the huddled boy, who remained curled in a ball, on board. "I've got him."

"Rachel, get some food and water. He's probably dehydrated." James pushed the raft away, sending the rickety pile of wood and barrels spinning into the night.

"I'm on it." She disappeared into the ship.

"We'll probably need a blanket, as well—" Barrett's words were interrupted by the kid, who suddenly unfolded himself and wriggled out of the crew member's arms. What was even more surprising was the ugly black pistol he pointed at the man, the weapon large in his small hands.

"Chuò! Chuò!"

"What the hell?" Stuart, for all his supposed indolence, took a step forward, only to have the muzzle of the pistol swivel to cover him. He raised his hands, not alarmed enough yet to put his drink down.

"What's going on?" Barrett didn't take his eyes off the gun, estimating the distance between him and the boy, who couldn't have been more than ten or eleven years old. The boat hook was still in his hand, but he was careful not to draw attention to it.

"He told us to stop. He might be a decoy for pirates."

"Damn, we need to disarm him and warn the others." Stuart shifted his weight, drawing the boy's flat stare. At that, Barrett lashed out with the hook, trying to knock the gun aside, or even better, right out of the boy's hand.

Catching the movement from the corner of his eye, the boy ducked under Barrett's swipc and swung the gun over toward him, which spit flame as he pulled the trigger. Barrett felt a sudden stab of pain in his abdomen, and looked down to see an expanding spot of dark wetness on his shirt.

"Little bastard...shot me..." Barrett leaned against the railing as the steward leaped forward to grab the pistol, wrenching it out of the boy's grasp. Distracted, he didn't notice the shadowy form that came around the corner of the yacht and slipped up behind him.

Barrett tried to shout a warning, but Stuart and the crew member were talking at the same time, calling for the physician. Their shouts for help mixed with the foreign curses and cries of the wriggling boy. The steward's voice was cut off with a gasp as the shadow came up behind him and wrapped an arm around his throat, doing something that made the man arch his back, his expression a grimacing mask of agony. The other man, a short, wiry Asian dressed in shapeless black pants and shirt, stepped back and let his victim fall to the formerly spotless deck, now dappled with Barrett's blood. A large knife, its blade dark and gleaming wet, was in his hand.

"Shit!" Stuart hurled his drink into the man's face, the glass shattering against his cheek and making him drop his blade and clutch his face, screaming in pain. "Come on, buddy!" He grabbed Barrett and hoisted him up, slinging his limp arm over his shoulder.

"Rachel…don't let them get Rachel…" James found it suddenly hard to think. His free hand, clamped over his wound, was soaked in blood, and he knew if he didn't get help soon, he would die.

"Let's just get inside— Son of a bitch!" Stuart's frantic tone made Barrett look up to see three more of the invaders, machetes and pistols in hand, running toward them from the ship's bow. Shouts and screams could now be heard from elsewhere on the yacht, along with the thuds of running feet.

"Come on!" The Kirkall brother wrestled with the door, shoving it open and pushing Barrett through. Stepping over him, Stuart pushed the door closed just as a body thumped into it from outside.

"James, help me—I can't hold this against all of them—"

Barrett, however, couldn't even help himself, his vision fading to gray as the blood loss started to take its toll on him. He heard a scream from somewhere in the room, then felt footsteps beside him as the door slammed open, Stuart falling over him with a grunt.

The sound of rapid, shouted Chinese filled the room as the hijackers beat Stuart to the floor. Barrett felt himself supported by warm, familiar hands, and looked up to see Rachel's tear-stained face above him.

"What happened, baby?" She took his hand away from his stomach, stifling a gasp at the growing puddle of blood leaking out of him. "Oh, my God—James, we have to get hel—"

Before she could do anything, her head was jerked backward, and she was dragged away from him by her hair, screaming and grabbing her assailant's hands. Barrett was left to flop onto the floor, helpless.

"Leave…her alone…" he gasped, trying to muster the strength to crawl after her attacker, but unable to make his arms and legs work. The last sounds he heard were the thuds of fists on flesh and the piercing screams of his girlfriend before darkness overtook him.

CHAPTER ONE

"These *chulos* better show up tonight. Gettin' tired of feeling my rear end grow wider sitting all night waitin' on 'em."

Mack Bolan, aka the Executioner, turned from watching the dilapidated warehouse near the docks of the Los Angeles Harbor to shoot a wry look at his partner. "I'm sure they'll be here soon enough, Cal." His grin disappeared as he returned to watching the night. "If they want what we're selling bad enough, they'll be here."

The two men were dressed in expensive, casual clothes: silk shirts, linen pants and tasseled Italian loafers. Bolan checked his appearance in the visor-mounted mirror, smoothing his gelled black hair one last time. Ice-blue eyes stared back at him out of a tanned face.

They sat in a silver Cadillac Escalade, its rear shocks compressed from the heavy load in the rear, peering through tinted windows at their eventual destination. Bolan suppressed his smile as he glanced at Calvin James, a member of Phoenix Force, and his partner for this op. "You ready?"

The lanky African-American snorted. "I was born ready. Just make the call. And remember, these fuckers don't mess around. They sniff pork, we're both dead men."

"Well, then, it's a good thing we don't mess around, either." Bolan hit a speed-dial button on his cell phone and lifted it to his ear. "We're here… Same ride as always… Hell no, we weren't followed. Yeah, yeah." He turned to James. "Flash your lights."

James flicked the headlight switch on and off once, then again while taking one last look around to make sure no one was taking undue interest in what was about to go down.

Next to the warehouse, several large, rusty panel trucks rested in a parking lot, all encircled by a chain-link fence topped with barbed wire. The gate to the lot was closed and secured with a rusty chain. Bolan thought he saw a glint of shiny metal on the chain, but before he could take a second look, the warehouse's garage door rumbled up, revealing a cavernous, dark interior. A single light flashed on inside, casting a dim glow into the cloudy night.

"Let's do it." James put the SUV in gear and rolled forward.

Bolan fixed his partner with a searching gaze. "You followed my advice, right?"

"Yeah, although I still think we're courting suicide to go in not packing."

"We're arms *dealers,* not users—there's no reason for us to carry. Besides, the SUV's armored, so just get to it in case of trouble, remember?"

"Yeah, it's surviving the short trip in one piece that concerns me."

"I suggest leaving your door open a crack. That split second to work the handle can make the difference between life and death."

Now James glanced over at him, meeting Bolan's

calm, steady gaze. "Damn it, I never can tell if you're kidding."

"I'm not."

The gleaming SUV pulled up in front of a cluster of eight Latinos, all dressed in variations of the L.A. gangland look: baggy, low-riding jeans, white wife-beater T-shirts, or flannels with the top button fastened, even in the city's ninety-five-degree heat, and immaculate ball caps or bandanas tied low, almost covering their eyes. The light from the overhead lamp illuminated only the surrounding area, making Bolan's threat sense tingle a bit; they had no way of knowing who might be in the darkness, waiting to attack when the time was right.

The garage door descended behind them, cutting off the outside with a slam of metal on concrete. The gang members slowly fanned out in a loose semicircle around the Escalade, no one making a sound.

"Time to get into character." Slipping on a pair of blue-tinted, wire-rimmed glasses, Bolan took a breath, let it out and popped the door, swinging out and letting his Italian loafers hit the stained warehouse floor with a smack. The still air was redolent of gasoline and oil, making his nose wrinkle. He glanced around, taking in all the members in a quick sweep, and immediately sensing a difference in this gang. Other L.A. street gangs would be more relaxed making a buy on their home turf—smoking blunts, talking shit, posturing, the usual bull. This group was all business. In fact, Bolan was reminded of a pack, each one knowing his place and wholly intent on what he was about to do—whether that be consummate the deal, or beat the shit out of Bolan and James before killing them.

"Hola, amigos!" Bolan casually pushed the door

shut, stopping it just short of closing, talking all the while to draw their attention away from what he was doing.

"You guys sure picked an out-of-the-way place— Hey, hey, there's no need for that." His protest went unheeded as two of the *vatos* stepped forward and quickly patted down Bolan and James, paying particular attention to the collars, waistbands, ankles and groins. Bolan glanced at James, his eyebrows narrowing in a silent warning not to make any kind of sarcastic remark.

One of the gang members stepped forward. "*Hola,* Mr. Sabato. Pleased t'see you kept your end so far."

"I wouldn't be much of a salesman if I tried to put one over on my clients now, would I? So what's with the not-so-warm welcome?"

"None o'yer bus'ness. Let's see whatcha got."

"I like a man who gets to the point. Step around here into my office." Bolan's cover was a slightly motor-mouthed arms dealer—not his usual mode of operation, but he kept up the pretense as he led the gang leader to the back of the SUV. He hit the remote on his key fob, opening the tailgate to reveal four long olive-green wooden boxes. "Here they are."

He stood back as the banger motioned two of his men forward to haul one out. As they worked, Bolan and his glasses watched and recorded everything, scanning faces, identifying marks and tattoos. All of the members were inked, and all of them had the same mark on them: MS-13.

Mara Salvatrucha, or MS-13, was the fastest-growing gang on the West Coast, and probably in the United States, as well. Originally started in L.A. in the 1980s to protect newly immigrated El Salvadorans, the gang had grown to encompass about eight thousand members, all Hispanic, and its influence had spread like wildfire from California throughout the rest of the nation. Its members were loyal and utterly ruthless when it came to expanding their territory. While this made it easier for Bolan and his partner to arrange arms stings like this one, they still risked death every time they set one up.

One of the members looked up from the lettering stenciled on the crate. "Hey, man, these ain't submachine guns. Whatcha pullin' here, homes?"

"Hold on now, guys. Before you get all uptight, just wait and see what I've brought you." Bolan pulled a small pry bar from the cargo bed and handed it to the leader. "Go on, open it up."

The banger handed the tool to one of his own and stood back, watching as they opened the crate with a squeal of loosened nails. The cover flew off to reveal six unusual-looking weapons.

"Gentlemen, allow me to introduce you to the Steyr Army Universal Gun, or AUG P, compact version." Bolan reached down and pulled one of the futuristic assault rifles from the crate. The gun almost looked unbalanced, with a slot for a 30-round magazine halfway between the shoulder butt and the trigger, which was mounted on a swept-back handle with a large trigger guard that protected all of the fingers on the firing hand. The stock and handle were made out of a single molded piece of drab-green, high-impact fiberglass-reinforced polyamide 66, with a stubby black barrel jutting above a folding handgrip. The weapon looked like something out of a science fiction movie, even though the design had been manufactured since the late 1970s.

Now Bolan had their full attention. Their leader,

known only as Araña, or Spider, crossed his arms. The rest of the gang closed ranks around him, hands disappearing into their large pockets, tensing to act on a moment's notice if necessary. "We'd agreed on two dozen submachine guns. What the hell's this?"

"These *are* submachine guns, my friends, and with them I guarantee you will rule the streets." Bolan reached down to pull a translucent plastic magazine from the box and insert it into the butt. "Cops and SWAT teams are armored against 9 mm, but these guns use 5.56—more than enough to take them out if necessary."

Araña let his arms drop. "Fool, we ain't out to start no war with the po-pos. We just wanna protect what's ours."

Bolan and James exchanged sidelong glances, and he realized he had inadvertently erred by mentioning killing cops. "Hey, I didn't say you were going after them, but like you said, you want to protect what is yours, right? These babies fire 700 rounds per minute, and are perfectly balanced to be used with one hand, for drive-and-fire capability if necessary. The built-in scope is set at 300 meters, allowing you to outshoot any enemy you encounter, and lets you control the field of fire." He held the loaded, but not primed, rifle out to Araña. "Here, feel how light it is."

The young man accepted the weapon gingerly, grunting in surprise at its weight and stability. His fingers curled around the handle, staying clear of the trigger itself. Bolan stepped forward and pointed out features. "The bolt and ejection port cover can be swapped out to make the gun suitable for left or right-handed shooters, and the safety selector is also accessible from either side of the weapon."

"You said it can shoot full-auto? Where's the selector?" the gang leader asked.

Bolan nodded. "Glad you asked. You control the rate of fire by squeezing the trigger. Halfway back is single shot, and pulling the trigger all the way back engages fully automatic fire."

His presentation brought the other members closer, all of them entranced by the high-tech weapon. "Of course, you could remove that sight to cut its profile down a bit, that's up to you."

"And you're willing to sell these as originally agreed?"

"Not only that, but each weapon comes with four magazines, a muzzle cap, spare bolt for left-handed shooters, cleaning kit, sling and a mountable bayonet, if you have the desire to get up close and personal with your targets. That is, if you have the agreed-upon price, then we're good to go."

Araña nodded to one of the other members, who sauntered off into the darkness. Bolan resisted the urge to rock back and forth on his heels as he waited for the transaction to be completed. While he usually didn't need to abide by the legal necessity of having the money trade hands, it didn't hurt to make the exchange—it was a better lever to get the gang members to roll on each other later.

The tattooed thug returned with a brand-new duffel bag, which he gave to Araña, who unzipped the top and showed it to Bolan. Inside were well-used bills, all neatly banded. "Fifty thousand, as agreed."

Bolan reached in for one of the bundles and riffled through it as if assessing the count. "Looks good to me.

Your boys can move these other crates, and then we can go our separate ways—"

As if he had mentioned an arranged signal, the garage door began to open, making Bolan look over his shoulder, then at Araña, who stared at him with a frown. Bright spotlights flared into life from the outside, and the silhouetted forms of men appeared in the halogen glow.

"ATF! Everyone put your hands up!" a voice commanded through a bullhorn.

The MS-13 members exploded into action. Half of them took off into the darkness, the others yanked guns out of their waistbands and aimed them at the lights and shadows outside, diving to the floor or taking cover beside the SUV. Cal was nowhere to be seen.

"Chimado!" Araña yanked the cocking lever back and leveled the rifle at Bolan, who was already lunging at him, hands outstretched to grab the weapon before it cut him in two. He shoved the barrel up just before it could be aimed at his chest. Araña maintained enough control not to squeeze the trigger, ignoring the repeated commands to drop his weapon. Instead, he twisted the Austrian assault rifle to the right, nearly breaking Bolan's grip on it, and shoving him nearer to the SUV.

"Everyone in the building drop your weapons and raise your hands *now!*" The bullhorn wielder still barked orders as black-fatigue-clad men crouched behind their cars, weapons aimed into the warehouse.

"Are you trying to get us all killed?" Bolan gritted between clenched teeth.

"You set us up—bastard!"

"What? If anything, they followed your sloppy asses here!" Bolan lashed out with his foot, catching the smaller man in the stomach with his heel. His opponent groaned but didn't relinquish the gun. Screw this, Bolan thought, yanking back on the rifle one last time, then letting it go. The move caught the gangbanger by surprise, and he staggered back against the crates of weapons in the cargo bed of the truck. Bolan ran around the side of the Escalade, sprinting for the cracked-open passenger door.

"Drop your weapons or we will open fire!" the electronically enhanced voice shouted from behind him.

Bolan hooked the door, and yanked it open, only to find a banger already inside, his pistol shoved into James's face as he screamed at him.

"I said start this motherfucker right now!" The startled *vato* was cut off in midsentence as Bolan yanked him backward, throwing him to the ground. The man's pistol discharging as he hit the concrete floor.

The ATF agents didn't need any more provocation, spraying the SUV and the surrounding area with bullets. Bolan lunged into the passenger seat, shouting, "Close the back! Close the back!" as he ducked, praying that none of the bullets would ricochet around the inside and punch through him like a fist through paper. He heard the *punk-punk-punk* of small arms rounds impacting on the back and sides of the sport-utility vehicle, and huddled even farther over. Although Bolan had been shot before, he never liked it.

"I'm on it." James was also hunched in his seat. "So what happened to 'take cover in here,' huh?"

"I got delayed." Bolan's attention was drawn by the flare of headlights at the other end of the warehouse—large headlights. "You better start it up."

"What in the hell is that?" James twisted the key as the headlights suddenly grew larger.

"I don't know, but get us the hell out of its way!" Bolan grabbed for the wheel, twisting it to the right as James jammed on the gas, making the Cadillac leap forward as the oncoming lights grew even more blinding. The approaching vehicle, now recognizable as a huge, industrial tow truck, lurched toward them, striking them a glancing blow that rocked the luxury SUV onto two wheels before it settled back down with a crash of rubber and steel.

James looked back over his shoulder. "They're not trying to make a break for it, are they?"

Bolan's attention, however, was focused on the real escape. "Nope, it's a diversion. Hit your lights."

James did so, illuminating the back wall, where another door was sliding open enough to let out a lowrider, now crammed full of fleeing MS-13 members. Caught in the high beams, their jaws dropped in shock, then three of them pointed pistols and started shooting as the car angled its way out of the warehouse.

The Phoenix Force veteran tromped on the gas again and the Escalade shot forward, bullets starring its triple-laminated windshield. Bolan braced himself as they shot out into the fenced yard. The car screamed toward the back of the perimeter, trying to gain enough speed to burst through the chain-link fence.

"Can you stop them before they get out?"

"I'm sure as hell gonna try." James leaned over the steering wheel, trying to catch up with the retreating gangbangers, or at least get close enough to try to force them to stop. Although the car looked like a glittering piece of pimped-out Detroit trash, it had a kick-ass engine, because the bangers stayed ahead of the powerful SUV as it tore through the fence and into the street beyond. James stayed hard on their rear, bouncing over the curb and struggling to wrestle the massive vehicle back onto the road.

"On an open street, they're going to leave us in the dust." Bolan reached behind his seat and pulled out a strange-looking device that resembled a handheld flamethrower, only its nozzle was plugged, ending in a metal grid. "And if they get into traffic, who knows how many people they'll injure or kill before they're stopped."

"Hey, hey! Don't point that thing at our engine, okay?"

"Relax. Try to get closer to them." Flipping the power switch on the machine, Bolan lowered his window and stuck his upper body out, holding the device in both hands. The SUV surged underneath him, but the low-rider was slowly pulling away. The soldier would have only one shot before they were out of range. He snugged the weapon into his shoulder, aimed and depressed the triggering button.

The device made no noise, but he felt it vibrate in his hands as it released its invisible energy. Ahead, the gang car's engine suddenly died, and the vehicle immediately began to slow. The *vatos* cursed and screamed at the driver, who yelled back at them in frustration.

Bolan leaned back inside and tossed the device into the backseat, pulling his Beretta 93R pistol out from under his seat. "Damn, that thing is handy. Stony Man ought to license it to the cops to stop speeders."

"Yeah, and it also just fried their cells, so they can't call for help. Who knew EMP could be so useful."

James had produced his own pistol, a matte-black SIG Sauer P229. "Um, how are we gonna catch all these guys?"

"We'll have to round them up the old-fashioned way...." Bolan trailed off as he felt a warm circle of metal press into the back of his neck hard, pushing his head forward. He froze, his pistol now a useless lump of plastic and metal.

"All right, *cara de mierda,* move just an inch and I'll splatter your brains all over this car. Hand me your gun, slowly, and your friend's gonna stop by my homies' car, *comprende?*"

James had also frozen at hearing Araña's voice coming from the back of the Escalade. "Where the hell'd he come from?"

Bolan had wondered that exact same thing, but had already come up with the answer. Despite having an assault rifle jammed into his neck, his voice was calm. "Damn, you're one clever son of a bitch. I thought the *federales* got you back there. You climbed into the back of our ride, didn't you?"

"Shut up, *pendejo!*" The AUG rifle's muzzle quivered on his skin, and Bolan thought he was about to buy it right there. "I don't know who you guys are. Real gun dealers would have split like anyone else when the po-pos showed. You guys did me a favor by driving me out of here, but I sure as hell ain't gonna return it. Now hand over those fucking guns right now—" Bolan felt his head being shoved forward even farther "—you first, then the driver. Slowly."

Bolan considered trying to flip his pistol and shoot the *vato,* but the angle was all wrong, and a miss would only result in his quick and painful death. Besides, even if he did hit the gangbanger, the guy might pull the rifle's trigger by reflex, causing the same undesired result. He spun the Beretta on his index finger and offered it to the man butt-first. Out of the corner of his eye, he saw James raise an eyebrow in an unspoken question, and he shook his head slightly.

Not yet.

Snatching the pistol, Araña jammed it into Bolan's neck and set the rifle down. "Since you trashed my boys' wheels, we're just gonna take these, and the guns, and the money. Seeing as how you did me a solid by getting me out of there in one piece, if you're lucky, you might even live to watch us drive away."

James had pulled over to the side of the empty road, surrounded by small businesses and manufacturing plants that had either gone belly-up or didn't have a night shift, since their parking lots were all deserted. Bolan expected the ATF boys to come screaming by, or even for a LAPD helicopter to have seen the commotion and investigate, but that didn't seem to be the case here. It figured, he thought, when a person really wanted the police, they were nowhere to be found.

The rest of the gang had piled out of their dead car, but they couldn't see what was happening inside the SUV through the smoked windows. Bolan kept his hands loose, waiting for his opportunity.

"Both of you assholes get out, right now!" For the briefest second, the pressure on his neck lessened, and that was when Bolan moved. Wrenching his head and body to the side, he twisted and grabbed the pistol, forcing it to point at the ceiling.

"Goddamn you—!" Araña tried to push the gun down again, but James rammed a short punch into his cheek that made the punk's head snap to the side hard enough to bounce off the armored window. His grip slackened, and Bolan twisted the pistol out of his hand, then turned so he was facing backward, his chest protected by the Escalade's bucket seat back. Even stunned, Araña tried to go for the rifle again, but Bolan ended the disagreement by slamming the butt of his pistol into the thug's forehead twice. With the second blow, his eyes rolled back, and he slumped over on the seat, unconscious.

Through the windshield, Bolan saw the rest of the gangers slowly approach the SUV, many with pistols drawn, but held at their sides. He grabbed the AUG carbine from the back and checked the load, which was still half full. "Huh, he didn't spray and pray, I'm impressed. All right, let's take the rest of these bangers down. Ready?"

James had grabbed Bolan's pistol, tucking the second under his arm as he reached for the door handle. "Let's do it."

The two men exited on their respective sides, guns raised, catching the group by surprise. One guy raised his pistol, but Bolan was faster, and snapped off a shot that took the gunman in the chest and sent him to the ground with a strangled gasp, the pistol skittering away on the asphalt. Standing on the running boards, Bolan and James were protected by the armored doors, giving them both a height advantage and almost complete cover.

"Drop the guns or we drop you! Now!" James repeated the order in Spanish as Bolan swept the muzzle of the assault rifle across the group to reinforce his partner. First one, then the others tossed their pistols away.

"All right, everybody grab some ground," Bolan ordered. "I'm sure you've all been to lockup. You know the drill."

Bolan and James had just collected all of the pistols, patted down each gang member for other weapons and drugs and zip-tied each when three ATF cars roared up, disgorging agents with their pistols out, all shouting for Bolan and James to raise their hands.

The two men let themselves be frisked, only then letting the other agents know that they were working as undercover FBI agents on this sting. "Which," Bolan added archly, "you boys almost screwed up royally by charging in when you did."

The other agents weren't impressed. "Tell your boss to inform other agencies the next time he's got people working in the city. In fact, forget that, just tell him to keep his fuckin' nose out of our business. We've been tracking this gang for three months, and you think you can just waltz in and snatch them from under our noses? Nice try, jerkoff. We're taking the collar on these guys, and you Feebies can kiss my ass."

James and Bolan complained a bit more about the injustice of the situation; after all, it was good for their cover, since they had been assigned to keep moving up this branch of MS-13 to the national leaders. Now, however, they'd simply have to get the interrogation transcripts from the ATF once they were sent back to headquarters. Although they'd busted up this cell of the gang, their mission wasn't truly complete, not by a long shot. But after this, the two would have to lie low for a while, until they could reintroduce themselves into the underworld and try to find another way into the gang's hierarchy.

After exchanging a few more choice insults about the relative efficiency of the ATF and FBI, and extracting a promise to return the crate of rifles that had been left at the buy scene, James and Bolan were finally able to get in their SUV and drive off.

Once they were a dozen miles away, Bolan leaned over and checked their prisoner. Araña lay in the backseat, his hands and feet zip-tied and duct tape covering his mouth, his brown eyes burning with hatred.

"Sorry, amigo, but you have an appointment with some different people who are very interested in what you have to tell them. And don't even try to spew some kind of macho bullshit at me. By the time they're done with you, you'll be telling them the names of the people you beat up when you were a punk-ass kid back home in El Salvador."

James took a corner, leaning back in his seat as the tension of the mission started to wear off. "What do ya think the ATF boys'll say when they find out the leader is missing?"

"That he was smarter than his goons and rabbited out of there, found a hole in the perimeter and, if he's smart, is three states away by now. By the time they figure out the truth of it—if they do—he'll have vanished off the face of the earth." Bolan reclined his seat and slouched back, pleased at accomplishing their mission and staying in one piece. For now, it was time to relax and enjoy coming out on top again.

"Hey, find us a drive-through on the way to airport. Don't know about you, but I'm starving."

CHAPTER TWO

Hu Ji Han stood in his elegant office, staring down at the dark, gleaming water of Victoria Harbour that separated Chung Wan, Hong Kong's central district, and Tsim Sha Tsui, the southernmost point of Kowloon Peninsula on the Chinese mainland. The neon glitter from the skyscrapers all around him reflected off the black seawater, turning what should have been a placid, still stretch into a riot of flashing blues and reds and yellows, signs exhorting those that saw them to buy, consume, spend—live for today in hedonistic, self-indulgent pleasure, with little thought of what the next day might bring.

Fifty-three stories above the ground, ensconced in the Cheung Kong Center, the artfully designed skyscraper built on the grounds of the former Hilton Hotel and Beaconsfield House, Hu stared out at the monuments to capitalism and business surrounding him. He gazed down at the crowded streets of the city that existed like a cancerous growth on an otherwise healthy living being. He lived and worked deep in the pulsing, constantly beating heart of the beast every day, surrounded by its excess, its shallow, tawdry pleasures, the souls of his countrymen adrift in a sea of overindulgent products, drowning in consumption for its own sake. Hu accepted this portion of his fate, living within this cesspool, studying it, surviving it while avoiding being drawn in by its proffered pleasures.

Even after forty years, sometimes he was surprised to find the hate still burning so strongly within him.

To the rest of the world, he was a successful businessman, respected and admired for creating a company that filled a void in the region, that of recovery and restoration after natural disasters. From his small, one-man office twenty-three years ago, the firm of Life and Property Recovery, Incorporated, now had offices all over Southeast Asia and the world, and was branching out into urban development and infrastructure planning and construction. Hu's cost-effective solutions to humanitarian crises had made him a lauded figure throughout the region. One entire wall of his office was covered with various awards and photos of him being feted and commemorated by various groups and people, including two sitting presidents of the United States. Those meetings had galled him most of all, bowing and smiling at the haughty Americans, all of whom still strutted around as though they were the only superpower in the world, doing what they pleased, heedless of what others thought.

The U.S. companies, many of whom had headquarters in Hong Kong due to the relaxed business environment, were a particular affront to Hu, extending their poisonous influence farther into his country. They were so quick to take advantage of what the city had to offer, yet, when they had been truly needed decades ago, there had been no help forthcoming, not from them, nor from anywhere else in the world. It was this terrible failure on their part, and that of other countries, that kept Hu's constant desire burning deep in his heart, carefully concealed by layers of politeness, business acumen and genial diplomacy. But always, always, there was the voice in the back of his mind, constantly exhorting him. His grandmother had selected his middle name, *Ji,* meaning to remember or keep in mind, and that was exactly what he had done all these long years.

Never forget...never forgive...

Throughout his years growing up, all through building his business over the decades, Hu had never forgotten. And now, with the first part of his plan set in motion, he was only a few days away from sending a truly divine wind down upon the complacent fools and fatuous men and women that wasted their lives in meaningless busywork—soon…it would all fall into place.

The soft whoosh of the doors to his private elevator broke through Hu's reverie.

His personal secretary, Zheng Rong, walked to his side. Dressed in a tailored navy blue pinstripe business suit jacket and trousers, she had served him faithfully for the past five years without hesitation. Stopping three feet away, she bowed, a gesture he returned with respect, although he didn't turn from his contemplation of the harbor.

"Stage one is complete, sir. The decoy vessel is under our control."

"Were there any casualties?"

There was the barest pause before her reply made his head swivel in her direction. "Regrettably, yes. The men tasked to take the ship were overzealous during the assault. One man was killed, two wounded, and a woman was violated before she and the others were set adrift as originally ordered."

Hu clucked his tongue. "Have the perpetrators been identified?"

"Yes. The death came at the hands of a young boy, who was used as a distraction. I have questioned him myself, and believe him when he says it was an accident. As for the other, he is downstairs, should you wish to speak with him yourself."

Hu considered the offer, then turned to face her. "Take me to him. I would see this animal before he is removed from this earth." Only the slight tremor in his voice betrayed his anger.

Zheng turned and led him back to the elevator, which was just large enough to hold both of them comfortably. The ride down was noiseless, descending into the sublevels below the building, where Hu had paid a princely sum in order to have a private garage with twenty-four-hour street access. For a man in his position, the ability to come and go unnoticed was more important than many would think.

At this time of night, there was only one vehicle in the private lot, a slate-gray Range Rover that barely rocked back and forth on its springs as the prisoner inside struggled to escape. From where he stood, Hu could barely hear the muffled thuds as the captive man slammed against the interior.

"My apologies, sir, he awoke sooner than expected."

"No, that is all right. I would look into his eyes before you remove him." Hu led the way, walking forward with a bare whisper of his virgin-wool trousers. He paused at the back door of the luxury SUV, waiting for Zheng to open it.

When the door rose, the man inside froze, caught in the act of hammering his bare feet against the back window glass. Gagged and bound hand and foot, he had worked himself into a sweat, the foul odor making Hu's nose wrinkle.

"This will be cleaned once the cargo is removed."

The man tried to catch Hu's eyes with his own panicked ones, their normal almond shape distended by fear into wide, white ovals, marred by a swelling bruise under one. His split and puffy lips writhed as he tried to speak around the gag, the muffled pleas reduced to guttural grunts and cries.

"I would have rewarded you handsomely, enough to care for your entire family for years. Yet you let your base desires get the best of you during this first, critical operation." Hu leaned close to the man's blanched face. "And if I cannot trust you to carry out your orders on this simple task, then I cannot employ you any longer. But since you know too much about what I have planned for this city and the rest of the world, I regret to inform you that your termination must be permanent."

Hearing his doom, the captive man lashed out with his head, trying to butt Hu in the face. A blurred form rushed in and slammed the man into the backs of the third-row seats. Zheng retreated just as quickly, her open palm out, ready to defend or attack as needed.

Hu shook his head sadly. Now, when he had spent so long preparing to put his plan into motion, he couldn't afford any action—by himself or others—that would endanger the operation he had been planning for half his life. "It is foolish actions such as this that can endanger everything we have worked for. Have him removed as an example to the others that this sort of base behavior will not be tolerated. I trust you will come up with a suitable message for them."

Zheng smiled, her expression devoid of any humor or warmth. "Yes, sir. I have just the right lesson planned. They won't forget it, and he certainly won't miss what I will use to drive the point home." She closed the door on the gasping, crying man, his last mumbled pleas for what Hu assumed were mercy falling on deaf ears.

"Make sure he is never found."

"Of course, sir."

"When will we be ready to begin the second phase?"

"Once the lesson has been delivered, then it is a matter of locating the right vessels to commandeer. The men will need some time aboard to set the devices to ensure their proper destruction."

"Very good, you will keep me informed as to their progress. Also, is the diversionary force ready to go on my orders?"

"Yes, sir, their fee to the event has been handled through one of our shell corporations. There is nothing tying it back to us. They are encamped in the desert thirty kilometers south of Tiznit, and are awaiting the word to move out."

"Excellent. Please inform my pilot that his services will not be needed. I'll be resting here tonight. I will see you in the morning."

Zheng bowed again. "As you wish." She went to the driver's side of the SUV while Hu walked back to the elevator to return to his office—and the continued contemplation of the pit that was Hong Kong around him, and how best to cleanse it and the others complicit in a betrayal that stretched back more than half a century.

CHAPTER THREE

Eight hours later, Bolan, James and their prize were at Stony Man Farm, in the Blue Ridge Mountains. Jack Grimaldi had flown them out of John Wayne Airport on a red-eye back east, resulting in them enjoying a cup of real coffee—not Kurtzman's superstrong black swill—and watching the sun come up over the fog-shrouded peaks.

Bolan had decided to spirit Araña back to Stony Man Farm to avoid any federal entanglements. The Executioner and James decided to check out leads the cyberteam had before they began questioning their informant. The two men heard a whoop just as they walked into the computer room in the Annex.

"What do ya think that's about?" Calvin James asked.

"Akira either found the latest bootleg he'd been looking for, or he's actually on to something. Only one way to find out."

Akira Tokaido was one of Stony Man's youngest members. He was also its best computer hacker, slipping in and out of foreign government mainframes, through criminal syndicate firewalls and anywhere else intel was needed from cyberspace.

But when Bolan and James walked to Tokaido's workstation, his clenched fists weren't raised in triumph at his latest sneak-and-peek, nor was he crowing about his success to anyone within earshot. Instead, his dark brown eyes were glued to a large monitor, his fingers blurred over the keyboard.

"Heard you hollerin' in the hallway. What's up?" James asked.

Tokaido didn't take his eyes off the screen as he replied. "Shouted too soon. It's probably just a false alarm. For a second, I thought I'd found a link to the Sale in the Sands."

The name got both Bolan's and James's attention right away. Throughout the world, there were certain black-market events that Stony Man was constantly on the lookout for. The "Sale in the Sands" was one of them—a huge assembly of black-market weapon dealers that got together every other year to sell weapons, espionage technology, engineering and systems knowledge and entire mercenary groups to the right bidder. It had been on Bolan's list to check out for some time, but either other more pressing ops had come up at the same time, or the Farm had followed artfully disguised trails that had led them nowhere.

"Why do you think it's a no-go?" Bolan asked as he leaned down to survey the screen.

Tokaido leaned back and interlaced his hands behind his head. "Because, how would a low-life L.A. gangbanger get access to the triple-encrypted website that allows potential attendees access and the chance to put down their fifty-thousand-dollar advance reservation fee?"

"Fifty grand?" James whistled. "Damn, that's one exclusive club."

"That's not the half of it, brother." Tokaido tapped

more keys. "From what I can tell, that's only half of what someone needs to pony up to attend this little party."

"Wait a sec—you're telling me Araña had access to the site, that he was in, for all intents and purposes?" Bolan asked.

"Near as I can tell, yes. I've been tracking down every bit of conversation he's had regarding this, and from what I've gathered, MS-13 was planning to attend. They'd put down their money, and were awaiting confirmation of their account being created, as well as the second part of the password to wire the second half."

Bolan and James exchanged glances. "In for fifty grand, in for a hundred," the lithe black man said.

"Akira, I assume you can masquerade as Araña and finish the transaction?"

"Well, I *had* already begun setting up a slave system on his smartphone to see just how far down the rabbit hole I could go. I was just waiting for authorization—"

"Which you just got." Bolan straightened as his own cell phone buzzed. "Stay on this, and gather as much intel as possible. Cal, notify Phoenix to be on standby. If it's going down in the next few days, we may have to scramble to get wherever it is on time." He flipped his cell open. "Yeah."

"It's Hal." Bolan's long-time colleague and friend usually sounded either disgruntled, disgusted or dyspeptic, but this time his voice carried none of those overtones. Rather, Hal Brognola's voice carried an undercurrent Bolan had hardly ever heard—nervousness.

"Are you all right?" Bolan asked.

"Yeah, everything in Foggy Bottom is as per usual—

gridlocked and logjammed. Striker, I have a favor to ask you. How soon can you get to JFK?"

"Jack's sacked out, but Charlie's available. What's this about?"

"I can't talk about it like this, even over a secure line. Just get there as soon as you can, and call me. I'll direct you the rest of the way once you've landed in New York City."

"Hal—" Bolan turned away from the other men and lowered his voice "—you're all right?"

"Yeah, this has to do with the circles I run in. Just get up here, would you? It would mean a lot to me."

"I'm on my way." Bolan hung up and speed-dialed Charlie Mott, Stony Man's second pilot. "Charlie…yeah, it's me…prep the jet for a flight to JFK…leaving in the next hour…thanks."

James was watching him as he headed for the door. "What's up?"

"Hal needs me in NYC. I want you to take over Araña's interrogation. Find out everything he knows about the Sale in the Sands, and anything else MS-13's up to. I'll call in once I'm in New York."

"You got it."

CHAPTER FOUR

Xiang Po bolted upright in the bed, the soft cotton sheets puddling around his body as he choked off his shout of fear. Heart hammering in his chest, he looked in every corner of the small stateroom, searching for the furious, black-haired ghost that had been crawling after him, its bloody hands reaching for him from beyond the grave....

A dream—it was only a dream, he thought. He cocked an ear, listening for any sign that his outburst might have been heard by the other pirates. When no fist hammered on the door, he leaned back against the plush headboard and sighed in relief. He stared at the opulent room he'd been given as a reward for his part in taking over the yacht, taking in the soft carpet, the real wooden furniture, the faint smell of some kind of floral fragrance that had filled the room when he had first entered. All of this, as well as a wonder he had scarcely believed when he had first set eyes on it.

Just thinking about it made him shiver in anticipation. Xiang slipped out of bed, carefully drawing up the covers again—it would be a crime to leave such a luxurious abode unkempt. He grinned as he thought about the first night they had stayed aboard, when he had tossed and turned on the soft mattress, unused to such comfort, until he had wrapped himself in the topsheet and slept on the floor, which had still been more comfortable than any other bed he'd ever been in. Over the next few days, he had moved to the bed, and his rest had never been so peaceful—except for the damn dreams.

He crossed to the private bathroom, marveling again at how his bare, callused feet sank into the soft, ivory-colored carpet. Sliding open the narrow door, he gazed at the object of his desire—the small, tiled shower stall. When Xiang had first found it, he had stayed under the fresh, clean spray for fifteen minutes, using up almost all of the water on the boat. The other pirates had wanted to beat him for his mistake, but their leader, Lee Ming, had instead made him responsible for maintaining the desalinization system for the yacht as long as they were on board, which he had done scrupulously ever since. Xiang had overheard a conversation between Lee and another pirate, and learned that they might remain onboard for as long as a week, maybe ten days. It wasn't their normal operating procedure, but was to be followed until the next phase of their plan was to be put into motion. He didn't mind; this was the best he'd ever had it in all of his twelve years.

At least he thought he was about twelve years old; the truth was, he had no idea of his birthday, or where he had been born, or who his parents were. The pirate life was all he'd ever known, and he did what he had to do to survive among this band of criminals.

In the shower, he had just gotten the water adjusted to his comfort when a heavy fist pounded on the door. "Xiang! Where's breakfast?" a familiar voice demanded in guttural Cantonese.

"Shit!" The boy turned the water off and grabbed the nearest towel, wiping himself down and leaping for his clothes. Scrambling into them, he reached for the door just as the fist hammered on it again, making the entire frame shake.

"Coming!" He slid the door open to see the leering face of Guong Ho staring down at him, making Xiang's buttocks clench involuntarily. "I'd better get up there, otherwise the others will be mad at me, too." He tried to slip by the stocky, muscular man, but was stopped by a thick arm blocking his way.

"Why the rush, Po?" The man's stubby fingers combed through the boy's wet hair. "You look so much better cleaned up."

Xiang ducked under his arm. "You asked where breakfast was. I need to get to the galley to make it."

The large man hip-checked him into the wall with surprising agility. His thick fingers grabbed Xiang's neck as he leaned close to the boy. "You'd better get back into that bed if you know what's good for you—"

"Po? Ho? What's going on down there? Where's our meal?" A strong voice carried down the hallway. Guong immediately straightened and shoved Xiang ahead of him.

"I'm rousting this lazybones right now. Get moving, you!" His hand thudded between Xiang's shoulder blades, staggering the boy and almost sending him to the marble floor. "This isn't over, little one," he hissed under his breath as he followed Xiang to the galley entrance.

"Easy, Ho, you don't want to injure our cook. Let's go, Po, everyone is hungry and waiting." Although their leader's voice was pleasant enough, his face was all hard, lean planes, with a hooked beak of a nose under glittering black eyes. Xiang knew firsthand that his tone was the only soft thing about him. Lee Ming had killed their previous leader a year ago, and since then had mercilessly trained the small band of pirates to take on larger ships and cargo. He was the one who had come up with the decoy idea, which had worked perfectly for several hijackings—at least, until this last time.

Xiang slid past the pirate leader, shoulders tensed in expectation of a blow, but the man let him pass without interference. Once immaculate and gleaming, the kitchen and its appliances were filthy from the rest of the men coming and going at all hours of the day, leaving rotting food scraps and dirty dishes and bowls everywhere in their wake. The fetid smell made him gag, and he opened the small porthole window to get some fresh air in, then turned on the oven fan to try to clear the stench. With a sigh, Xiang realized he'd let things go unattended here for too long. He'd have to clean the whole area from top to bottom, before it could get any worse.

He checked the walk-in refrigerator, which contained supplies for twice the number of people currently on board, and grabbed a dozen and a half eggs, four pounds of peeled shrimp, crisp bean sprouts, fish sauce and everything else he needed for a giant batch of spicy egg *foo yung* with shrimp, a quick yet filling meal that would satisfy the chorus of growling stomachs outside.

For the next ten minutes, Xiang lost himself in the ritual of cooking, one of the few things he truly enjoyed, having picked it up from the last leader of their group. The soothing cadence of cracking, chopping and whisking was almost able to distract him from the shocked look of wide-eyed pain on the American's face when the bullet had hit him, the man's face still haunting his sleep. Soon the savory smell of cooking egg and shrimp filled the galley, overlying the stink of spoiled food. Xiang also heated plenty of water for tea, finding the last of the leaves in a container underneath the small galley table.

When it was finished, Xiang scooped them into two large bowls—the last clean ones he could find, and reheated the last of the scallion pancakes he'd made the previous night, which had somehow escaped the ravenous men's notice. Piling everything on a large tray, along with bowls, cups and chopsticks, he carefully carried it out to the rear sundeck, where the men had gathered to eat. The tray was so heavy it made his arms shake, but Xiang didn't complain or stop moving for a moment, knowing that his only option was to make it to the table with his burden intact.

He emerged from the hallway into a bright morning, with a canopy covering the rear area to ward off the already blazing sun. Out here, the smell of the savory breakfast was overpowered by the salt tang of the ocean. Xiang didn't look around, but kept his eyes on his goal—the table. He was only concerned once, when Guong Ho feinted as if he was going to rise and come after him. His movement was noticed by Lee, who frowned.

"Don't make the boy drop our breakfast, Ho, otherwise we'll have to make you cook, and everyone knows what a lousy chef you are!"

The rest of the pirates roared with laughter while Guong hunkered down in his chair, flushed and glowering. Xiang set the platter down, and the men swarmed over the food like starving sharks, scooping out large portions with their bowls and eating with the chopsticks, or just their fingers. After glaring at Xiang with a dark stare that promised revenge for the perceived insult, Guong Ho dug in, as well.

Xiang stood away from the table, waiting for the men to finish. He noticed that almost all of them had raided the closets of the former occupants. Since the clothes were American, they had been modified, with khaki and linen pant legs rolled up, and many sleeves shortened by a knife blade. Only Lee Ming wore clothes that could even be considered appropriate, having modified the captain's uniform to fit his slender frame. Xiang frowned. The makeshift outfits could fool a passing ship, but anyone coming onboard would see through the poor disguises in an instant. Normally they sold a ship after stripping it of anything valuable in a few days, but since they were staying this time, the danger increased with every day they remained onboard. Xiang knew he couldn't say anything about it, since Lee would take that as an affront to his leadership. He'd just have to be vigilant about having an escape route open in case they were caught.

The men had just about finished their breakfasts, leaning back and belching in satisfaction, exchanging smiles and jibes about how much each other had eaten. Xiang waited for Lee to finish, knowing the harsh penalty for attempting to clear the table before their leader was done, when one of the men assigned to monitor the radio walked out of the communications room.

"The demon woman has contacted us—she is coming in for a meeting."

Xiang was secretly pleased at seeing Lee stiffen slightly upon hearing the message. So, there were people even he feared, the boy thought. It was easy to see why, however. A visit from the demon woman was always fraught with peril. The last time, she'd taken Lee aside for a whispered conversation, then he had pointed out Gouhou Cheng and Xiang. She had sternly interrogated Xiang about the events during the hijacking and he'd done his best to assure her that his shooting the man had been an accident. But she had taken Gouhou away with her. That had been two days ago, and they hadn't heard anything about or from him since.

Lee let his chopsticks clatter on the table. "When?"

"She will be here in ten minutes. She said all of us should be here on the deck when she arrives."

"That stuck-up bitch." Lee's nostrils flared, and Xiang knew his anger had just risen another notch. Their leader hated kowtowing to the woman, but he swallowed his pride and followed her orders so that the pirates could earn the promised reward for all of this work, a prize far beyond stealing ships, even ones such as this. Xiang had no idea what was necessary to obtain it, but Lee, in one of his rare, expansive moods after drinking a half-bottle of wine one evening, had hinted that it would be enough to let them quit the pirate life forever, to enable them to live like normal people for a change. That was why he'd pushed the men so hard to do their assigned jobs well, so that no one would imperil their chance to leave this life behind.

"Xiang! Clear this mess away. The rest of you, go clean yourselves up. We must look presentable when she arrives."

The boy jumped to obey, stacking the bowls and loading them onto the tray. Picking it up, he carried his pile into the galley, stacking them in the sink and filling it with hot water to soak them. He took a quick look at himself in the mirror, patting his hair down with water, then scurried back on deck, making sure to stay as close to Lee Ming and as far from Guong Ho as possible.

The rumbling throb of a powerboat could now be heard reverberating over the calm ocean, and Xiang looked off the port side to see a slim, forty-five-foot-long cigarette boat approaching, cutting through the water like a sleek, silver-gray dolphin. It turned sharply toward the yacht, powering down as it closed in. Lee Ming nodded for two men to meet the powerboat. A few minutes later, the demon woman stepped aboard.

Xiang, along with the rest of the men, shifted uneasily in her presence. She was impeccably dressed in a western-style suit, with a cream silk blouse under matching dark pinstriped blazer and pants. Despite the heat, she didn't sweat, and her hair was restrained in what looked like an ivory holder and draped her left shoulder. She carried a small, alligator-skin briefcase in her right hand. Her eyes were concealed behind dark blue designer sunglasses that lent her face an alien, insectile quality. Whenever he saw her, a strange mixture of feelings cascaded over Xiang: fear and anger and another emotion that he couldn't quite identify.

Setting the briefcase down on the table with a thump, she didn't waste time with greetings. "Why haven't you repainted the boat? It has been three days since you took it, yet it still looks the same."

Lee Ming concealed his anger under a calm, lazy affectation. "It is difficult to do such work when we are being interrupted by pointless meetings with you all the time."

She smiled, her white teeth flashing in a vulpine grin. "This meeting is anything but pointless, asshole.

I have your next assignment, but first, an object lesson for you and the rest of these dirty pigs."

Now she had all of the men's attention. Of course, calling Ming an asshole and the rest of them dirty pigs would do that, Xiang thought. One or two of them tensed, as if they were going to try to jump her, but Lee froze them in place with just a look. He returned his attention to the woman, who stood by the table like a statue, watching them all from behind her dark sunglasses.

"Please, continue." One could almost miss the gritted strain in his voice, he covered it well.

"In here is money for resupplying the boat, as well as getting the damn thing painted. It had better be done in the next two days, or we'll find another crew to handle this operation. And if you doubt my word—"

She popped open the locks on the briefcase, opened it and took out a small lacquered box inlaid with gold filigree. "I brought you a gift from my superior." She set it on the table in front of Lee. "Open it."

Even Xiang knew that opening a gift immediately after receiving it was bad form, but since it was more of an order than a request, Lee didn't have a choice. He reached out and undid the tiny metal clasp with one hand, then flipped the cover open. The men behind him gasped in surprise, but Lee showed no hint of any reaction at all.

Xiang carefully sidled closer to the table, overcome with curiosity. He had just gotten a glimpse of something that looked sort of like a dried fleshy finger when Lee slammed the cover shut, his fingers curling into a fist over the box.

The woman continued as if she didn't notice his boiling rage. "We dropped off the rest of him on the way here. I imagine the sharks dined well. My superior was very displeased with his actions when you took over this boat. He trusts there will be no further incidents like the one that cost Cheng his life."

Xiang, like many of the other pirates, gaped at her in shock. The woman had overseen one of the most grievous insults to a Chinese person by denying him a proper burial. But instead of acting ashamed, she stood tall and proud, as if pleased by what she had carried out. Xiang hadn't been overly fond of Cheng, as he was a drunkard and a bully, but even he wouldn't have considered the thought of doing something that heinous to the man's body.

The woman stood over Lee, as if daring him to reply. The silence stretched out for many seconds. Finally, the pirate leader looked up. "We shall do everything you require. There will be no further...incidents."

"Good. You will also need to recruit more men. My superior has decided that we will be taking two vessels for the mission, not just one."

The shock of the "gift" was replaced by the surprise of this new directive. Even Lee's eyebrows raised at this. "Taking over one ship was going to be difficult enough, but two—"

"I did not ask for your opinion, I told you what you must do. If this is a problem, then I can find other men willing to undertake this mission, rendering all of you—" her gaze, even through the sunglasses, raked across everyone "—as expendable as that pig there." She waved a hand at the box. "Get this boat repainted, get more men, preferably some with large ship experience, and be ready to move in two days. We will contact you with further instructions then."

Lee swallowed, his fisted hands having disappeared under the table. "Everything will be ready as you have requested." His voice had gone low and very soft. The pirates edged away from him; they knew exactly what that tone meant. Xiang slowly crept back to his place near the hallway entrance; when the time came, he wanted to have his bolt hole close at hand.

"Good. And no more fuck-ups, or you'll all join your friend as shark bait. Well, except for some parts, perhaps." She grinned again, turned on her heel and descended back to the boat. With a muffled roar, the powerboat pushed off, then turned and disappeared into the distance, shrinking until it could no longer be seen, and its engine noise was nothing but a loud memory.

Lee sat at the table for a long minute, then took the box and hurled it overboard, contents and all. "I swear, we will complete our job, but before we do, that bitch will be dead."

He rose with such force that his chair toppled over, skidding on the hardwood deck. "Let's move, all of you! Get underway, head for the island! We'll show them just how we get things done!"

He stalked into the main room as the rest of the men scrambled to obey his orders. Xiang ducked into the hallway to the galley and began cleaning the pots, wondering just how much harder their plan was going to be now.

And what exactly did the demon woman mean by two ships?

CHAPTER FIVE

Three and a half hours later, Bolan turned his rented Escalade off the Henry Hudson Parkway onto a forested road, leaving the whoosh and roar of the highway behind as he traveled into a secluded forest park.

He looked out the window at the well-kept lawns and stark trees just beginning to bud in the spring season. He hit his earpiece, speed-dialing Stony Man Farm as a building straight out the Middle Ages came into view, complete with a stone tower rising over the foliage. After the call was routed through a series of cutouts, an operator at the Farm put him through to Tokaido.

"Speak to me."

"This is Striker. What am I coming up on?" After getting the address from Brognola, Bolan had sent it to Akira Tokaido to gather info during the hour-long drive from JFK to Long Island.

"Hey, Striker. You just entered Fort Tryon Park. That would make the building you're coming up on part of the Cloisters." Bolan heard keys tapping. "It's a part of the Metropolitan Museum of Art, is dedicated to the art and architecture of Medieval Europe, and was opened in 1938 to the public—"

"I'm familiar with New York landmarks, so that's enough of a history lesson, thanks." Bolan watched the red tile-roofed building grow larger as he approached.

"Wonder why Hal suggested this place, instead of any one of a dozen in D.C. that would be as discreet?"

"Offhand, it seems to be about as far from both NYC and D.C. as you could get. Since it's so isolated, anyone trying to follow either of you would stick out like the proverbial sore thumb."

"Right." Bolan had known Hal Brognola far too long to suspect the man of trying to lure him into some kind of trap, but that didn't mean there weren't others who wouldn't attempt the same using Hal as bait. "I'll check in with you afterward."

"I've downloaded a site map to your phone. You sure you don't want eyes in the sky or ears on the ground?" Tokaido asked.

"Thanks, but I think I'll be fine. Striker out." Disconnecting his call as he pulled into an empty space on the graveled parking lot, Bolan took a few seconds to scan and memorize the grounds plan Tokaido had sent him, as well as look around, his trained mind evaluating entrances, exits, hard points, cover. He also took a moment to check his casual rig. His Beretta 93R was nestled in a Galco belt holster at the small of his back, easily concealed by his camel-colored sport coat. Keeping the pistol hidden from casual view, he drew it, checked the load and replaced it before shrugging into his jacket.

He strolled up the driveway to the diamond-shaped main hall, dropping a twenty-dollar donation to the organization that maintained the building. Exits at each point led to a medieval book collection on his right, into what was termed the Romanesque Hall straight ahead, and to the Late Gothic Hall on his left, which led to the garden.

Bolan walked into the larger hallway to his left, not

sparing a single glance at the rich collection of artwork adorning the walls. Stepping out into the garden bathed him in the golden light of the late-morning sun, which washed the nearby wall and ground in its warm, glowing radiance.

The garden grounds were arranged in a traditional style, with the large rectangle formed by the walls divided by framed footpaths into four equal areas, each filled with a profusion of plants and color that created a heady mix of floral scents. In the center of the garden, a stone fountain burbled, and next to it, staring into its trickling waters as intently as if he was trying to divine the future, stood Hal Brognola.

Bolan walked to him slowly, his boots making enough noise on the gravel to alert the other man. He took in the big Fed's appearance as he approached. Normally comfortably attired, if a little rumpled, he now looked as if he had been traveling for the past day or so and hadn't gotten much sleep. His hands were in the pockets of his slacks, but Bolan couldn't tell if he was holding something in one or both of them, or just clenching his fists.

He was a yard away when Brognola spoke. "Hi, Striker." His usually warm, reassuring voice was thin and reedy, more evidence of the stress he was under.

"Hal." Bolan strode to his side and looked into the bottom of the fountain. The face staring back at him, even distorted by the rippling water, made him pause. His oldest friend's features were ashen-gray, with red-rimmed eyes surrounded by puffy skin, attesting to his lack of sleep. His graying hair, usually neatly combed, ruffled in the light breeze.

"Hal, are you all right?"

Brognola nodded, holding up a forestalling hand. "I'm fine. It's just been a very busy past twenty-four hours, that's all." He rubbed his tired face with his hands. "Finally I just had to get away for a little bit—but of course, the business at hand always intervenes. That's why you're here."

Bolan had a far less philosophical view of his endless war. It always came down to him versus the evil in the rest of the world. Usually Brognola was right there alongside him, fighting the good fight. To see him shaken this way was anything but normal. Bolan tried to snap him out of it by getting right to the point. "What's this all about?"

Brognola took a deep breath and raised his head, staring into Bolan's ice-blue eyes with his own rheumy ones. "In the course of my work in D.C., I've gotten to know people throughout the city. One family in particular—the Kirkalls."

Bolan's eyebrows rose in surprise. "The manufacturing Kirkalls? That's quite a connection to keep out of sight, particularly on the Hill." The soldier kept up on the movers and shakers in D.C., and also recognized the surname as a former director of the CIA about ten years ago. "I assume Morgan is part of the family, as well?"

"Of course. Despite our proximity to projects on both sides of the political fence, our families have always been friendly. Morgan's granddaughter, Rachel..." As soon as he said her name, Brognola gritted his teeth, forcing his next words out. "Those heartless bastards."

"What happened?"

"It's a short story. After the spring term, Morgan's son, Robert, took his family on an around-the-world cruise, a reward for everyone for their accomplishments during the semester. Apparently they had just left the Philippines when their boat was attacked by pirates. According to Robert, they were after the yacht, which will fetch several hundred thousand on the black market. But during the hijacking, Rachel's boyfriend was shot and died of blood loss soon after. Their bodyguards were subdued, and Rachel was raped by one of the pirates. More than once, that's all anyone will tell me. Afterward, they put everyone, family and the crew, into one of thc speedboats and set them adrift after disabling the engine. They were out there for a day before a Japanese freighter found them and brought them to Singapore. As soon as he found out, Morgan sent his private jet to bring them all home.

"When I found out, I went to the hospital right away. But when I first saw Rachel in that hospital bed, I realized there was nothing I could do. I've known Robert for most of his life, but I'd never seen him cry out of sheer helplessness until I saw him that morning." He rubbed his stubbled chin. "I got as much information out of him as I could, under the circumstances. Assuming that the pirates haven't ditched the boat already, they've probably already modified it, replaced the transmitter and are hiding somewhere in the thousands of square miles of ocean in that area, perhaps in one of the hundreds of islands throughout the region."

He stared at the wall across the garden, as if seeing a place somewhere beyond the garden, beyond the city. "Rachel once was an intern on the Hill. She's so different from the girl I knew even a month ago. I know she'll recover from this—she's strong, like the rest of her family. But she'll never be the same again. As I was leaving, I saw Morgan—he asked…no, he begged me to do what I could to find those responsible for this. He can't possibly be involved in any way. If it were found out, the repercussions would destroy his reputation and damage the family's. I told him that I would do what I could, and then set up the meeting here, with you.

"I could use my Agency contacts. I know a few people who could get the job done. But I don't want to drag them into this. Last I knew, they were stretched pretty thinly across the region, and sending one off on a personal vendetta, even for me, seems pretty high-handed."

"But you wouldn't hesitate to request a favor from a friend in a position to do so, would you?" Bolan said without a hint of rancor. He knew what it was like to lose people, to see them hurt in the line of duty. To see them dead for just trying to do the right thing. A terrible crime had been inflicted on this young woman, which would no doubt haunt her for the rest of her life.

Brognola turned back to him. "We go back a long way, Striker. I know I have no right to ask this of you—and I certainly don't want you going to any special lengths on my account, or for some former CIA director—but if you have a mission that comes up in that area in the near future, I'd appreciate it if you or one of the others would keep an eye out for the ship or any of the men. Robert's taking his own steps to find them—he wouldn't say how, despite my best efforts to find out—so anyone you send may find some competition there." He held out a flash drive. "Here's everything I could get—facial sketches of the pirates, the specifications on the yacht, all of it. I hope it can help in some small way."

Bolan took the small drive and pocketed it. "I can't promise Morgan or you anything, Hal, but I'll see what

I can do for you, even if that means just locating these people so you can pass the intel on to Robert."

"Thanks, Striker."

A cloud had blocked the sun, casting shadows over the garden, stealing the warmth away from the area. "Are you fixed for getting back to Washington?"

"Yeah, my car's in the lot." A wry smile quirked the big Fed's lips. "Don't worry. I'm a bit somber these days, but I still remember to know not to leave the area together."

Bolan smiled as they left the garden, heading back into the Late Gothic Hall, where he shook Brognola's hand before heading back to his SUV. He pulled out of the parking lot, merging with the freeway traffic back into the city. After five minutes of travel, Bolan plugged the USB drive into an adapter on his cell and hit the hands-free function, speed-dialing a number that would connect him to the Farm.

"Speak to me."

"This is Striker."

"How's Hal?"

"All right." Bolan filled Tokaido in on the general parameters of the task, leaving names out of it. "I'll square it with Aaron. You're my man till we see this through. I'm sending you files on the ship and the perpetrators. Start isolating general traffic in the area, satellite passes, law enforcement bulletins, whatever you can find." "Aaron" was Aaron "the Bear" Kurtzman, head of the Farm's cyberteam.

"Okay. You do realize that this'll be like searching for the proverbial needle in a haystack?"

"More like one ship out of a few thousand, but I'm

sure you're the guy to do it. Any word from Calvin on our subject?"

"He's in the middle of the session now, using that new scopolamine derivative he stumbled across. Probably have a report ready for you by the time you get back."

"And how's your infiltration coming?"

Bolan heard a deep breath on the other end of the line. "As far as I know, we're in. I just got the code of the account to wire the other half of the money. The event starts in four days."

"Good work, Akira. Ask Aaron to contact Charlie and have him prep the jet. I want to be wheels-up as soon as I hit the airport."

"You got it."

"Striker out."

With the balls in motion, Bolan disconnected, his mind turned to the logistics of such a personal mission, and how to execute it against the framework of a larger one.

CHAPTER SIX

Ninety minutes later, Bolan leaned back in his white leather chair of the Gulfstream G650 that Brognola had arranged to ferry him to New York City and back, grimacing in frustration.

Although there were plenty of crimes going on in the South China Sea—smuggling of drugs, knock-off merchandise and humans, illegal fishing, sweatshops—there didn't seem to be anything on Stony Man's radar that would necessitate actually going to the region. Even the fringe Japanese terrorist groups had been lying low recently. It was almost…

Too quiet, Bolan thought. The all-too-apparent lack of activity ironically seemed to point at something going on.

A chime from his combat laptop signaled an incoming videophone message. Bolan opened a window to answer it, and saw Tokaido's smiling face.

Bolan didn't mince words. "I assume you've got something for me?"

"Yeah. Whoever pulled that file together included every possible scrap of information about the yacht they could find, even down to service records, so my job wasn't too difficult."

"And?"

Tokaido tapped keys, and another window opened on

Bolan's screen, showing the lines of a yacht out at sea through the powerful camera of a spy satellite hundreds of miles overhead. The ship's coordinates were in the upper right corner of the window, roughly 160 nautical miles northwest of the Philippines. As he watched, a speedboat raced in from the north, pulling up to the rear of the large pleasure craft. The detail from the picture was enough to show a dark-haired woman getting off the speedboat, dressed in business attire and carrying a small briefcase.

"Who's that, and why is a businesswoman meeting with what are supposed to be pirates?" Bolan asked

"The pirates are very real. We found a satellite in the area two days earlier that caught the takeover on the periphery of its camera. They're definitely hijackers, although they haven't followed the usual pattern of either stripping and sinking the boat or modifying and selling it. Instead, they've stayed on board for the past two days. And now the woman comes aboard, a very unusual piece to this puzzle. We ran her picture through our database and found this."

A newspaper article from the *Hong Kong Standard* appeared next to a blow-up and enhancement of the woman's face. In the picture accompanying the article, an older gentleman was accepting some kind of honor from another suited businessman, the two shaking hands and smiling for the cameras. "The man on the right is Hu Ji Han, a noted businessman and philanthropist in Hong Kong. The man he's shaking hands with is the chief executive of the city. The woman—" the newspaper photo magnified to reveal her sitting in the first row of the assembled visitors' area "—is his personal secretary."

The back of Bolan's neck tingled with the distinct feeling he got when his instincts told him something much bigger was going on. "Why do I get the feeling that she's not shopping for a discount watercraft."

"Hardly. Mr. Hu could buy half the Chinese navy if he wanted, with enough money left over to raise another few skyscrapers in downtown Hong Kong."

"What do you have on him?"

"Chinese national, sixty-four years old. Rose from nothing to create his business, which specializes in disaster recovery and infrastructure rebuilding. It's one of the top companies in the nation, notwithstanding the rumors that Mr. Hu overextended himself during the building spree before the Olympics. However, he doubled down on ailing U.S. banks and national companies, such as Ford, Citibank, et cetera, during the fallout from the loan disaster in the U.S., and emerged even richer than before."

Bolan's mouth quirked in what might have been the beginning of a smile. "Well, then, I doubt he's planning to branch out into actual crime. Legal theft is so much more profitable, as everyone saw recently. Still, this is the highest of high society meeting with the lowest of the low. There's a bigger picture going on here, and we need to find out more than just this little bit."

Tokaido smiled. "I figured you might say that. What'd you have in mind?"

Here came the tricky part. While Bolan had investigated the death or abduction of relatives of high-powered Washington players before, he didn't intend to run a revenge mission to satisfy Brognola's vendetta. However, if the opportunity arose to eliminate these people while they were committing another, even more serious crime, that could work just as well. But he needed a handpicked member with extensive time in Asia to handle this. Bolan knew exactly whom he could call upon for this mission.

"Get me our contact information on John Trent. My plan's still to stop off in Africa to investigate the Sale in the Sands. Hopefully Trent will be able to take a bit of a vacation and take a look into whatever is going on in Southeast Asia, not to mention the infiltration of this pirate group." Bolan's gaze went back to the open video window, where the woman was leaving, reaching down with one hand to enter the boat, her other hand outstretched to keep her balance.

Her empty left hand.

"She left the briefcase behind." He peered more closely at the picture, but it faded into static as the satellite passed out of range. His head snapped up, his ice-blue eyes staring back at his computer hacker with steely resolve. "They're up to something, and I want to find out what."

"I'm forwarding you Trent's number right now."

"Good. Meanwhile, continue expediting the arrangement for Morocco. There'll be a few unexpected guests attending the convention this year."

"What, you mean you're not going to pose as an MS-13 member looking for hardware?"

Bolan shook his head. "No, I want you to spoof that invite to a mercenary leader cover identity I've been wanting to get out there for a while. I discussed it with Gary Manning a while back, he can fill you in on the details."

"Okay, I'll give him a call and get to work. No rest for the wicked, apparently."

"Nor for the righteous, either. Striker out." He signed off and brought up John Trent's home number, letting the internet dialer connect him.

JOHN TRENT FACED OFF against his five opponents, all of whom were arrayed around him in a loose circle. Confident and loose, he stood right where he was, not moving a muscle. He was aware of the position and likely initial attack method of each of his foes, and was ready to counter whatever they might throw at him.

As if on an unseen signal, all of them charged at him at once, intending to overwhelm him with their superior numbers. John blocked the forward punch of the one in front of him and moved aside just enough to redirect the force of his blow, knocking the man off-balance and sending him stumbling into the thug next to him—taking both of them out of the fight for a moment. Trent stepped forward into the opening they left even as he felt a hand grab the collar of his jacket.

Instantly he spun into the man's attempt to grapple with him, confusing his attacker for a moment, and also interrupting the other two men's attacks. Face-to-face with the third man, Trent wrapped his left arm around the man's right, breaking his grip while bringing his right hand, fingers stiffened, up into the man's throat before he could block it. The man would have staggered backward, except for Trent's hold on him. He used his control of the man to push him into the other two, making them dodge their ally instead of attack him.

By now the first two had recovered, and were coming after Trent again. He ducked the overhand strike of one and punched him in the groin, sending him to the ground. His partner tried bringing his interlaced hands down on Trent's head, but he avoided the blow by leaning to one side, then grabbed the man's hands and pulled him into a throw over his leg, ending the takedown with two lightning-quick strikes to the man's left temple.

Two down, three to go.

Trent rose to his feet as the three eyed him warily, aware of what he could do, but not willing to give up just yet. The three sized him up for another moment, then all came at him at once. Trent met the one on the left's front kick with a block that levered his foot up and into the middle man's arm, knocking his punch away. Trent pushed up higher and away, making the man fall backward on his buttocks. Without stopping, he shot his elbow into the temple of the middle man, dropping him, then ducked a knife slash from the last man, coming up inside his reach and trapping the weapon hand in a wrist lock that let him control his attacker's movement, taking him down to the ground. Trent disarmed the man, popping him in the jaw with the butt of the knife, then rose to take on the first guy again, who had gotten to his feet and was coming after him again, this time with a leaping high kick.

Again Trent moved into the attack, stabbing the man in the groin with the blade of the knife and taking him out of the fight.

The whole encounter had taken less than ten seconds.

Trent's five "attackers" all got up from the ground and bowed him, straightening their *gis* as they did. Trent bowed back to them before turning to the other students of his advanced *ninjitsu* class.

"As you have been learning ever since you began this martial art path, *ninjitsu* is no one way, it is using whatever method, move or means that is effective to defeat one's opponent. In the demonstration you just saw, I used a variety of moves to keep my opponents off balance and off target. Usually, however, when faced with five-to-one odds, I would disable them enough to escape and find the nearest police officer."

That comment brought chuckles from the class. "Okay, let's split into groups of three and practice two-on-one sparring. Use everything you've been taught, both as attackers and defenders. Do fifteen rounds, five for each person in each position, then move up to knives and clubs. I'll be coming around to instruct as you work."

The class split into smaller groups as Trent's assistant approached him, holding a cell phone. "*Sensei,* I'm afraid you have an urgent phone call. The caller says he is an old friend from the farm."

Trent looked at him, black eyebrows raised in surprise. "Hmm. I'll take it." He took the cell phone and walked to a corner of the dojo. "This is John Trent."

"Mack Bolan here, John. I won't bore you with small talk and will get right to the point. How would you feel about helping me out again?"

CHAPTER SEVEN

Hu Ji Han positioned himself and addressed the ball on his tee, a four iron held firmly in his gloved hands. A momentary pause, then inhale as he swung the club back and exhale as he brought it down, the power flowing from his shoulders and waist into the club head, smacking the ball into the clear blue sky. It sailed over the azure ocean water to land in the center of the fairway, roughly two hundred yards from the green.

"Excellent shot, Mr. Hu." His golfing partner, an impeccably dressed man with a polished Oxford accent, inclined his head in approval. The two men, along with their caddies and a junior member from each company, were on the third hole of the ocean nine at the Clearwater Bay Golf and Country Club. The day was perfect for the challenging course, including this par four, 460-yard hole that required the players to angle a shot over a stretch of the South China Sea to even have a chance to line up their approach to the green and make par.

"Thank you." Golf normally calmed Hu's mind, although this day his thoughts were in disarray. He was meeting with the representative of this particular company to ensure that the final pieces of his opening gambit were ready to be introduced into play. He was playing well enough, but the course was merciless, and the slightest lapse of concentration could cost him.

His partner, one Rhys Davis-Smythe, took his position and addressed his ball. He was several inches taller than the short Chinese man, and whipcord-lean. Hu couldn't tell if he had always been in sales, since he had noticed scars on Davis-Smythe's hands before he had pulled his gloves on. Plus, he was always alert to everything that was going on around them, from other groups playing in front and behind them to even the noisy call of a seagull as it took off into the stiff breeze. None of this seemed to affect his game in the slightest, as evidenced by the crushing shot he hit, following the same route Hu had, and winding up fifty yards closer to the green.

"A superb shot, as well, Mr. Davis-Smythe." Usually fiercely competitive, Hu was willing to lose this round, as long as it ensured that he got what he wanted. That didn't mean that he was going to make it easy on his opponent. Hu handed his club to his caddy and began strolling toward his lie. "Have you ever played the ocean nine before?"

Davis-Smythe inclined his head toward Hu. "I confess that I have not had the pleasure before your very gracious invitation. It is a beautiful, if challenging course."

"Indeed. I appreciate that you could make time in your schedule on such short notice to join me today."

"As you are probably aware, Mr. Hu, you are one of our most important customers at the moment. When you extended your invitation to join you here, my superiors let me know that I had no other duties save making this appointment. I am pleased to say that this does not feel even remotely like business."

"That is good to hear." The Englishman was reserved

and cool, yet Hu found himself liking the man. From the moment they had met, he'd showed the proper respect to both an elder and a top customer. He took a moment to look out over the sea, watching the ship traffic come and go around the city. "I agree with your sentiment, but unfortunately, I'm afraid that business must intrude upon what has been a very pleasant outing so far. Let us hope that it won't intrude too much. You are a very worthy opponent, and I would hate to distract you from our game."

Again a slight nod from Davis-Smythe. "By all means. I was fairly certain that this wasn't a purely social call. I will endeavor to answer whatever questions you may have, and anything that I cannot speak to I will look into upon my return to the office, and have an answer for you not later than the end of the day."

"Excellent. To begin, please give me a current status report of the assets in play," Hu requested as they approached his ball.

"Well, sir, the mission you requested certainly tasked the majority of our available personnel, but I am pleased to report that we were able to mobilize and transport more than eighty percent of our active personnel within forty-eight hours of the finalization of the contract. Currently there are 357 men awaiting orders to strike the designated target location."

"Excellent. Please detail the vehicles and equipment that you plan to use to achieve my stated objectives."

"Of course. To begin with, we have mortar teams ready to entrench in their designated zones to supply preassault fire to soften up the target before the main assault. Our support aircraft are two Boeing AH-6 gunships, armed with 30 mm chain guns and 2.75 mm rocket pods. The ground forces will launch their initial assault in a dozen M1117 Guardian ASVs, each equipped with a 40 mm grenade launcher, a .50-caliber machine gun and an M240H medium machine gun. Also, there will be more than a dozen Humvees mounting both wire-guided TOW missiles and turret-mounted .50-caliber heavy machine guns, to achieve maximum fire penetration, supporting the individual combat units. As the majority of the attendees will be carrying light arms at best, we expect to achieve a kill rate of at least eighty percent."

"Most impressive. And what about the additional mission we had discussed?"

Davis-Smythe cleared his throat. "Yes, well, as the vast majority of our men are currently tasked under the primary mission, we have had to outsource the two teams for that one. However, I am pleased to let you know that we have two top freelance teams under contract for each target. We have worked with each group before, and can highly recommend them. They are under contract with us, and are bound by our insurance and liability."

"Very good."

"Just to verify, the men's orders are to set the autopilot, set the munitions that they will bring on board, and then debark from the ship, leaving it aimed toward the harbor to detonate when it reaches its final destination?"

"That is acceptable, as long as the freighters make it as close to shore as possible. That is key."

"I will inform our men of this and ensure that they execute your directives to the utmost of their ability."

Hu nodded. "Excellent. The recommendations I received when investigating whom to contract to handle these tasks were most accurate. I'm also very pleased with your readiness and efficiency." Satisfied with the answers he'd received, Hu addressed his ball again with a six iron, drew back and swung. His shot arced high and landed on the far end of the green, approximately twenty yards from the pin.

"Another excellent shot. Given the generous terms of the contract you signed with us, Force Forward made absolutely every effort to meet your requests, and we are very pleased that you are satisfied with the results so far. I trust that our people will continue to live up to the high standards that you expect." Davis-Smythe began walking toward his own ball again. "Are there any other questions that you have?"

"Not at this time. If all goes well, I should be able to give you the go-ahead instructions within the next forty-eight to seventy-two hours."

"Very good, sir."

Hu's cell phone vibrated in his pocket as they walked. "I'm afraid it is my office calling. If you will excuse me for a moment, gentlemen." He walked several yards away, then answered. "Yes?"

"It is done," Zheng Rong's calm voice replied.

"Excellent. We should contact our other parties. No doubt they are getting restless, as well."

"Yes, sir, however, I would not do so on an unsecured line. May I suggest that you do so when you are back in the office? I will get in touch with each of them and set up an appropriate call for each."

"That would be excellent, Ms. Zheng. Is everything else proceeding as we desire?"

"Yes. The men are preparing themselves right now. All we need is for the right pair of vessels to come along, and we will be ready to go. I have been reviewing the shipping schedules, and have identified several likely possibilities. I have also marked several vessels that will be suitable for the longer-range aspects of your plan. A complete report will be available for you upon your return."

"Very good. I will return later this afternoon." He disconnected and rejoined his foursome to head to their various shots. "Gentlemen, let us proceed. On the way, Mr. Davis-Smythe, perhaps you can enlighten me as to how you are enjoying your time in our city?" As he spoke, Hu spotted the other man's shot land on the green, less than five yards from the pin, where he had been consistently hitting all day.

Smiling at the challenge, Hu prepared himself for a demanding round of golf.

CHAPTER EIGHT

“Ladies and gentlemen, this is your captain speaking. I have just been informed by the tower that we are cleared for our final approach, and will be touching down in the next few minutes. We appreciate your patience during the delay, and hope that you have enjoyed your flight with us. Flight crew, please prepare for landing.”

John Trent relaxed in his business-class airline seat, sparing a pitying thought for the folks crammed back in coach after their fifteen-hour flight. Returning his seat to its upright position, he stowed his tray table then turned to the window, looking down on the hustle and bustle of Hong Kong, the southern jewel of China.

Skyscrapers dominated the landscape, reducing the still-thick forests surrounding the sprawling city to tiny green trees. The morning sun glittered on the water, its rays refracting into thousands of brilliant diamonds that lit the harbor, interspersed with dozens of ships that plied the waterways, from the classic, trendy tourist junks to the ponderous, massive cargo ships and tankers that sailed through the strait daily. Everywhere he looked, Trent saw a thriving city, even amid the oppressive overall global recession that had sapped the business center’s strength. Although the economic markets had receded from their lofty highs of a few years ago, in Hong Kong, it still looked as though business was quite good, at least on the surface.

Resting his head on the comfortable seatback of the Cathay Pacific jetliner, Trent let his mind drift to the last time he'd been here. He had wanted to see more of Asia besides Japan, and had traveled the large country for a year, during which he had soaked up much of the local culture and language as he could. He already spoke fluent Mandarin Chinese, but his journey had taught him the conversational aspects of the language that were so different from American Chinese. Trent suspected that that, along with his Asian appearance, were two of the reasons he'd been picked for this mission.

The jet banked one last time, turning to come back over Hong Kong Airport. The building itself was on a reclaimed island that had been made by combining two smaller pieces of land into one big one. The main structure itself was arranged almost like a stick man with his arms outstretched, his splayed legs being the aprons where the airplanes taxied in to disgorge their passengers. It was an attractive building, the long roof made of some kind of scalloped silvery-gray material that flowed up and down, inducing a pleasant sense of calm. The entire island was a mass of constant activity, with planes coming, going, being towed into position, and tiny figures scurrying everywhere to make sure they took off on time. Trent settled in for the landing, closing his eyes and going over the information from the thick file he'd spent most of the flight reviewing, getting up to speed on Southeast Asia, the pirate situation and the lay of both the land and water, as it were.

The jetliner touched down without incident, and twenty minutes later he was walking through the terminal to catch the airport express train to the mainland. The interior of the airport continued the harmonious architecture he had seen from the air, with the walls, ceiling and furnishings all colored that same silvery-gray, like a fog bank given tangible shape, then molded to create an calming oasis to prepare the tens of thousands of travelers for a peaceful journey, no matter whether they were coming or going. Indeed, looking around, everyone seemed in good spirits, with no loud voices or obnoxious behavior, just a crowd of people from all around the world moving to their destination. The hum of conversations around Trent—in several different languages—underscored his entry in this foreign land.

"Terrence!"

Trent spotted a tall man dressed in a brown sport coat and chinos with lean, foxlike features under short brown hair waving at him. He was holding a sign that read, in both traditional Chinese and English, Terrence Wu—the alias Trent was using.

I was supposed to meet my contact on the mainland, he thought, every sense on alert now. Trent quickened his pace, dodging a group of brightly dressed German tourists walking around with bemused expressions on their faces and tiny cameras in their hands. "Good to see you, David—"

"You, too, Terry." David McCarter grinned as he folded the placard in two and tucked it under his arm as he turned to face Trent. "Welcome to Hong Kong."

Unsmiling, Trent turned to head toward the luggage carousel. "What's with the change in plans?"

The commander of Phoenix Force, Stony Man's global threat response team, kept smiling. "You should have a message on your phone. We thought it would be best to meet you in the terminal and accompany you back on the train."

Trent checked the screen of his phone to find that there was a message waiting for him. He just hadn't seen the small flashing symbol or heard the gentle tone in all of the commotion around him. "Hmm, just a moment." He slipped on his earpiece and played the message.

"Hello, Mr. Wu, this is Daniel Gray from Asia-Global Shipping. I've spoken to my superior, and it was decided to have me meet you at the airport. I look forward to making your acquaintance this afternoon."

Trent nodded. "I'm just not thrilled with abrupt changes in the schedule, that's all."

"I know what you mean, however, our targets are on the move, and it may be necessary to insert you more quickly than we had thought. That is, if you're ready."

"No time like the present."

"Good to hear. Most people require a good night's rest before they're able to function well here."

"Fortunately, I adapt quickly." That, and Trent had caught a few hours' sleep on the flight over. Picking up his luggage, one medium-size suitcase, more than enough for him to live out of for several weeks if necessary, Trent looked for the sign to the train. "Let's go."

They walked through the terminal to the express train entrance. "Is there anything you can tell me on the way? Are we working with anyone else on the team?"

"No, right now it's just us." McCarter casually glanced left and right while appearing to look for the oncoming train. "As for the info, let's wait a bit. It's best to do this away from others."

"Fair enough." The sleek train arrived in front of them, the doors sliding open to let out a steady stream of travelers. McCarter motioned Trent to proceed, then followed, making sure they weren't being tailed.

"Don't worry, no one's taking any undue interest in us." Both men glanced over their shoulders at the platform one last time, just in case.

The interior of the car was modern and comfortable, with the baggage holders walled by Plexiglas so travelers could keep an eye on their luggage. McCarter directed Trent to their individual bucket seats.

"How long is the trip into the city?"

"It will take us about twenty-five minutes to reach the Central District, and from there it will be only a few minutes to your hotel."

True to McCarter's word, they arrived at the Central District Station exactly twenty-five minutes later, then took a small SUV to the Island Pacific Hotel. Trent checked in, and the two men headed up to his room. Once inside, McCarter swept the walls and furniture with a small device.

"Okay, we're clear. I can fill you in on what we know so far, then we should probably get you outfitted for your trip to the Philippines."

"Striker brought me up to speed before I left, so unless anything has occurred in the past fifteen hours or so, I should be good. The islands are where the target is currently?"

"Exactly. They are in the process of modifying their stolen yacht at a small harbor outside Manila where the authorities are happy to look the other way for the proper fee. We have surveillance on them there already, and have also been watching their employer's office here in Hong Kong. If necessary, we'll be investigating that avenue, but as far as you're concerned, you will be infiltrating the group to learn what their plan is and take whatever steps are necessary to make sure they don't succeed."

"Works for me. When do I leave?"

McCarter handed him an envelope. "Here is your Chinese passport and other identification papers, along with your cover identity. I don't have to tell you what leaves this room with you and what doesn't. You can head down as soon as you're ready. The faster you infiltrate their group and gain their confidence, the quicker we discover exactly what they're up to."

"Definitely." Trent filled a glass with sparkling water from the small refrigerator and took a long drink, feeling much better now that the mission had started in earnest. "On to the Philippines, then."

CHAPTER NINE

Xiang dangled over the side of the boat on a wooden seat attached to two ropes that stretched up to a winch on deck. A paint mask, modified with layers of duct tape to fit his small face, covered his mouth and nose, making the already humid air even thicker with every breath. One hand gripped the rope nearest to him to steady himself, the other held a paint sprayer.

"Lower…a bit more… Stop!"

His feet dangled only a few inches above the placid ocean water. Adjusting the mask again, Xiang sprayed the hull of the boat, coming as close to the water line as he could without painting into the water itself.

The money the demon woman had given them would have bought a more professional job, provided they could have found a dry dock that could handle such a large craft and wouldn't ask any questions. But Lee had decided to keep as much of the money as possible as personal profit, so they had improvised by finding a natural bay on the leeward side of the wind that could hold such a craft, then hanging several men over the side and painting the hull with electric sprayers. It would look terrible when they were through, but Lee had said it wouldn't matter. The disguise only had to last through the next couple of days.

Leaning back, Xiang swung closer to the curved

bow at the front, timing his swings with quick, accurate bursts of sky-blue paint from the gun. He was enjoying this. The sun was up, the water was calm, and no one had bothered him since he had started. Perhaps later he could even go for a swim, remembering to be always mindful of sharks.

With one final sway, he stretched out to finish off the last part of this section of bow, and was about to holler up for someone above to move him when he heard the chime of a cell phone on deck. Xiang froze when he heard who answered.

"Yes?" It was Lee Ming. "Yes, the boat is drying even as I speak… I don't even know why you care, it's not going to be around for much longer… Then there's nothing to worry about, it's been taken care of… In the next twenty-four hours…? Good, 'cause the men are getting restless… Of course I have enough people… They are, and they will do as I say, that's why… You want the job done, don't you…? Then listen to me when I say it will be… Good… Don't worry, you'll get everything you want…. All the destruction you can handle… You just be sure that the money is waiting for us once we deliver… All right, we'll be waiting for the go-ahead."

Xiang held his breath, not sure if Lee could hear him, but certainly not wanting to take the chance of being found there. He was certain that conversation wasn't meant for anyone to hear, especially not him.

"Xiang! Guong! Feng! Where are you?" Lee's voice carried over the rest of the yacht as his footsteps faded away. As soon as he judged it safe, Xiang pushed up his mask, gripped the cord of the paint gun in his teeth and shimmied up the rope. The moment his eyes cleared the bow railing, he looked for Lee, but didn't see him, or anyone else on the bow. Tossing the paint gun onto the deck, he scrambled after it, snatching it as he rose and trotted toward where he thought Lee had been going.

Rounding the corner of the yacht's main room, Xiang came upon him talking to Guong Ho and the third man, Feng Shen. "We'll need at least nine more men, ten preferably, and as many as possible should have some kind of ship skills—freighter, yacht, whatever you can find. It shouldn't be too hard getting the people we need here." Sensing someone behind him, Lee turned to Xiang. "Where the hell were you? I was shouting all over the boat!"

The boy waved at the front part of the boat, not too close to where he'd overheard the conversation. "I was painting."

Lee's hand shot out, smacking the boy's head hard enough to spin him halfway around, and making Guong smile. "Next time I call you, you'd better find me as fast as you can, or we'll see how quick you can run with a broken leg. These guys are going into town to find us some more hands. Go with them, and buy enough food to last twenty men two days." He gave Xiang a roll of bank notes. "That should do it. Take the launch and be back before dawn."

Xiang followed the two men to the back of the boat, where the twenty-three-foot tender had been taken off the aft deck and lowered to the water. He climbed down, careful to keep an eye on Guong as he did so. Once there, he went to the bow of the ship and curled up on the seat, wrapping his arms around his legs and watching Guong watch him as Feng started the engine and roared out of the cove.

"JOHN AND DAVID HAVE BOTH touched down at Manila's airport."

"Okay, keep me informed as things happen." Forty thousand feet over the Atlantic Ocean, Bolan sat in his passenger chair of the Gulfstream, prepping for the Morocco op. Although not personally handling the South China Sea mission, he'd wanted to keep track of Trent and McCarter as they set up their insertion. It wasn't a matter of trust—McCarter could handle himself in any situation around the world, bar none, and Trent was supremely capable in his own right. However, the fact was that John Trent was a civilian undertaking this infiltration as an ad hoc part of Stony Man at this time, and the Executioner wanted to make sure he was as comfortable as possible under the circumstances.

Right now, his computer screen showed a pair of dots, transmitting from the men's GPS locators in their cell phones, moving through a layout of the dilapidated, outdated Terminal One, a few miles south of the city itself.

"Target status?" Bolan asked.

"Long-range surveillance says two men and a boy left the ship about an hour ago to head into town. They're being followed at the moment, and John will make contact with them to ascertain the situation and insert. David will serve as backup and overwatch."

"So far, so good," Bolan stated.

"You need any assistance for the Morocco op?"

"Our flight path is clear to land at Marrakesh-Menara International Airport, and we'll arrive there in another seven hours. Once there, we'll receive the final coordinates for the bazaar and use Land Rovers to get there. Everything's one hundred percent, Akira, but thanks. Keep an eye on our boys, and I'll let you know if anything else comes up."

"You got it."

Bolan spent the next ten minutes making sure the proper cover story had been inserted into various websites and chat rooms around the world. For him to pull off this impersonation, there had to be a convincing jacket planted on him and his men—that of a ruthless and effective mercenary group that would do whatever a client wanted—as long as the price was right. While skimming an article in a soldier of fortune webzine out of Brussels, Belgium, he was interrupted by a call from Tokaido.

"Our boy's made contact with the surveillance team, and they're setting up a sting operation to draw one of the targets in. We'll know more in a few minutes, when another satellite comes over."

"Sure would be better to have real-time camera views." Bolan silently cursed the lack of available equipment in the Philippines capital. It was so much easier to run urban ops in, say, London, where the city was wired with cameras practically on every corner, allowing almost real-time viewing once they'd piggybacked onto the system. Unfortunately, many areas of the world lacked this convenience.

"Yeah, well, you get the Third World governments to invest that much in their citizens' safety, and I'll chug an entire pot of Bear's coffee. Looks like they're splitting up. I think Trent's going in now."

Leaning forward in his chair, Bolan watched the operation unfold from a very unusual vantage point—several thousand miles away. The dots were like watching a crude video game, only this one used real guns. Real bullets.

And the possibility of very real death.

CHAPTER TEN

As soon as the speed boat had pulled up to the dock, Guong and Feng had jumped out and walked off toward the nearest street to hail a taxi.

"Hey, what about the food?" Xiang had asked, knowing it would be very hazardous to try to procure the needed items by himself.

"Lee told you to get the supplies. You figure it out," Guong had replied over his shoulder. "We need to find more men. Get what you need and wait for us, we'll be back before sunrise." And with that, they'd jumped in a car and were gone, leaving a fuming Xiang behind.

Tying up the boat, he considered his situation. Lee Ming wouldn't accept failure under any circumstances, and Xiang couldn't blame the two men, as much as he wanted to, because that would cause them to lose face to their leader, and they'd take it out on Xiang later. The only option was to go forward and figure out a way to get the job done by himself.

Looking around to make sure no one was watching, he concealed the money in a hollowed-out space he had made in the heel of his right sandal long ago. Then he slipped into the bustling city streets, using every trick he knew of to stay out of sight of the police and other potential criminals. At this early evening hour, the streets were crowded with hundreds of people, from the girls outside the brothels trying to attract customers, to taxi drivers carrying slumming tourists or citizens around the less-attractive parts of the city.

After finding a store that could supply him with everything he needed—rice, dried noodles, jars of pickled vegetables, even fresh fish and other seafood—and haggling with the shopkeeper for twenty minutes, he'd purchased everything necessary for the next two days. Now there was only the problem of how to get the large quantity of food back to the boat, particularly with his very limited funds.

While he was pondering his dilemma, a brightly colored jeepney, one of the local public transportation vehicles on the island, rolled up to the corner, the driver stumbling out and grabbing at a young woman barely out of her teens who had been sitting in the passenger seat. Laughing and joking with her, the man turned off the vehicle and secured the wheel with a lock and chain wrapped around one of the canopy poles over the open driver's seat, then they staggered toward a nondescript, two-story building that was obviously a brothel.

The moment he saw them, the plan formed in Xiang mind, and he was on his feet, moving toward the couple. When he was a few yards away, he lurched forward, throwing up his hands to stop himself from falling over and colliding with the man hard enough to make him stagger.

"You clumsy bastard!" the drunken driver clouted him on the side of the head. Xiang saw it coming, but didn't want to keep the man on the street any longer than necessary, so he took the blow instead of dodging it, letting out a wail and running off. Behind him, he heard the man cursing, but the woman hung on his arm, distracting him from further pursuit. Moments later, they stumbled into the brothel.

Rubbing his head, Xiang opened his other hand, which contained the man's keys to his green-and-yellow striped vehicle. It's not like I'm stealing it, only borrowing it for a while, he thought. With furtive glances at the doorway, he shuttled the crates and sacks of food into the back of the jeepney. As soon as it was loaded, he hopped into the front seat, unlocked the steering wheel and drove off.

Or at least, he attempted to. Although Xiang knew how to drive, the large steering wheel and stiff manual transmission made controlling the large vehicle difficult. He was forced to lean on the horn more than once to warn passersby of his presence, particularly when the half jeep, half bus seemed to have a mind of its own, lurching from one side of the street to the other. Luck smiled on him, as he didn't hit a single car on his way to the dock, although he had more than one hair-raising near-miss.

At last he saw the long concrete berths of the dock in front of him, and pulled up to the speedboat with a sigh of relief. Watching up and down the docks for signs of anyone taking an interest in him, Xiang began unloading the supplies.

He was almost finished when a white car with blue lights mounted on its roof and familiar red-and-blue stripes along the side pulled up next to the jeepney. Xiang stiffened, then continued offloading, hoisting another sack over his shoulder and walking to the boat while going over his limited options. He couldn't run. They might impound the entire boat, and then he wouldn't just be in trouble, he'd be dead. His only real hope was to bribe them, perhaps, but he had also heard horror stories about the local police running kidnapping rings, with their favorite targets being Chinese kids, since they were often children of wealthy parents. If he was taken, however, Lee Ming would cut him loose without a second thought, and when the kidnappers learned he didn't even have parents, he would be of no use to them and he would end up just as dead.

Hopefully I can bluff them into leaving me alone, he thought, putting the sack of rice into a storage bin and turning back to the jeepney, which now had both officers walking around it, shining their flashlights into the back.

"Hello, may I help you, Officers?" Xiang asked.

One of the policemen turned to him, while the other continued his inspection of the vehicle. "Where's the driver of this vehicle?" he asked in Filipino.

Xiang had spent adequate time in the islands to pick up enough of the language to communicate, although it wasn't pretty. He pointed down the general direction of the docks. "He have business over there. He come back in thirty minute."

"That's a nice boat you got there. What's a kid like you doing out here all by yourself? Where's your parents?"

"My father and uncle go to city to—" the boy tried to find a polite way to say they went looking for prostitutes "—sample nightlife." Xiang tried to put what he thought was a knowing smile on his face. "They gone for few hours, but with you guys here, no worries."

The two officers exchanged glances, then the one asked, "Did they pay their docking fee?"

Xiang relaxed a bit, since the conversation seemed

to be taking a normal turn in the officer's request for a bribe. "I do not know. How much payment?"

"One hundred."

Xiang pulled out the bills he had left, and came up with eighty pesos. "I only have this much." He held out the small sheaf, which was snatched out of his hand.

The cop quickly counted the money, then looked at his partner again. Neither of them looked particularly happy. The second, silent partner reached into the back of the jeepney and took out a bottle. Xiang's heart sank as the officer held up the bottle of Gineva San Miguel gin that he was going to bring back as a special gift for Lee Ming, although it had cost almost twice as much as normal, due to his age. He cursed inwardly for not having unloaded it right away.

The first officer's face brightened when he saw the liquor. "This will do nicely in lieu of the rest of the payment. Besides, boys shouldn't have liquor in their possession. That's more than a fine, it could get you arrested."

Xiang grinned and nodded, not having any other choice.

"You say the driver's returning in a half hour?"

He nodded again, aware of the suddenly cool sweat on the back of his neck, even in the evening heat. If the officers decided to stick around, there might be real trouble when Guong and Cheng returned.

The first officer continued. "A half hour, eh? We'll be back, and if this vehicle isn't gone, we'll have a few more questions for you. Understand?"

"Yes, Officer. Thank you, Officer." Xiang resisted the urge to bow to them, and concentrated on getting the rest of the supplies unloaded as quickly as possible.

The pair of policemen got back in their car and headed down the pier.

Xiang secured everything in the storage lockers of the boat, filling them all to almost overflowing, and closing each one with an effort. Checking to see that the police car hadn't doubled back to watch him, he jumped into the driver's seat and fired up the jeepney again.

The drive back was easier, although it took longer, with the traffic having grown thicker in the past hour. Xiang stopped a block away from where he had "borrowed" the vehicle, wrestled it over to a corner, causing horns to blow and shouted curses from the vehicles around him, and locked it up again, even wrapping the chain around the pole just as he had found it.

Hiding the keys in one hand, he strolled down the busy sidewalk to the brothel where the cabdriver had been. The man was back out on the street now, cursing to anyone who would listen and waving his arms wildly in the air. Xiang's luck was holding. He either hadn't called the police yet, not wanting to have to explain why he wasn't on his usual route, or he had called and they hadn't arrived yet. Either way, he could return the keys and get out before anyone was the wiser.

He walked up to the driver, who was arguing with his lady about what had happened. After clearing his throat loudly twice, Xiang had to reach up and tug at the man's sleeve to get his attention.

The driver looked down at him with disdain. "What! What do you want, *gago?*"

Xiang let the insult pass; the man had inadvertently helped him, after all. "You look for jeepney?"

"Yes!" The man's emphatic affirmative made Xiang smile. "What do you know about it?"

"It one block that way." Xiang pointed down the street the way he had come, then tossed the keys at the man and took off in the opposite direction, ducking and weaving between people on the crowded street, while the man yelled for someone to stop him. Rounding a corner, he slowed to a fast trot, then cut across the lane at an opportune moment, darting between two cars and blending into the shadows as he moved farther away from the crime scene.

Twenty minutes later, Xiang was a few miles away from that street, and heading back to the dock at a brisk clip. As he approached, he noticed a familiar police car cruising the area, and he melted into the night until they had passed, ducking from the bright beam of their spotlight.

The dock appeared deserted, with only the slap of the waves against the concrete heard as Xiang came up on the boat again. Breathing a sigh of relief, he was about to jump into the boat, head below and grab some much-needed sleep, when a low whistle of admiration made him freeze with one foot on the runner and one still on the dock.

"That's a nice boat you got there."

Xiang heard the implied threat in the speaker's voice, and slowly turned to see four young men approaching, all of them having come out of nowhere, just like he had. They were all lean, with short haircuts, sleeveless T-shirts and baggy cargo pants or shorts. With a sinking heart, the boy realized what they were after—the boat itself.

CHAPTER ELEVEN

"Kid's got balls, that's for sure."

Secure in the second story of a building five hundred yards away from the dock, Trent had on a pair of headphones as he watched and listened to the kid's encounter with the police, admiring the way he kept his cool under their scrutiny. The long-range microphone brought him every word with crystal-clear detail.

"Yeah, he's a scrapper, all right." McCarter stood next to him, keeping an eye on the departing police car. "You still comfortable with the original plan?"

Trent didn't take his eyes from the field glasses. "Well, we didn't want the police involved, but he's already taken care of that. I still think our scenario at the dock would work best. I want to set up a bit closer to him first, observe him for a bit. Perhaps I can find a way in while he's in town. If not, we'll just go to plan B."

"All right, just stay in touch. This area of town is not known for genteel manners."

"I'll keep that in mind." Handing McCarter the binoculars, Trent left the building and got in their car, a five-year-old Hyundai. He'd pulled out just in time to see the kid hauling on the steering wheel as he drove the jeepney back into town.

Now where's he going? he wondered, tailing him at a discreet distance. It grew more difficult the deeper they went into the neighborhood, with the cramped streets and bumper-to-bumper traffic slowing their progress to a crawl. However, he was able to keep the large vehicle in sight amid the smaller cars and trucks. After a few miles, the kid shoved his way to the side of a road, in front of a cluster of ramshackle houses that were little more than simple huts with patched-together walls and corrugated tin roofs. The air was thick and heavy with car exhaust, cooking food and the mingled smells of the throngs of people on the streets.

Trent watched as the kid locked up the steering wheel, then got out and headed down the street. As jammed as the traffic was, it was easy to follow him to a gesticulating man who was protesting loudly near a local house of pleasure. Trent only caught one word in five, but from the guy's loud exclamations, it sounded like something had been stolen from him. The kid walked up, waited a bit, then tugged on his sleeve. Whatever he said got immediate attention, for the man replied instantly. The boy said something else, pointing back the way he had come, then tossed something shiny at him and took off down the block, weaving in and out of the crowd.

"Shit!" Leaning on his horn, Trent tried to follow as best he could, but lost him in the thick clusters of people on the side of the street. He turned right at the first intersection, where he thought the kid had gone, but saw no sign of him. He drove down the block as fast as he could, scanning both sides of the lane, but didn't spot the boy anywhere.

Trent hit his earpiece. "Lookout, this is Alpha, I followed the target into the city, where he ditched the vehicle, but lost him in the crowd. I'm returning to set up street-side near the boat."

"Affirmative. I told you he was a scrapper. Best watch your step around this one."

"Right. I'll report in once I'm in position. Alpha out."

Trent chuckled as he navigated the packed streets back to the harbor. Although he hadn't gotten a really good look at the kid yet, and even though he was a criminal for all intents and purposes—a criminal who had shot someone, according to the report he had read—he had still liked what he saw. The boy had enough scruples to return that guy's vehicle when he didn't have to, he thought. Out here, that says a lot about him.

He drove back to the quiet dock, the return trip taking longer than the drive out, found a convenient spot about one hundred yards away from where the boat was anchored and settled down to watch and wait. After only a few minutes the boy reappeared, walking down the concrete jetty toward the speedboat. He trudged along more slowly now, his shoulders slumping tiredly, and was about to board the boat when something caught his attention. Trent sat up a bit higher.

From out of the nearby shadows came four young men, dressed in casual clothes, with predatory smiles on their faces. They approached the boy in a loose semicircle, trapping him between the boat and themselves. Trent saw a momentary look of fear cross his face, then he squared himself to meet his assailants.

"Lookout, this is Alpha. Are you running plan B right now?"

"Negative, we're awaiting your go ahead. Is that uninvited company?"

"Damn it, I'm moving to intercept. Keep observing,

and be ready to reinforce if necessary. Alpha out." Trent popped his car door and got out, breaking into a run as soon as he was upright. Plan B had been to send McCarter to pose as a drunken man out for a good time. He'd see the kid alone, make fun of him, then be stopped by Trent, who would have happened to come along. However, this new group apparently hadn't gotten the memo on the plan, and was making its own move.

His feet slapping the pavement, Trent slipped through the shadows until he was only a few yards away. He heard raised voices, the lower sound of the young men's contrasting with the higher-pitch of the protesting boy. Trent peeked around the corner. The four men had boxed the kid in and were about to escalate their threats into physical intimidation. For his part, the kid wasn't giving an inch, even though he had to be scared for his life. Trent knew he would have been scared, too, at that age, even as a trained ninja.

Whistling a tuneless melody, he rounded the corner, heading straight for the confrontation as if he didn't even see them. His unorthodox move had the desired effect. All four men, along with the kid, stared at him in surprise. The ringleader immediately moved to stand next to the boy, his hand on the boy's neck, holding him in place.

Trent followed up with his temporary advantage. "Hey, guys, what's going on?"

The leader of the gang flashed a phony white smile. "Nothing to concern you, old man. We were just discussing a boat ride, isn't that right, little one?"

Trent saw the punk's fingers squeeze the boy's neck. The kid stared at him with wide eyes as he spoke. "I was just explaining to these men that I'm not available for hire this evening. They've been very persistent, however." He gasped as the man next to him tightened his hold, making him rise on his tiptoes.

"Well, it seems you all should be moving along, then. The boy just said he doesn't have time to take you sightseeing."

The three other young men slowly spread out to flank him, while their leader kept talking. "Like I said before, this doesn't concern you, old man. I'm sure we'll reach a price that will be right for him, so why don't *you* keep on walking?"

A worried voice whispered in Trent's earpiece. "Alpha, this is Lookout, we've got you in sight. Are you sure you don't need assistance?"

As if scratching his back, Trent reached behind himself and gave the signal for McCarter to remain on standby. He knew what the Brit's idea of assistance entailed—four shots from a suppressed HK G3 rifle. He adjusted his feet so they were shoulder width apart, his arms loose and relaxed, his hands and fingers ready to move on a moment's notice.

"I'm afraid that I can't do that. The kid doesn't want your business. He already told you that, so I'm gonna tell you one last time—move along."

The leader shook his head. "You must be as dumb as this kid—*urkk!*"

He was interrupted by the "dumb kid" planting an elbow straight into his crotch with all the force he could muster. Even as the ringleader folded, his hands clutching his groin, he managed to choke out, "Get him!" right before the boy whipped a bare foot into his nose, the crack of breaking bone plainly audible.

Two of the thugs moved toward Trent; the other one

went for the kid. A knife appeared in the first guy's hand as he lunged forward, leading with the blade in an attempt to stab his opponent. Instead of dodging, Trent met his charge, blocking the knife thrust to one side with his left wrist while placing his free right hand over the other man's knife hand and lifting up with his blocking arm, trapping the man. Startled, his attacker pulled away, but as he did so, even though he tried to keep his grip on the blade, he left his weapon in Trent's hands. Not hesitating, the operative stabbed the guy in the kidney as he passed by, making him stagger and cry out in pain. That would keep him out of the fight while Trent handled the second punk, who wielded a bicycle chain, and approached more cautiously.

Trent stayed on the balls of his feet, his arms out, hands open. He didn't want to prolong this contest any more than necessary, especially since the kid had been trapped by both of the other men. Instead of waiting for the man's attack, the *ninjitsu* master stepped inside his radius, and drove the butt of the knife into the base of the man's nose. The blow didn't drive shards of bone into the man's brain, as was commonly depicted in movies, but it did break his nose. It caused an instinctive recoiling at the intense pain, the man's eyes watering profusely as he staggered back, his weapon forgotten for a moment. Trent grabbed his hand and bent it back in a painful wristlock, making him drop the chain, all pretense of fight forgotten.

"Get away while you still can." He shoved him to the ground and scooped up the chain. The guy he had stabbed had fallen to the ground a few yards away, whimpering softly as he clutched at the spreading dark stain on his bright shirt.

Trent turned to the other two, who were both on the boy, the fourth man holding the boy's arms tightly behind him, rendering him helpless, although his feet kicked weakly at his captor. The leader had regained his composure, although he was moving a bit more gingerly, and hunched over with each step. He took out his frustration on the kid, socking him with short, sharp punches to the head and stomach. The boy took the abuse in silence, vomiting a glob of bile as the blows rocked him back and forth.

Trent's stomach knotted with fury, but he pushed it aside and concentrated on staying in control as he tossed the chain away and approached the three. The leader had just delivered another blow to the boy when he spotted Trent coming up like a silent wraith behind his partner. He opened his mouth to warn him, but it was too late.

Before either of them could react, Trent slipped an arm around the other Filipino and thrust the knife into his back, angling the blade up to penetrate the ribs and find his heart. The man convulsed once, then relaxed his grip as death overcame him. Released, the kid sagged to the ground, his face a bleeding mess.

"Who the fuck are you? What do you want?" The leader backed away, his strength having left him with the defeat of his henchmen.

Trent sprang forward and grabbed the man's wrist. "I want you—" he broke the man's pinky finger, eliciting a yowl of agony "—to stop beating up children." Trent bent a second and a third finger at impossible angles, feeling them crack in his grip. He let the cowering man drop to the ground, clutching his hand. "If I find out you're still assaulting people, I'll come back and break the rest. Now get the fuck out of here, and take your punks with you."

The would-be criminal staggered to his feet and scrambled to his bleeding buddy, who was now looking ashen and pale. Together with the third man, he grabbed his wounded comrade and the trio lurched off into the night.

Trent ran to the boy, who was curled on the ground, unconscious. He hit his earpiece. "Lookout, this is Alpha, I've got a bit of a mess here."

"Acknowledged, clean-up is on the way. Do you need assistance with the target?"

"Bring a kit, I want to treat him for shock and give him an antibiotic. I'll be on the boat." Scooping the boy up in his arms, Trent took him aboard, setting him down on the padded bench. Turning on the cockpit light, he searched for a first-aid kit, finding it under the driver's console. He opened it and shook out the emergency survival blanket, wrapping it around the boy, knowing its heat-trapping properties would help retain his body heat, even in the humid night.

A nondescript panel truck pulled up to the dockside, and McCarter jumped out, whistling at the crumpled form on the quay. "Well, that's one way to stop him."

"They might have killed the boy if I hadn't. Get this cleaned up quickly. Those cops might be back any minute."

"Right." The Brit shook out a thick, black plastic body bag, rolled the body into it, then zipped it shut and hoisted it over his shoulder, lugging the deadweight to the van and throwing it inside. "Here." He tossed the kit to Trent, who took out a small hypo and selected a strong antibiotic, filling the syringe, tapping it to make sure it was free of air bubbles, then injected the boy in the arm. He moaned softly at the sting, but didn't awaken.

Meanwhile, McCarter sprayed the area with a chemical that would break down the blood left by the fight into an unrecognizable, quick-drying stain that would set in a few minutes. He came over long enough to spray Trent's hands and clothes, as well, to ensure no evidence of the fight was left on him, either.

"Sorry, kid, but you gotta be my alibi, otherwise I won't get aboard." Trent selected a fast-acting stimulant, broke the single-use needle open and injected the drug into the boy's bloodstream. He waved McCarter off. "If you're done, get out of here. I'll be in touch."

The lean Brit nodded. "Watch your back." He got in the van and drove off, disappearing into the night. Seconds later, the same police car appeared, cruising slowly along the pier. When it saw the light on in the boat, it pulled up and stopped, the two officers getting out and shining their lights on Trent.

"What's going on here?" The first officer's light alternated between the boy's swollen face and Trent's. "What happened to him?"

"I left my son here to watch the boat and get supplies while I ran into town. When I came back, there were a couple of toughs harassing him. I drove them off, but he was hurt in the scuffle. I'll take care of him."

"You sure? He looks pretty badly hurt." The officers moved closer. "Where did those attackers you say hurt your boy go?"

Trent frowned at the question and waved at the long pier. "I don't really know. I was more concerned about him." He turned back to the boy, dabbing antiseptic on the cuts on his face.

"Uh-huh. Let me see your hands." In spite of his calmly voiced request, Trent noticed that his free hand was close to the butt of his holstered pistol.

Trent stopped his ministrations and held out both hands, backs out, revealing no skinned or bruised knuckles. "Satisfied?"

A gasp from behind him made all of them start. Trent turned back to the boy, who had come awake with a shudder, grabbing the blanket and pulling it around himself.

Trent went back and sat next to him. "Son, how are you feeling?"

"They tried…they tried to steal the boat, Papa."

"I know, son, but we stopped them, and you were very brave."

"Papa, I hurt…my face hurts, and my stomach, too."

"You just rest for a bit, and I'll make sure you're taken care of."

"Okay…" The boy's voice slurred suddenly. The stimulant was temporary, and its effects were already wearing off. Trent turned to the officers. "Gentlemen, I think the best thing will be to get him back to my yacht, where my crew doctor can take a look at him. If there's nothing else?"

McCarter's voice sounded in his ear again. "Alpha, you have a group of men approaching the boat from the northeast. They're hanging back because of the police car."

The cops still took a little more convincing. "He's breathing all right. Okay, sir, but you make sure he gets proper attention."

"Of course I will. Good night, Officers, and thank you."

The two policemen moved off slowly, casting wary looks back at him, but they eventually got in their car and drove off. Trent turned back to the boy, whose head was lolling on the back of the seat. "You're gonna be okay, I promise. Just another minute or two more."

Turning away again, he tapped his earpiece. "Lookout, where's that group of yours?"

"They're still hanging back. Probably making sure the police have really left. Just stay there. I'm sure they'll be on you soon enough."

"Right. I'm going to discomm now, so keep an eye out in case I get in over my head."

"It'll be like I'm looking right over your shoulder."

Trent knew McCarter was correct. Standard observation protocol meant that he was backed up by long-range firepower. If the shit did hit the fan, all he'd have to do was hit the ground and activate his earpiece, and when he stood back up, he'd be surrounded by dead bodies. Not the best way to infiltrate the group, Trent thought: Hi, how are you, I'd like to join up— Oh, and here are the bodies of your friends I met along the way.

He heard the clump of approaching footsteps and leaned against the far side of the craft, just in case he had to make a quick water exit.

"What the— What the hell happened here? Who the fuck are you?" Trent's interrogator fired questions at him in rapid Cantonese. The nine others clustered around him radiated their own unspoken message of immediate, barely restrained menace. The ringleader, a thick Chinese man with broad shoulders and corded muscles, jumped to the deck, making the entire boat shake. "I asked you a question, goddammit."

"Hey, I was just minding my own business, when I saw these guys roughing up the kid. I think they were about to steal your boat. I jumped in and drove them off, then decided to stick around until someone came back. He got smacked around pretty good."

The leader looked at the kid as if noticing him there for the first time. Reaching out with a thick-fingered hand, he grabbed the boy's chin and turned his head, letting light from the cockpit illuminate his cut and bruised face. He muttered something that Trent thought sounded like, "Lucky I didn't do this. It'd be much worse," then shook him roughly, making the boy moan in pain.

"Hey, lay off—" Trent's protest was silenced by the man holding his other hand up.

"You're two seconds from feeding the harbor fish, so shut the fuck up. Xiang, wake up!"

"Wha—what? Ow!"

"What happened here? Answer me!" The big Chinese man shook the boy harder. Trent clenched his hands into fists at his side, but didn't make a move, all too aware the rest of his thugs would enjoy beating him into hamburger at the slightest provocation. They looked like a stereotypical group of pirates—hard, tough men—only here there was some internal rivalry, many of them eyeballing the rest, which meant this crew hadn't been together very long. Trent filed that fact away for future reference.

"Just like he said. Four guys tried to rob me. Gonna steal the boat. He stopped them. Think he killed one—"

"No shit." The surly man eyed Trent with a glimmer of new respect. "That true?"

Trent schooled his features to remain calm. He'd been trying to keep that out of the discussion, but suddenly saw how he could use it to his advantage. "I might have—it all happened pretty fast. Stabbed one guy in the back. He was bleeding pretty badly. Might be dead by now. All I know is that he won't be bothering you either way."

The men on the pier nodded and whispered to one another. The leader jerked his thumb toward the dock. "All right, get the hell out of here."

"Wait!" the kid protested through bruised lips. "Take him with us. He could be useful...."

"Is that so?" The hardcase looked Trent up and down, taking in his shapeless pants and shirt and comfortable, battered sneakers. "What's your name?"

"Liang Dai."

"What are you doing in the Philippines?"

"Besides not stealing your boat, you mean?" The jibe brought a smattering of laughter from the group of men, and even the big guy cracked a brief smile. "Whatever needs doing—if the price is right."

"If the kid's telling the truth, he can certainly handle himself," one of the men from the group said, swaying a bit as he spoke, as if he'd had too much to drink. "Besides, we still need another guy—"

The leader turned and glared at the speaker, freezing his mouth in midsentence. "You should excuse my friend. He has a tendency to talk when he shouldn't. However, that's a good point. Where you from?"

"Furthest back I know was Shanghai, from there, just about anywhere from New Zealand to Japan, and anywhere in between."

"Do you have experience with ships?"

Trent figured yes was the right answer; it was just a question of how big to go. “I hitched a ride here on a freighter from Australia, must have been 150 meters easy. I know my way around.”

The big man nodded, and Trent knew he’d answered correctly. “All right, you come along with us, and we’ll see. Everyone get aboard, we’re out of here. You got anything ashore you need to get before we go?”

Trent shook his head. “I travel light.”

“Good to hear. Assuming the boss likes you, your luck might have just changed for the better.” The big man moved to the helm as the rest crowded aboard, with the last man casting off. “Then again, if you fuck up, it’ll get a lot worse.”

The inboard engines moved the boat into deeper water, and as soon as he could, the leader shoved the throttle forward, making the bow of the boat leap up as they headed out to deep water.

For his part, Trent leaned back on the bench seat and tried to look nonchalant, but his gaze kept returning to the battered boy, wondering how a kid had got himself into this kind of situation.

CHAPTER TWELVE

Hu Ji Han ran trembling fingers through his gray hair, feeling the cooling sweat on his scalp. He had seen and survived much during his lifetime, had done much to thrive and build his empire up from nothing. He had wrestled with labor, supply, expansion pains and the continual cyclical up and downs of the construction market. He had experienced fear, greed, anger, ennui, panic and glee many times throughout the decades, but this latest emotion that coiled in his belly and stayed there, writhing like a pit of snakes, was one that he had never felt before.

Anxiety.

It was almost as if he could feel the spirit of his grandmother standing nearby, watching…waiting for the plan to be set into motion.

Standing, he stretched his aching back, feeling the knots in his muscles and spine send stabbing pain throughout his neck and shoulders. A long steam and massage was in order, but there was one more item of business he had to take care of first. Hu touched the intercom button on his phone. "Zheng, please come to my office with a clean phone."

He gazed out at the skyline around him, steeling himself for the task he was about to set into motion. For days, a part of him had warred with the implacable spirit of his grandmother, still relentlessly pushing him forward, instilling in him this desire to carry out the revenge she was unable to do in her lifetime. From when he was a small child, she had whispered in his ear.

They must not be allowed to get away with it, Han....

Our own government stood by and did nothing....

Their apologies mean nothing, they are simply mouthing empty words, false feelings....

Only when they and the others have suffered as we have suffered....

Only then will they all know the true pain of what they have inflicted on us....

As he grew older, Hu had learned more about his grandmother's obsession, and he had come to agree with her, having really very little choice in the matter. There was only one time when he even attempted to discuss the issue from a different point of view, after he had graduated from college, and was about to embark on his first business venture. The vehemence in her voice had matched the blazing fury in her eyes as she had slapped him across the face.

"Do not ever think that what the callow Americans did to end the war in any way repays the sacrifices our country made during those bloody years! The deaths in Hiroshima and Nagasaki pale in comparison to the bloody torture I witnessed, to say nothing of the indignities and barbarism forced upon me and my fellow countrymen and women!"

Hu had never tried to dissent from her view again. It didn't matter, anyway. The Japanese government had brought shame on his family, and the Chinese government, along with the rest of the world, had compounded it by allowing the rape of the city of Nanking to go on for months, back in 1937.

World War II had allowed the atrocities inflicted on the civilian population, left after the Chinese army had fled, to be hidden for years. When the war was over, books and films had at last brought the cruelty to light—the impaling of infants on bayonets, the mass rapes, the wholesale slaughter of men, women and children by cruel, rampaging, bloodthirsty Japanese soldiers.

Scholars and military historians had debated the charges, and of course the Japanese government had denied that anything even remotely close to the described events had happened. Hu's grandmother never gave the debate a second of credit. "Of course they wish to disprove what they think may or may not have happened all those years ago—but they weren't there."

She, however, had been. She had seen it with her own eyes, experienced the degradation and brutality with her own body, and had never forgotten what had happened there, and who was responsible for it. She had survived after seeing her husband killed, seeing two of her three daughters slaughtered for sport by a Japanese infantry patrol pillaging in her neighborhood. She had been raped repeatedly, then left for dead, escaping with her life by assuming the pose of the lifeless, later crawling out of a pit of dead bodies, naked and bleeding.

She had told the story to Hu countless times, until he could almost recite it from memory. "From that very moment, I was reborn. I knew I had been granted my life to visit the vengeance of everyone who fell before those bayonets, to silence the endless screams of the women and children who were defiled by the invaders, to quench the hundreds of thousands of souls who still cry out for retribution. I hear them every day, and it is my mission to answer their pleas. Since I cannot do this thing myself, it will be up to you, Han, to carry out this most sacred task for me. I am counting on you.

"You must punish the two nations, the Japanese for the atrocities they committed against us, and the Chinese for doing nothing while it happened. Also, you will inflict punishment on the Americans and the British for standing idly by while the heinous crimes continued. Only then will the souls of the dead find the peace they deserve."

With the sudden death of his father and mother—his grandmother's third daughter—in a car accident when Hu was six years old, she was the only family he knew. So he nodded solemnly, and listened while she poured out the hate and bile she had kept deep inside for years, absorbing it all, until he was thoroughly indoctrinated into her point of view.

And all this time, her presence hovered over him, just out of view, like a restless spirit doomed to exist on this plane until he fulfilled the destiny she had set him on. And now, all these years later, the time had come for him to complete the circle, with the added benefit of enriching his own company at the same time. For Hu was nothing if not thrifty, and if he could reap additional benefits from the whirlwind he was about to visit upon both lands, then why shouldn't he?

At last, it was time to set the final stages of the plan into motion. In one fell swoop, he would avenge his grandmother, along with the hundreds of thousands that died at Nanking, and become even richer and more powerful in the process. Everyone would win. Well, except for the governments of China, Japan, America and Great Britain. But they have all brought this disaster upon themselves, and it is only just that they should reap what they have sown, he thought.

Walking back to his desk, his eyes fell on the picture of his wife, smiling at him. He trailed a finger over her face, imagining the softness of her cheek, the warmth of her gaze. He had met her early during his career, when she had applied to be a secretary at his firm. Her keen business acumen had caught his attention, followed by a most unexpected emotion, that of falling in love. Pei had been with him for the past three decades, helping guide and grow the company to its present state. She had also been the last barrier to his enacting this plan, for if it had failed, and he had been caught, he wouldn't have wanted her to suffer in the court of public judgment. But with her death last year from ovarian cancer, now there was nothing holding him back.

"Forgive me, dear wife, for what I am about to do." Gently, he took her picture and laid it facedown on the desk.

The elevator doors slid open, and Zheng walked in, resplendent in a traditional crimson silk dress, slit up both sides to her knees. She carried a small leather briefcase. Sitting in a chair on the other side of the desk, she set the case on her knees, opened it and produced a small cell phone with a black box attached to it. She switched it on and handed it to Hu. "It is ready."

He took a deep breath, letting the tension flow out of him with his exhalation. As nerve-racking as the previous call had been, the next two would be even more so. He checked to make sure the black box was working as it should be, then pressed the number one on the pad, which dialed a prearranged number.

It rang four times before being answered. “Yes?”

“We are almost ready. Is everything prepared on your end?” Hu tried not to think about the person on the other end hearing his words as though spoken by a woman, for that was the purpose of the box on the phone, to ensure that his voice would be disguised so well that no one would be able to tell who was speaking on the other end.

“Yes, the proper statements have been prepared. Once it is done, they will be sent to the appropriate places. All we need now is the key event to release them.”

“In the next twenty-four hours, you will have it. We will be in touch once it is done.”

“We look forward to hearing from you.”

Hu disconnected the phone, then pressed the number two button, calling another arranged number.

“Hai?”

“Speak Cantonese, if you must.”

“It is time, then?”

“Yes, it is time. You will have all you desire within twenty-four hours. Look to the news, and you will know when to release your statement.”

“Very good. Thank you.”

Hu didn’t answer, but turned the phone off instead, removed the black box and closed it, making sure the device was completely powered down. He held it out to Zheng. “You know what to do.”

She nodded, taking it and the voice modulator from

him, wiping it down and placing it in the briefcase. She would take it to a construction site to destroy it with acid, to ensure no one would ever be able to connect the phone with those calls. Zheng had also rerouted the call through several cell towers to further confuse anyone trying to trace the call.

"Will there be anything else, sir?"

Hu leaned back in his chair, mopping his forehead with a silk handkerchief. "You will need to make the final call to our friends in the south, then I think that will be all for the day, Zheng. Please make sure that the masseuse is on standby. I will have need of her services a bit later. Now I just wish to be alone."

"Of course, sir. Good night."

Hu wished her a pleasant evening, as well, dimmed the overhead lights and sat in the dimness, pondering the inexorable chain of events that had been set in motion. It had taken all of his skill, and a not inconsiderable amount of his capital, to make contact with the people who were going to provide the cover for the destruction he was about to visit upon four countries.

The representative from the splinter Uighur separatist movement in the western part of China had initially been very wary about even talking to the mysterious woman who claimed to be able to provide them with an event that would guarantee their cause would be on the lips of every nation in the world once it happened. Long overshadowed by the more media-friendly Tibetan struggle for freedom, Hu knew the Uighur group was torn between its sincere desire to get its cause out into the mainstream media and its suspicion that their organization was being set up by the Chinese government and lured to their own destruction.

He couldn't very well have a face-to-face meeting with the leaders, for the good of both sides. Instead, he had used the only leverage he had—money. Several hundred thousand yuan, all in cash, and three small shipments of arms later, he had established an uneasy alliance with them; all had been done very carefully and was completely untraceable to him. Now they were his cover, and would take credit for two of the incidents he had set in motion, one against Hong Kong and the second against Shanghai. In any event, the association only had to last for another day at most. They would get what they wanted, and Hu would get what he desired, both publicly and privately.

Regarding the second call, the splinter group of Aum Shinrikyo, the Buddhist group that had attacked the subways with sarin gas in 1995, had been much more receptive to his overtures, despite his not being a member of their cult. The organization had declined in numbers since the group had first re-formed itself into the group calling itself Aleph, then fractured further over goals and organization. It had taken absurdly little effort to convince them that he was an exiled member of the group living abroad since the tragedy in 1995. Not the gas attacks themselves, which, as Hu stated, were necessary to begin the overthrow of the repressive government and install the rightful ruler of the nation to the throne, but the fact that their leader, Shinyo Asahara, had been caught and executed.

The hardcore cult members had come over to his side with almost laughable ease, agreeing to take responsibility for the disaster that was coming their way. They thought the failure of the government to stop what was about to happen would cause the people to rise up in revolution, and they would somehow be able to step in, take control and install their own leader on the throne.

Hu didn't care what they planned to do; he was only concerned with making sure that he had a cover for the attack on Tokyo Harbor. Again, everything had been done through several layers of cover. Hu was positive there was absolutely nothing to link him with this group. The Japanese government, however, will be on their own, he mused. Throughout his company's history, they were the only nation he had never done business with, even when the earthquake had rocked their country in 2011.

But as soon as what he had put into play happened, the Chinese government, needing to ensure that Hong Kong remained a bastion of banking and commerce, would rush into the city with aid and money.

As for the others, Force Forward was all too happy to provide men to take over loaded freighters on their way to the harbors of New York and London and carry out his plan, striking at all five major capital cities.

And as for the others, well, the U.S. and Great Britain had funds enough to handle what was coming their way. And if they didn't, then they, too, would learn the hard way about trying to care for their people without the proper supplies.

And my company will be first on the scene to provide assistance and rebuilding material and personnel to aid in these terrible tragedies, he thought. Who would possibly suspect the leader of such a humanitarian company could be behind such an event? He was covered from every conceivable direction he could think of.

Soon, an age-old grievance will finally be laid to rest, he thought, a smile creasing his aged face as he visualized his beloved grandmother's spirit finally finding the rest she deserved.

Soon, Grandmother, he thought, *soon enough your most fervent wish will be a reality....*

CHAPTER THIRTEEN

Trent kept his face expressionless, but couldn't help stealing glances at the boy huddled in the seat of the powerboat as it raced across the ocean.

Every slap of the hull on the water must be like another shot to the ribs, he thought. But he couldn't really do anything about it, especially given his position as one of the new men. He noticed the stocky pirate at the helm also glancing at the boy every so often, a strange expression on his face, halfway between anger and possessiveness. I'd better keep an eye on him, Trent noted, careful not to lock gazes with the other man.

So far he'd stayed apart from the others; not out of aloofness, but because he knew he wasn't an accepted member of the group yet. For all he knew, the rest of these men knew one another from previous crimes they had committed. He'd taken the first step toward proving himself, but much like a pack of wolves, he was on probation for now, and they wouldn't hesitate to destroy him at the first sign of weakness. The good news was that his story about the would-be hijackers, bolstered by the boy's muzzy agreement, seemed to have served as his entry into the group. Now it would just be a matter of surviving long enough to find out what the hell they were up to, and do what he could to stop it.

A cluster of distant lights against the moonless night

revealed itself to be a long luxury yacht. The stocky man throttled the speedboat's engines down as they approached, bringing the craft around to the rear of the large pleasure boat.

Trent whistled. "You guys certainly know how to travel in style."

The drunken man who had spoke up before looked at him with a bleary grin. "This is traveling incog… incog…undercover, so no one knows who we are."

Trent just nodded, not sure what to make of the guy. Out of the corner of his eye, he saw the stocky Chinese man try to scoop up the boy in his arms, but the kid wriggled free and stood up, unsteadily, but under his own power.

"I'm fine…." He stumbled to the boarding deck, almost slipping off when the speedboat rolled away from the yacht, but catching himself just in time. The stocky man glared after him, his expression like that of a cat who had just lost the canary he'd been stalking, but knew where it was going, and would find it later for sure.

Yeah, definitely gonna have to keep an eye on this guy, Trent thought. Although he knew he probably shouldn't take any actions that might jeopardize his mission, he also knew something was wrong with the man's unusual interest, and he sure as hell wasn't going to let a kid get abused on his watch if he could help it.

The heavyset man motioned for Trent to grab a box of food before he boarded, and he did so, stepping onto the ship amid the rest of the new crew. The other men were meeting those already there, some politely, some with back slaps and shouts of greeting as men recognized each other. Trent stood off to one side, keeping his mouth shut and his eyes open, waiting for the real meeting to begin.

After several minutes, a slender Chinese man with whipcord muscles stood on a chair and gestured for silence. It took a while, until the stocky one bellowed for quiet, his bull roar silencing the noisy men as quickly as if he had clapped a hand over each one's mouth.

"Thank you, Guong. Men, I welcome all of you aboard the *Patriot's Pride.* Some of you I know from previous jobs, some of you are new to me. But all of you know that when Lee Ming has a job, there is guaranteed profit for everyone!"

His voice was drowned out by the raucous cheering of the group of men around him. After a few seconds, Lee held up his hands again. "And this one is no different. In fact, this one could be the big one, the one that will let each of you get out of this life once and for all."

"But why would we want to do that?" a voice from the back shouted to general laughter.

Even Lee smiled at the jest. "Well, Chi, you can do whatever you want with your share, but I expect you'll probably blow it all on gambling and whores in Singapore!"

Another round of cheers greeted this suggestion. Lee held up his hands again. "However, this job carries both high reward and high risk. All of you know that our so-called occupation is getting more difficult lately, with the authorities coming down harder on us, and sending poor, working men like you and I to prison—or to death."

The crowd rumbled angrily. Trent had to give the guy his due; he was an excellent orator, holding the motley men in the palm of his hand, letting them blow off steam by cheering their coming profit or focusing their anger on society, then reeling them back in again.

"But after this job, like I said, you will have enough money to take off, head to Australia, Mexico, wherever you like. Oh, and I almost forgot. Each of you will be getting a *full* share of the profits directly, not one to divide among the crew."

This time the cheering and stamping of feet was almost deafening. Lee gave them a few seconds, and this time the pirates quieted without him even having to lift a finger. "However, this will be the most dangerous job we've ever done. We'll be hijacking two fully loaded cargo ships, and sailing each to a special destination. Once the ship has reached its final berth, we'll be paid for our efforts, and then all go our separate ways—only much, much richer than when we met tonight!"

Another round of cheers. "In fact, I've just received the call letting me know that the operation is under way. Our target is a ways away, so tonight you can relax and enjoy yourselves, but come morning, we'll begin preparations to carry out the biggest heist the South China Sea has ever seen!"

Lee Ming stepped down amid the jubilant crew, many of whom were uncorking bottles of wine and champagne as the gathering quickly devolved into an impromptu party. Lee's attention was caught by the stocky Chinese man he had called Guong, who took him to the side and spoke to him, pointing at Trent at the end of it. Lee nodded, patted him on the shoulder and headed his way.

Trent straightened, not sure if he was about to be congratulated or killed. He accepted a cup of what appeared to be champagne from one of the revelers, sipping it appreciatively as he waited.

Up close, Lee Ming appeared every bit as formidable as he had when he was molding the pirates together with his promises of modern-day treasure. His features were handsome enough, consisting of dark brown, almond-shaped eyes under a short, broad forehead, with long hair tied back at his nape. High cheekbones accented the Asian cast of his face, with a small mouth and pointed chin, made more so by his mustache and V-shaped goatee.

"Guong Ho tells me we have you to thank for saving our boat and provisions."

Trent eyebrow lifted in surprise. He hadn't expected the broad thug to actually tell the truth. "Your guard looked like he was in trouble. I simply stepped in to help."

"Very kind of you." The man's features were inscrutable.

"Well, I was hoping for more of an opportunity to come of it, and by the looks of it, I guessed right."

The leader stroked his chin. "And what if this had been a boat run by a rich person from the West?"

"If they'd taken me on board, I would have worked here until I'd gotten the layout of the place, then robbed them blind and left at the next port."

The leader chuckled. "Xiang made the right call when he said bring you on. My name is Lee Ming." He held out his hand.

Trent took it, pumping twice. "Liang Dai."

"A pleasure. Guong also tells me you have some experience on larger ships."

"A berth on a freighter is a good way to see the world."

"A sailor and a philosopher, eh? Well, Confucius, as you heard, we're about to take over two very large ships. What do you say to that?"

Trent smiled at last. "I say, when do we start?"

XIANG STAGGERED DOWN the narrow passageway, all of his flagging energy focused on reaching his room, getting inside and locking the door before someone else beat him to it and threw him out.

He ached all over; from his foot where he'd planted it in the crotch of that slippery bastard who'd tried to steal the boat; to his arms, which had been wrenched behind his back when the second man had grabbed him; to his stomach, ribs and face, which had taken the worst of the beating before his rescuer had done whatever he'd done to the man, who had immediately let go of him.

As he'd fallen to the ground, Xiang had watched through puffy eyes as the man had caught his abuser, and done something to him that had caused extreme pain, judging by his victim's shrill yelps. Xiang didn't remember much after that. He thought he had seen a van drive up and park by the boat, and the man talk to someone else, but that memory was elusive, and he wasn't sure he hadn't simply dreamed that part in the first place.

Then, suddenly, he had been awake—strangely awake, as if he'd just taken a hit of speed—in time to see Guong and the others come back. He'd remained lucid enough to recommend they take the guy on. Anyone who could go four-against-one and win had to be good at just about anything else he did, too. The one thing Xiang did remember was when the man had picked him up off the ground and carried him aboard the boat. For those few, all-too-brief seconds, he had felt safe, protected. Then Guong had come aboard, and the feeling had disappeared as swiftly as it had come.

Xiang knew better than to trust that feeling, however. This guy probably was no better than the rest; just more skilled at killing people. He'd probably extract his own price for saving Xiang before too long, for that was always the way of this life; something was never given for nothing.

With the last of his strength, he reached the door to his small stateroom, leaning his aching head against the cool wood. Fumbling at the latch, he finally got the door open, almost falling through it. Staggering in, he shoved the door shut and made it to the bed just as his exhausted legs gave out underneath him.

Semiconscious, he lay on the cool sheets for a long time, the dim sounds of some kind of cheering celebration on the aft deck drifting to his ears. Only when a heavy fist pounded on his door did he jerk awake with a start.

"Xiang? You in there?" The question was followed by the sound of metal scraping and clicking near the doorknob.

Guong! And he was breaking into his room! Xiang thrashed around on the bed, trying to get his legs to work. He got to his feet and headed for the one place he could hope to hide—the tiny bathroom. Once inside, he pressed himself into the niche shower stall, his back against the wall. Breathing shallowly, he twitched the curtain out just enough to hide his body, hoping the brutish pirate would just give the bathroom a cursory glance.

The bedroom door popped open, and Xiang saw light

appear, then disappear as Guong closed the door. The boy held his breath, straining to hear as the predator moved into the bedroom. He heard the rustle of the sheets, then a heavy footstep coming toward the bathroom. Xiang tried his hardest to become part of the cool tiles at his back. He heard the partition door slide into the wall behind him, and felt Guong's presence enter the room, a heavy, dark cloud of negative *chi* filling every corner of the small space.

Xiang knew he was too worn out to fend him off this time, but a part of him still wasn't willing to give up without a fight. If he wants me this badly, he's gonna have to pay for it, he thought wearily, balling up his fists.

The door to the bedroom opened, startling both of them. Xiang had the presence of mind to freeze right where he was as Guong stalked back to the doorway. "What do you want?"

"Oh, I was just looking for that kid." Xiang heard the new man's voice. "He'd been beaten pretty bad. I helped out the doctor on my last berth, so I thought I'd take a look at him."

"He don't need any help from you. He'll be just fine."

"Ah, good to hear it. Also, your captain was looking for you. Said he wanted to go over the assault plan."

The man was interrupted by a thump that made the whole room shake, followed by Guong's low growl. "He is *not* my captain. I work with him, understand?"

The new guy's voice sounded strained, as if he had to labor to suck in enough air to reply. "Got it. My mistake."

"And don't you forget it." There was another, smaller

thud, followed by a fit of coughing and footsteps stomping off. Still, Xiang didn't move from his hiding place.

"Jesus, what an ass." The man remained in the doorway, his silhouette casting a black shadow on the cream carpet. "Kid, if you're in here somewhere, you're welcome, but watch your back from now on, okay?"

With that, the shadow disappeared as the man left, closing the door behind him and walking down the hallway. Xiang waited for several minutes, listening as hard as he could for any kind of trick, or that one of them was still hiding in the room. Only when he was sure they were both gone did he step out of his hiding place. Pausing only long enough to wedge a chair under the doorknob, he made sure his knife was hidden under his pillow, then curled up under the sheets and was unconscious before his head hit the pillow.

CHAPTER FOURTEEN

"Man, this place is unbelievable."

Calvin James's awestruck statement was pretty much shared by the rest of the Phoenix Force team, and even Bolan himself.

They were all outfitted in the disguises suitable to their cover stories. Bolan, as the mercenary group leader, was dressed in tailored, pressed fatigues, complete with a black beret. Gary Manning and Calvin James, both similarly dressed, were his two bodyguards, with Rafael Encizo and T. J. Hawkins serving as floaters in sport coats and slacks, keeping an eye on the other three from a distance, and ready to move in to assist in the event of trouble.

Each man wore state-of-the-art tinted sunglasses to shield their eyes from the harsh African desert sun. The sleek glasses served a dual purpose, as well. Hidden inside the arms and around the frames were microcameras busily recording everything and everyone the five operatives looked at. Along with wirelessly transmitting the data to a hard drive built into each of their belts, it was also being burst transmitted back to their vehicles as a backup.

And there was plenty to see. The Sale in the Sands field covered at least forty acres, and that didn't include the airstrip that had been created by one of the foreign defense tech companies showing off its "instant bridge-landing strip" composite material that could be laid down over any terrain and hardened by running an electrical current through it to form a solid surface capable of supporting up to 40,000 pounds.

Everywhere Bolan and the Phoenix Force looked, there was a company, either foreign or a few that were based in the U.S., offering any kind of technology and weapon under the sun, from personal defense systems and body armor to larger weapons and equipment, all the way up to armored vehicles and aircraft.

The shoppers were there, as well, a who's who of dictators, mercenary leaders, drug lords and even military officers from developing nations shopping for items to add to their country's arsenals.

"Good thing we didn't bring McCarter here. No doubt he would have tried to smuggle something in, and we would have been blown right from the start," Hawkins mused over their private satellite phone network.

"Well, the letter was very strict about their 'no-weapons' policy," James replied.

"All right, let's tighten it up," Bolan said even while grinning at the thought of the hot-headed Englishman trading insults with the perimeter security. The security at the site was very professional and strict. When they'd landed, a package had been waiting for them. Inside were laminated identification badges with their aliases and holographic bar codes. The accompanying letter gave them the website and an individual code to access the coordinates of the bazaar site. It stated that they had one hour from touchdown to access the coordinates and provide the makes, models, color and license plate of the vehicles they would be attending the arms bazaar in. If they failed to provide any of this information within the stated time frame, the invitation would be automatically rescinded. Bolan got online right away, submitted the required items and grabbed the info.

The five men had taken their pair of brand-new Land Rovers deep into the African desert, three hundred miles from the nearest town. As they had driven in, Bolan had spotted what looked like an unmanned drone keeping tabs on them in the distance.

Once there, they'd parked as directed on a large field and walked up to a checkpoint with several gates, getting in line with everyone else. When they had reached the front, their badges were scanned with a portable reader, and they were asked seemingly innocuous questions such as where they had come from or the like. Bolan figured that since the IDs didn't have pictures, they were using face-to-face examination to see if anyone was acting nervous or uncomfortable about being there—and might be a law enforcement agent in disguise.

Next came the search line, where everyone, no matter who they were, was scanned with portable metal detectors, and even patted down when necessary. Those who had been to one of these before submitted with varying degrees of grace, new invitees reacted with different levels of indignation and anger, but only one group, a quartet of ebony-skinned men in olive fatigues and red berets, was turned away for not submitting to the efficient search, and had been escorted away by the ever-present pairs of men with black-and-red armbands and carrying HK MP7 A1 personal defense weapons.

As Bolan had gone through the various security levels, he'd admired the slick execution of the operation. Even among such a wide-ranging group of individuals, the fact that this had been organized and pulled off without any of the world's law-enforcement agencies getting wind of it was a feat that bordered on incredible. Even if one had managed to gain access to it, getting enough personnel to mount any kind of serious operation organized and on site to take it down would have been nearly impossible.

He had been a bit worried about their sunglasses. But as they were turned off until all the men were inside the grounds, there was nothing to arouse suspicion. Even while they were unable to take overt action against any of the men or groups they saw represented around them, Bolan and the Phoenix Force members were gaining a wealth of information regarding the criminals, despots and military strongmen who were in attendance here.

"Whoa—isn't that Juan Aguilar? I thought he'd been killed in the most recent cartel clash in Sinaloa?" James muttered as he watched the linen-suited man, his head covered in a straw fedora, as he and his entourage examined the wares of an Indian small-arms dealer.

"Apparently he didn't get the message," Rafael Encizo replied, keeping tabs on the people around them while James recorded the group. "I just saw three members of Basque Fatherland and Liberty walk past us. I'd heard they'd been lying low in Cuba for the past few years. I'd love to find out if that's still the case."

Bolan stopped at the tent of a company supplying customized gun systems that could be hidden in anything, from a briefcase to a book to a watermelon. "We'll have plenty of time to run down everyone we get video on once we get out of here," he subvocalized.

"For now, the most important piece is to make sure that we get as much footage as we can or as many people as we can."

"Hell, maybe next year we can set up our own table, hand out cards, get some booth babes and see what kinda business we attract," Hawkins drawled.

"That's not a bad idea, T.J., but for the time being, I'm more interested in finding out enough about the people here to put as many out of business as possible." Bolan kept his eyes constantly scanning, and noticed an Arab in a keffiyeh and flowing robe sitting under a canopy on a rug amid traditional pillows eyeing him.

"Heads-up, we have someone scoping us." Bolan met his stare for a long moment, then the Arab waved him over. "I'm going to see what this guy wants."

"Do you know him?" Gary Manning asked.

"Never seen him before. Floaters, keep an eye out." Bolan walked over to the man and bowed slightly, his eyes flicking to the left and right, looking for henchmen in case this was some kind of assassination attempt.

"*Asalaam Aleikum,* good sir! Please, sit and join me." The man waved his hand at a nearby pillow. He was around fifty years old, handsome, with deep brown eyes and short black hair flecked with gray and a matching mustache.

"I'm afraid that you have the advantage of me." Bolan fluidly sat cross-legged on the nearest pillow.

"Advantage—hardly. My name is Mansoor Qasim Uthman. May I offer you some tea?"

"Thank you, but no. I'm Max Carthwell, owner of Situation Threat Evaluation and Response, Inc. Or STEAR for short."

"Ah, you are private security, then?"

"That's one of the services we provide."

"Only one?"

Bolan gave him a thin-lipped smile and offered a card. "You can find more information about us on our website. Forgive my bluntness, but why did you call me over here?"

Uthman smiled broadly. "I have been coming to this sale ever since it began, sometimes to buy, sometimes to sell. Lately, I have come to observe. The people here, they know me, and know I pose no threat to them. One of the things I enjoy doing is seeking out new people, those who are attending for the first time. As I have been here for years, there is little I do not know—"

"And more likely even less people that you don't know." Bolan let a hint of humor slip into his eyes. "Let me give you the two-minute pitch, then." He outlined the various services his fictitious PMC company could provide, including—in veiled terms—intimidation, private courier or armed escort, smuggling, corporate espionage, kidnapping and assassination.

"Of course, certain services don't come cheaply. However, all of our men are ex-military, with more than sixty percent former special forces from all branches of service."

Uthman laughed and nodded. "If your references are as good as you say, then you should have no trouble finding work here."

"Let's hope so. Ever since the Blackwater debacle, many people are looking more closely at PMCs and seeing them as more of a potential public-relations hindrance than a help. However, the right companies only have to gain—if they hire the right PMC from the start."

"Excellent, Mr. Carthwell!" Uthman extended his

own business card. "I will take a look at your website, and if I like what I see, I may be in the position to refer you to a few of my associates who are often in the market for a group such as yours. Feel free to mention that you have met me. That will often serve to smooth over any hesitation on your potential employer's part."

Bolan inclined his head as he rose to his feet. "You're very kind, particularly to someone you've just met."

Uthman's genial expression didn't change, but his warm brown eyes turned dead-cold. "The fact that you're attending this particular event means that you handle *all* types of situations. You're obviously our kind of company, otherwise you wouldn't have made it this far." He spread his hands out. "Dealing with these types of people, in these types of businesses, it pays to know as many as possible. Who knows, in the future, it may be me calling upon you and your associates to handle a task."

"I hope that is the case. It has been a pleasure, Mr. Uthman. I hope we'll be seeing each other again very soon."

And if I have my way, you can count on it, Bolan thought, turning to leave the cool confines of the canopy for the hot, dry afternoon air.

Manning and James fell into step behind him. "Good talk?" James asked.

"Definitely." Bolan stared at Uthman's card for several seconds, making sure the glasses recorded all of it, before handing it to Manning. "Akira, I want to know everything about this guy. If even half of what he said was true, he's well-connected in the criminal underworld. And I want him—"

A familiar sound pierced Bolan's consciousness,

halting his words midsentence. He didn't have to listen to the high-pitched whistle to seek out and head for the nearest cover, Manning and James right on his heels.

"Floaters, get to cover—" was all he had time to say before the tents and desert all around them erupted in explosions of fire, sand and smoke.

CHAPTER FIFTEEN

After a refreshing six hours of sleep, Akira Tokaido was back on duty at his computer. In the dimness of the Stony Man computer room, he conferenced with David McCarter as the Phoenix Force leader executed a raid on Hu Ji Han's penthouse office.

Once Trent had made contact with the pirates, McCarter had boarded a rented Gulfstream for the quick hop over the South China Sea back to Hong Kong, where he'd prepped for the insert. While he waited for the operation to begin, Tokaido filled him in on what they'd found so far.

"The masseuse gave him a rubdown at 9:15 p.m., then he retired for the evening, leaving the building at 9:35 p.m. for his home in the hills above Hong Kong. Interestingly, we intercepted two brief cell phone calls from the vicinity of his office, one to a member of an Uighur separatist movement in western China, the other to what we suspect is a splinter of the old Aum Shinrikyo cult of the mid-nineties in Japan. I've got transcripts and translated audio files downloading now. I'm attempting to triangulate a location of the person on the other end of each call, but that may take a day or two, and in the case of the Uighur, even longer, but I'm looking."

Tokaido played each call for McCarter while reading the transcription. The Phoenix Force warrior hissed with impatience as he listened. "Any idea who the woman is? His secretary?"

"No, the voice doesn't match. Given the state of voice disguising technology today, it could easily either be her or him using a device to conceal their voice. Besides, it's all so vague. They talk of 'events' and 'announcements,' as if they know they're being listened to, which, given both these groups, they certainly should be. I don't know about you, but I'm getting tired of playing catch-up on whatever's going on."

"Well, if John can't uncover what's going on aboard that ship, perhaps I'll have more luck in Hu's office."

"Let's hope so. You're green-lit. Throw this up on screen, if you don't mind."

"Like having a bloody nanny watchin' over my shoulder," McCarter grumbled, but activated his head-mounted camera anyway.

A window appeared in the upper right corner of his monitor, and Tokaido enlarged it until it took up half the screen. He saw a typical parking garage through one of the building's own security cameras. One of his biggest points of pride was that he could break into any commercial security and maintenance program at will, overriding any or all systems as needed. He boasted that he could literally move a herd of elephants from the lobby to the top floor of a building without anyone being the wiser, and if Bolan or any of the other Stony Man warriors had requested it, Tokaido was sure he could come through. For this mission, the job was almost absurdly easy.

Several cars were scattered around the deserted parking lot, and the computer hacker watched as a security vehicle with tinted windows made its rounds. As soon as it was off the floor, the driver's door of a stretch limousine popped open, and a black-clad figure emerged. Tokaido knew that the central security patrol was only seeing an empty parking floor, with a loop cut in of the normal floor, right down to the advancing time-date stamp. For them, no one would be there all night.

McCarter crept to a small set of elevator doors. "Hu's exclusive elevator. Even doing a lot of the work with his own country, he had to pay a substantial sum to get that installed," Tokaido noted.

"I'll bet," McCarter whispered.

Tokaido leaned back in his chair and watched as the Brit brought the elevator down by the simple expedient of pushing the button, as the hacker had already subverted the system. The doors opened, and McCarter began the swift ascent to Hu's office.

"Sure beats climbing down from the roof, I bet. Too bad all insertions aren't this easy."

"Don't jinx it." McCarter stood stock-still as the elevator whisked him up to the penthouse office. "Target's still unchanged?"

"Right, the freestanding computer in his office that doesn't even appear to have a modem in it. Since we've been through his regular files, you can ignore the computer on his main desk. We're assuming the information we're looking for is on that second one."

"I assume there wasn't anything pertinent in his regular records?"

"Just the usual—a Chinese billionaire is getting richer."

The elevator reached the destination floor, and the doors opened. Tokaido monitored the screens giving him access to the security system as McCarter began creeping inside. “Okay, the laser system is powered down, the room is yours.”

“Good.” McCarter straightened and strode to the computer sitting alone on a desk off to the side of the room. Pulling a hardened flash drive from a pocket on his sleeve, he inserted it into the USB port on the front of the computer.

“All right, accessing the computer system…sure hope there aren’t any surprises here—”

“You hope?” McCarter said, keeping an eye on the elevator doors as the infiltration program attempted to do the same thing to the computer’s hard drive that he had done to the building.

“Relax, the sec suite should handle anything that might pop up. Just give it a few seconds to make its sweep. The next security round is in four minutes, by the way.”

“Well, if this little doodad is as good as you claim, I should be out of here by then.”

Tokaido nodded at the by-the-book mission.

McCarter’s head snapped up as he looked at the elevator doors.

“I’ve got activity in the shaft, what’s happening over there?”

“The elevator’s going down—didn’t you lock it out?”

“Yeah, but just temporarily. No one should be coming up at this hour, and we don’t want them to think something’s malfunct—”

“Well, someone’s sure as hell coming up now!”

“Have you finished loading the data yet?”

“No, the damn thing’s only three-quarters full. Probably gonna be another ninety seconds or so.”

"You may have to abort. Find a good hiding place, and be prepared to get to it quickly. Otherwise, try to get as much as you can."

"No shit."

Tokaido was on the edge of his seat, unable to do anything but watch.

The elevator doors slid open, and a slender figure walked into the large office. She paused, as if waiting for something to happen—or if sensing the presence of someone else there. A frown crossed her face, and she pulled out a cell phone.

Tokaido and McCarter realized it at the same time, but the professional soldier said it first. "Lights. Hit the motion sensors!" he subvocalized.

The hacker brought them up, the recessed lights coming on just as the woman brought out her cell phone. She stepped back into the elevator, watching as the lights slowly dimmed, then stepped out again, watching the lights flare into full brightness. Evidently satisfied, she continued into the room, heading straight for the large desk in the middle of the floor—exactly where McCarter had chosen to hide.

"Too close." Tokaido breathed. "Did you get the flash drive out?"

"Yeah, but I couldn't shut the computer off."

Tokaido zoomed in the camera on the desk. Sure enough, the amber power light glowed steadily in the dimness. "Let's just hope her boss is forgetful."

Unfortunately, it didn't seem as though she was going to leave any time soon. Tokaido frowned as she settled into the chair, back straight, hands on the keyboard in perfect typing position. He held his breath, as he expected the woman to scream at any moment upon contacting the operative under the desk, but she hadn't moved an inch yet.

"What's she up to? Surely she's not working this late at night?" he muttered, bringing one of the cameras within the suite up to view what she was working on. A view of the computer screen and the work the secretary was doing appeared. She was doing exactly that—setting up his schedule, confirming phone appointments in the U.S.

After ten minutes, she powered down the computer and turned off the small desk light. She strolled across the floor toward the elevator, but her steps slowed as she turned toward the second computer.

"Here it comes—get ready, David."

"Shit, I've been ready ever since that chick walked into the room. She's got great legs, that's for sure."

The secretary slowly walked over to the computer, eyeing it warily.

Tokaido watched with bated breath.

With a sigh and a shake of her head, the woman turned the monitor on, powered the computer down, then turned the screen off again. Chuckling to herself, she walked back out of the room.

Tokaido leaned back in her chair and exhaled. "That was closer than I would have liked. Get out of there."

"No need to tell me twice, mate. Just gotta plant my bugs, and I'm gettin' out." McCarter unfolded himself from underneath the desk and crept to the elevator doors. A minute later, they opened again, and he stepped inside.

Tokaido stayed with him until he was clear, then the Stony Man hacker accessed the downloaded contents of the flash drive through a cell phone transmission.

"What's in there?" Aaron Kurtzman asked.

"Looks like another set of books, this one keeping track of all of the graft and bribes he's taken and paid over the years. A nice piece of evidence if you're cracking down on corruption, but not a lot of good for what we're looking for."

"You sure? It's not encoded or anything?"

"I'm running the standard tests right now. If anything extra's in there, I'll find it." Tokaido set his decryption program to run and massaged his temples. "So far, it looks like this was a dead end. Looks like the ball is back in John's court."

"Looks that way. Let's hope he comes up with something soon."

Yup, Tokaido thought, wondering just when that was going to happen.

CHAPTER SIXTEEN

Bolan dived to the dirt as huge gouts of flame and smoke threw geysers of sand into the air. The explosions walked straight through the arms bazaar, devastating people, tents and equipment everywhere. Men and women ran, screamed and died as the bombardment continued, reducing much of the bazaar to rubble.

Shielding his head with his arms, Bolan barked into his mike. "Akira, Akira, can you hear me? Akira, come in, over." The link to Stony Man was only to be used in an emergency, and a surprise mortar attack from nowhere certainly qualified.

Only silence greeted him. Had the satellite communications somehow been disrupted? But connecting with Stony Man was the least of his problems at the moment.

"Phoenix Force, report!"

"Manning here."

"James here."

"Encizo here."

"Hawkins, ready to rock."

"Everyone all right?" Bolan asked. The four warriors confirmed their uninjured status.

"Who the fuck's raining the fire down on this place?" James asked.

"No clue. That's only one thing we've got to find out. But first we have to create an evac strategy."

"Yeah, I'm definitely open to suggestions," Hawkins said.

"Wait a minute." Bolan looked back at Uthman's tent. The flap, now riddled with shrapnel holes, billowed in the wind caused by the shelling, but he saw no sign of the portly man. "Everyone regroup near the Arab's tent."

As shells continued falling, Bolan rolled to the side of the tent and squirmed underneath the flap. The interior was empty, with only scattered pillows on the rumpled rug. But something still didn't look right to Bolan.

Rustling at the front of the tent made him whirl to see Manning and James duck inside. Bolan held a finger to his lips and pointed at the rug on the floor. The two Phoenix Force warriors immediately split up, Manning flanking left, James right. Bolan crept to the corner of the rug and pulled the whole thing back in one swift movement.

No gunfire erupted from underneath, but they all saw the outline of a trapdoor with no handle on this side in the sand. Standing behind it, Bolan stomped on the hidden panel with his combat boot. "Uthman, this is Max Carthwell!" he shouted over the din outside. "I'm not here to kill you. I want to help get you out of here!"

A voice came from one of the pillows. "What assurance do I have that you won't kill me if I open the door?"

As Bolan picked up the pillow and felt the hidden speaker inside, he saw Encizo and James crawl under the back wall of the tent. "Believe me, if I'd wanted you dead already, you would be. Besides, I wouldn't be a very good bodyguard if I killed my own client, now, would I?" The ground around them shook from a shell landing nearby, and everyone crouched on the ground. "Time's running out. Either stay here and hope a shell doesn't land on you, or take your chances with us!"

There was a moment's pause. "I'll give you one hundred thousand U.S. dollars to escort me safely out of here."

"One million. U.S."

"Five hundred thousand, no more. That is for safe passage to the nearest city."

"Done. Do you have any weapons in there?"

"No. I would be killed if they ever found them. Arming yourself and finding a vehicle is your problem."

"Great." Bolan's head snapped up at the sudden silence.

Manning peeked cautiously out through a hole in the tent flap. "The mortars have stopped."

Bolan frowned at the shelling's cessation. "If this is more than a simple hit-and-run, the enemy force'll probably come in to kill any survivors. Did anyone see anything that could be used as a weapon?"

James nodded. "Assuming it didn't get blown to bits, there was a crowd control and suppression vehicle four tents down that looked like it could at least protect us long enough to upgrade to something more robust."

Bolan nodded, too. "All right. T.J., Rafael, stay here and keep watch over our new client. Gary, Calvin, let's go get it."

Leading the other two men to the tent flap, he pushed it aside and peered out. Destruction was everywhere around them. The shattered remains of tents listed in the breeze or burned from direct hits by the shells or from being set on fire by red-hot shrapnel. Bodies were everywhere, some lying motionless, covered in blood, others beginning to move if they could. The stench of cordite, blood and smoke hung heavily over everything.

In the distance, Bolan heard the rumble of approaching engines. "Tangos are about three klicks out." Although his hands itched for a weapon, Bolan knew he'd have to forage for anything he could come up with along the way. "Let's move out, and if you see anything usable, grab it."

The three men headed into the carnage, alert to every noise or movement around them. The cries of the wounded were starting now, groans and screams shattering the stillness.

"There, that big tent ahead." James pointed to a large canopy that was half knocked down, as if a circus had abandoned their big top right before the show.

"Let's go." Bolan was just beginning to accelerate into a jog when a figure out of a nightmare stumbled toward him.

"Help me...please help me..." The man had been severely lacerated by shrapnel, which had sliced his face into bloody ribbons, removing his eyes, lips and ears along the way. He reached out to Bolan, who evaded his clutching grasp and swept his feet out from under him, grabbing his tattered suit jacket to help him to the ground.

"Stay here, we'll send someone back for you." Prying his hands free of the man's grip, Bolan kept moving.

"Damn, Striker, shouldn't I—" James's question was cut off by the big man.

"No sense treating him if we're all going to die in the next few minutes." Bolan kept moving, darting from ruined tent to ruined tent. "We're almost there. The only way he's gonna survive is if we do."

By now they were at the downed end of the large tent. Bolan raised the heavy canvas and held it for the other men to duck under. After everyone was inside, he entered, as well, going from the hot, bright outside to the hot, dark inside of the tent. He stepped around overturned tables as his eyes adjusted to the dimness. The tent seemed abandoned, with no dead or wounded in here, only a broken pole that had held up the right side of the tent next to a large vehicle that appeared undamaged.

Manning, ever practical, shone a small penlight around. "This will do."

The vehicle he was illuminating was a boxy beige beast, around nine feet high, that rested on four huge tires. It had a turret with a bent barrel on top, but the rest of the APC looked ready to go.

"A Fahd 240/30," Encizo said. "Egypt was pumping these out to quiet the rioters last year…look how well that turned out."

Manning slapped the side of the Fahd. "Built on a solid, reliable Mercedes-Benz chassis, this one should get us out alive." He looked over at Bolan. "Unless you have another plan in mind?"

Bolan grinned like a shark and he climbed into the commander's seat. "I'd prefer to go out with guns blazing, however, right now we're getting the hell out of here. Let's pick up our cargo, and if any targets of opportunity arise, we'll deal with them at that time."

Manning climbed into the driver's seat and fired up the Mercedes-Benz OM366 LA4 engine, which roared into a steady purr. After making sure the entrance of the tent was unobstructed, James got inside and sat in the first troop seat in the rear compartment. Manning hit the rear hatch for the other two men to come in, when a shrill and definitely feminine scream was heard from the rear.

"Hit it, Gary," Bolan said as he turned in his chair. "What's going on back there?"

"Found a stowaway, sir." James walked forward, holding the arm of a pretty young woman with short blond hair, dressed in a mussed charcoal-gray jacket and slacks. Although her mascara was smudged with tears, at the moment she was struggling to free her arm from James's firm grip.

"Let me go—if anything, you people are the trespassers here. You're stealing this vehicle!"

Bolan reached over to drop the armored panels over the front windshields. "Miss, please shut up for the moment. Cal, see if you can possibly get us a link to Akira." He hit his earpiece. "Rafael, T.J., come in."

"This is Rafael, go."

"We're coming to get you in sixty. Have Uthman and anyone with him ready to go."

"Roger that."

"Who are you people?" was all the woman got out before Bolan clamped a hand over her mouth.

"I won't ask you to shut up again. My name is Max Carthwell, and I head a private security company called Situational Threat Evaluation and Response. Right now, that's exactly what we are doing—responding to a huge situational threat by getting the hell out of here. If you wish to come with us, great, if not, we'd be happy to let you out when we stop, which will be right about—now." Bolan leaned forward in his harness as Manning brought the eleven-ton vehicle to a halt and opened the back door again.

"Calvin, help our passengers get aboard." The sound of approaching engines was even louder now.

"And leave me here? Are you crazy? Look, I can help you. My name is Kristianna Lofgren, and I'm a salesperson with the Kader Factory. I know this APC inside and out."

"Good, is there *any* kind of working armament on this vehicle?"

"Well, it was designed for show, so I'm afraid that there's no real live ammo. We were planning a demonstration of the three forward-mounted 81 mm electrically operated grenade launchers on the turret using smoke grenades. However, they only fire toward the front of the vehicle. Fortunately, the gas tanks are almost full, giving us a range of about 450 kilometers."

"Great, assuming we can outrun them, we're set." Bolan exchanged a wry glance with Manning. "Better than nothing. How are we doing on time?"

"Ten seconds left." Manning was interrupted by the sound of feet pounding up the rear hatch again.

"Passenger and two bodyguards are secure. Close the back door and go, go, go!"

Manning had already hit the button, and as the ramp closed, they heard the sound of bullets hammering the armor plate. "Everyone sit down and hang on!" The Phoenix Force warrior hit the gas, making the big APC leap forward.

"T.J., get on the turret and see if it's operational at all. Watch our six. Calvin, make sure the passengers are secure. It's gonna be a bumpy ride," Bolan called.

"We got company!" Hawkins shouted from the turret. "A pair of Humvees with what looks like .50-caliber machine guns are coming up fast!"

"What's this thing's armor rated for?" Manning asked without taking his eyes from the debris-strewed lane they were careening down.

Lofgren replied, "7.62 mm."

"That's gonna be a problem," James said. The words were barely out of his mouth when the rattle of a machine gun could be heard over the roar of the engine, just as Manning cranked the wheel hard right. The APC swerved, blowing through another tent already on fire, and making it burst into fiery wreckage as the huge tires sent laptops, a flat-screen television and burning canvas everywhere.

"Still on our six!" Hawkins reported. "One's coming up right behind us!"

"Everyone hang on!" Manning shouted.

Bolan had just enough time to push the saleswoman toward a seat when Manning slammed on the brakes. Caught by surprise, the driver of the Humvee tried to swerve out of the way, but his right front fender caught the back left corner of the Fahd, slewing the 4x4 around.

Manning shifted into Reverse and cranked the wheel, backing into the side of the Humvee before the driver could get out of the way. The huge APC shoved the smaller vehicle across the sand, both engines screaming as the Humvee driver tried to get out of the way of the Fahd.

"What are you doing?" both Uthman and Lofgren cried out at the same moment.

"Trying to improve our offensive capability," Manning answered. "Or at least take it away from them."

"The other one's coming at us, nine o'clock!" Hawkins

said as the chatter of machine gun fire drowned out his words, along with the peculiar clanking of metal being penetrated by high-velocity slugs. The Fahd slewed left as Manning fought to control it while trying to evade the shooter and still keep the first Humvee engaged.

"Last burst tracked high, but he's setting up for another shot!" Hawkins said.

Manning grimaced. "Playing tag with them's only gonna get us shot to pieces, and we can't outrun them! We can't keep sitting here. If more show up, we're dead men driving!"

"Let the other one go and take the shooter on headfirst. If we can disable him, maybe we can create enough of a hole to escape through before they regroup." Bolan leaned back to the passenger compartment. "Everyone should probably hit the floor. There's likely to be rounds passing straight through this compartment shortly." His announcement was followed by a mad dash by everyone to hit the metal deck.

"Kristianna, is there anything special T.J. needs to do to operate the grenade launcher?" Bolan asked as the APC began a wide turn, the large tires flattening anything in their path.

"No, if he's familiar with a vehicle-mounted system, it's pretty much the same."

"Okay, T.J., you're on our only weapons system. The second you spot that Humvee, open up on it!"

"With pleasure!"

It took Manning a bit of jockeying, and running through another half-destroyed tent to get them in position, but finally he had the APC lined up enough for Hawkins to begin lobbing the smoke grenades at the firing Humvee.

"Screw this!" Manning said, ducking in his seat as he stomped on the gas. The Fahd leaped forward, heading straight at the Humvee. The chattering .50-caliber gun stitched rounds all over the front of the APC, coring the bulletproof plates and starring the bullet-resistant windshield. Hunched in the commander's seat, Bolan felt a round snap by his head, and hunkered down a bit more.

"Yeah! Got 'em!" The triumphant shout from Hawkins was followed right afterward by Manning's shouted warning.

"Brace for impact!"

CHAPTER SEVENTEEN

Bolan glimpsed the approaching Humvee, its windshield wreathed in the smoke pluming from one of Hawkins's grenades, which had somehow gotten lodged on the hood. Before the driver could swerve or brake, the larger, heavier Fahd was upon it.

The two vehicles came together in a rending crash of metal. With its angled front, the APC launched off the Humvee's hood and lurched into the air, landing on its two right wheels, and teetering there for a heart-stopping few seconds before crashing back down onto all four.

"Where's the Humvee?" Bolan popped back up and looked around for it. He knew how tough the vehicles were. If there was a chance to have stopped it without disabling it, he wanted to follow up and seize the vehicle before reinforcements arrived. And there was still the second Humvee to contend with....

"Spun out on the right—three o'clock!" Hawkins said from the turret.

"Calvin, Rafael, with me!" Bolan sprang up and shoved the door open, hitting the ground and running toward the stalled Humvee, which was still wreathed in smoke from the grenade. A large cloud of dust and sand had been thrown up by the collision, and he used it to full advantage as he stalked the vehicle. The left front fender was crumpled, the driver's-side windshield was cracked and the top left corner of the passenger compartment was crushed, but otherwise the 4x4 was undamaged.

As Bolan approached, the passenger door opened up and a man emerged, half stepping, half falling out, blood streaming down the side of his face, a pistol in his hand. Bolan was on him before he could realize what was happening, stripping the pistol from the guy and putting a bullet into his brain. Throwing the body aside, Bolan stuck the pistol inside the compartment, aiming for the general location of the driver's seat, and pulled the trigger three times. He was rewarded with a scream of pain.

Encizo appeared from the other side, shaking his head. "Driver's door is jammed."

"Not a problem." Bolan risked ducking for a quick look inside. The driver was dead.

"Get him out of there," Bolan said as he cleared the backseat.

"Where the hell's the gunner?" Encizo asked as they wrestled the dead man out of the driver's seat.

In answer, a body slid down from the top of the Humvee, landing in the sand in an awkward tangle of limbs, the man's head lolling at an unnatural angle.

James appeared above them. "Dead—neck broken. Gary must have tagged him with the tire in the crash."

"The dust cloud's settling." Bolan took off the man's helmet and goggles and tossed them to James. "Man the Fifty. If we can sucker that other Humvee in by chasing the Fahd, take 'em out."

"Got it." The lanky black man clapped the helmet on his head and pulled the goggles down. He finished the disguise by stripping the dead gunner of his camo kerchief and pulling it over his nose and mouth, obscuring his entire face.

"Rafael, tell Gary the plan and have him head north-northwest." The Cuban warrior ran to the APC and jumped inside. Moments later, the back door clanged shut and the vehicle began accelerating out of the fire zone. Bolan gave him a five-second head start, then began pursuing.

The radio in the Humvee crackled to life. "Scout Two, report. What's going on out there?"

Bolan grabbed the mike, speaking loud and fast. "This is Scout Two! We have dead. Repeat, we have dead! Am pursuing resisters now, with Scout One to follow!"

"Who is this? What's your name, soldier?"

Bolan clicked the mike's button several times as he replied "Trans…break…ng up. Still…pursuit—" Then he replaced the mike and ignored the repeated requests for identification. "Might buy us a little time anyway."

"Anything's possible." James ducked to make sure the turret's range of motion was clear, and took a look around the rear compartment of the Humvee. "These guys mean business. Not only do they have the Fifty up top, but they have a loaded M249 back here, ready to go."

"Good to know." Bolan didn't glance back, concentrating on keeping the Humvee moving forward in the shifting desert sand, which could turn from dunes to hard-packed ground in only a few yards.

"The other Humvee's coming up fast!" James shouted from the open turret.

"Good, they took the bait. Make it look good, Cal."

James worked the action on the .50-caliber gun to clear it, and began firing short bursts at the fleeing Fahd, kicking up sand on either side of the swerving APC as Manning tried to evade the bullets. Bolan kept an eye on the approaching Humvee through his bent side mirror and the one on the passenger side, which was undamaged. “Get them a little closer, Calvin—and don’t hit Gary!” he called out as a burst of bullets came a little too close to the left rear tire.

“No shit, although it’s harder than it looks to miss on purpose!”

“The good news is that this ought to bring ’em in close enough to take out.” Bolan had appropriated the driver’s sidearm, a Beretta M9 pistol, which was now stuck into his belt. Goosing the accelerator, he pursued the escaping Fahd as it cleared the last hurdle, a low ring of sand dunes, and headed for the endless desert beyond.

The second Humvee had pulled up almost alongside Bolan’s vehicle, the gunner on top targeting the Fahd’s right rear quarter with aimed bursts from his own M2HB. Manning was still holding his own, but more bullets were hitting than missing now.

“Where’s that ambush, Cal?”

“Slow down a bit—let him draw alongside!” James said in between his own bursts.

Bolan eased up on the gas just enough to allow the other vehicle to pull even with him. Apparently thinking the Fahd was getting away, the other Humvee driver burst ahead of his partner, the gunner tracking the larger vehicle for another burst.

“Well, that helps.” James only had to traverse his turret ninety degrees to line up the other Humvee in his sights. Seeing movement out of the corner of his eye, the turret gunner started to turn and look at the other Humvee when James depressed the trigger of the .50-caliber heavy machine gun.

The turret gunner died before he could even register what had happened; the AP slugs pulverized his upper chest and head, literally blowing him away. James avoided hitting the heavy machine gun itself and walked his fire down into the passenger compartment, sending at least twenty rounds into the back, in case there were any hardmen there, then hammering the driver's door with another long burst.

Bolan heard a panicked voice on his radio, the copilot trying to contact the driver of the other Humvee and begging him to stop firing. As he yelled into the mike, the driver started to turn away, but Bolan turned with him, allowing James to destroy the driver's door and to continue firing into the front of the compartment.

"Stop the engine!" Bolan shouted up to him, and James obligingly put a burst through the Humvee's hood and left front tire. The slugs mangled both, making steam burst from the front, and the crippled vehicle immediately began to slow down. It jerked to a stop with a horrible grinding noise, and a jet of black fluid spurted out from underneath the engine compartment.

The radio burst with excited chatter again, but Bolan wasn't paying attention, swinging the Humvee around and pulling up to the disabled vehicle. "Let's get that Fifty off and on the Fahd."

James was already out the door and climbing onto the wrecked vehicle, examining the pintle mount for damage and beginning the process of unfastening the post with the Browning machine gun on it. Bolan scanned the horizon for potential pursuers, keeping an ear on the radio transmissions of the enemy. With Encizo's help, James was almost finished when Bolan heard a transmission that made his blood run cold.

"Base to Airstrike One, Scouts One and Two are not responding on their radios. Move forward and investigate their position at the following coordinates, over."

"Acknowledged, Base. Airstrike One moving to investigate."

"Move it, guys, we're gonna have air support on us in a few minutes!"

Wrapping the still-hot barrel in his jacket, the stocky Cuban hoisted the eighty-pound gun over his shoulder, picked up a full box of two hundred rounds with his free hand and ran to the Fahd, which had circled around to pick him up. James also left the destroyed Humvee, sprinting back to their captured vehicle and leaping up to the roof. Having left the turret, Hawkins was standing on top of the APC and grabbed the machine gun as Rafael hoisted it up to him.

"Incoming at eight o'clock!" James traversed his turret to the southwest, raised his gun to its maximum elevation and opened fire on the small helicopter that was skimming the dunes. The Boeing AH-6 nimbly dodged the incoming rounds and retaliated with a barrage of rockets from its underwing pods.

"Get us the hell outta here!" James ducked into the rear of the Humvee as Bolan stomped the gas pedal to the floor, making the Humvee leap forward. On the Fahd, Hawkins and Encizo were still improvising their mount for the captured machine gun while Manning was trying to put some more distance between them and their aerial pursuer. The 2.75-inch rockets hit the ground a scant twenty yards behind them, spraying the escaping Humvee with shrapnel and sand.

"Jesus, that was too close!" James said, poking his head out to try to spot the Boeing again.

"Yeah, well, get used to it, since we're probably going to be the bait to take that helicopter out."

"What else is new?" James frowned, then pointed at the roof of the Fahd. "What's Rafael doing?"

Bolan looked up to see the Phoenix Force warrior flashing both hands at him, ten fingers, then five more. He'd moved to Channel 15.

The Executioner turned the dial until he caught the Canadian's calm voice. "Commander Carthwell, do you copy, over?"

"I'm here, Gary. We're going to fall back and engage that chopper to see if we can take it out. You get our passengers to Marrakesh and on the plane. If we're not following you when you arrive, give us three hours, then depart the country immediately—that's an order."

"Yes, sir. Let's hope it doesn't come to that."

"Yeah, you and me both. Carthwell out." Bolan hung the mike back up and wrenched the Humvee's wheel hard left, sending a rooster tail of sand into the air as he turned back south to duel with the helicopter.

"You realize we're probably heading to our deaths, right?" James asked as he checked the ammo feed for his .50, then scanned the sky for the chopper.

"Maybe so, maybe not. When you engage him, run that Ma Deuce dry, and make sure the pilot sees you doing it. Obviously, if you can take him down while doing it, that would be great."

"You're the boss. Shit, here he comes again!" Bolan heard the racket of the approaching helicopter again, then Calvin opened up with the M2. "Right, hard right *now!*"

Bolan cranked the wheel, slewing the Humvee over as a line of shells burst in the sand on his left.

James traversed his turret as fast as he could, but the nimble helicopter was able to literally fly rings around the slower Humvee. "Only a matter of time before he tags us!"

Bolan could still see the Fahd on the horizon, although it was rapidly increasing the distance between it and the Humvee. "Need to buy them a few more minutes..." He cranked the wheel left this time, aiming the vehicle at a tall sand dune. The Humvee spun its way up the hill, pausing for a moment at the top, then plunging down the other side, the Boeing in hot pursuit.

James whirled the turret around, tracking the helicopter as best as he could and shooting at it until the trigger clicked. "That's it! We're empty!"

"Okay, now—" Bolan's reply was cut off by a stream of bullets walking across the Humvee's hood, punching large holes in the steel. The engine disintegrated with a shriek, making Bolan duck as fluids sprayed the windshield.

"They got us dead to rights!" James said.

"Climb out onto the roof and surrender—"

"You want me to do *what?*"

"Trust me, Calvin. I got your back! Just make sure you tell me which direction the chopper's at when you got up there!"

"All right, man. Sure hope they want prisoners and aren't just out to kill us." Bolan saw James's legs disappear as he scrambled out onto the roof. "He's coming around to the rear of the Hummer. Whatever you're gonna do, do it fast!"

In those few seconds, Bolan had grabbed the M249 Squad Assault Weapon and made sure it was ready to go. Everything would depend on the next couple of moments, including making sure he was able to get the weapon up, out and deployed properly.

"He's at four o'clock...five..."

Bolan didn't reply, but instead simply popped out, the SAW clutched in both arms. James had been spot-on. The Boeing was drifting into the six o'clock position, and all Bolan had to do was drop the barrel on the round cockpit and squeeze the trigger.

At less than one hundred yards, the stream of 5.56 mm bullets shattered the cockpit glass and shredded both the pilot and copilot as Bolan swept the muzzle of the light machine gun back and forth across the cockpit. The Boeing jerked back, rose into the air for a moment, then sideslipped and fell toward the ground, Bolan hosing it with bullets the entire way. Only at the last second did he raise the SAW and drop back into the passenger compartment of the Humvee as the helicopter's blades chopped into the earth and shattered, followed by the impact of the aircraft itself a second later. The resulting explosion sent a black plume of oily smoke into the air as the rockets and machine gun ammunition began to cook off for an agonizing minute. Finally, however, the wreck quieted, save for the crackling of the fire as it consumed the fuselage.

Bolan poked his head back out to take a look at the downed helicopter, which was fast turning into a pile of scorched metal and melted plastic. "Cal?"

"Here, man." The Phoenix Force warrior's head

popped up from below the front of the ruined Humvee, and he let out a long whistle at the destruction Bolan had wreaked. "Very nice work."

Still carrying M249, Bolan climbed out of the Humvee and surveyed the desert around them. "Same to you. Unfortunately, we got a long walk to Marrakesh."

"Or not." Calvin pointed to the north, where the Fahd was rumbling toward them.

Shaking his head, Bolan set out in a jog toward the APC, with James falling in beside him. When they reached the vehicle, Manning stuck his head out.

"Though you could use a lift, Commander."

"Absolutely, but what happened to following my orders explicitly?" Bolan asked as he climbed aboard.

Manning shifted the Fahd into gear as he replied. "Well, they didn't expressly state we were to leave the fire zone, so Rafael and T.J. had been angling to get a shot at that Boeing with the M2 when you took it out. It was then that I realized that I didn't have my full compliment of passengers that you'd instructed me to drive to Marrakesh, so I had to come back to collect the remaining two."

Bolan leaned back in his seat, enjoying the fact that James and he wouldn't have to leg it back to the city. "Like I said, excellent work following my orders to the letter, Gary."

CHAPTER EIGHTEEN

Trent's eyes cracked open, wincing at the harsh sunlight streaming through the windows, so bright it practically seared his retinas. Pushing himself up on the couch he'd been dozing on, he stared at the remains of the party all around him.

The new hires had drank and celebrated themselves into oblivion. There were empty and broken bottles lying everywhere, along with unconscious and sleeping men in chairs, settees and sprawled on the floor. The room was mostly quiet, the still air broken only by intermittent snoring. But as Trent watched and listened, he heard the steady thrum of the yacht's powerful engines as they propelled the boat forward. We're on the move, he thought. Time to check in.

Rising, he picked his way through the debris until he reached the door. Sliding it open, he poked his head out and looked up and down the hallway, exiting only when he was sure it was empty. He crept down the narrow, wood-paneled passageway, freezing only once, when he heard footsteps on the roof above him. The lack of activity was a bit disturbing; Trent had gotten the impression that Lee Ming ran a tighter ship than this. However, if it also made his job easier, he certainly wasn't going to complain.

Searching for a place to report in undiscovered,

Trent had a brainstorm. He located the nearest bathroom, evicted the unfortunate soul who had taken refuge there, claiming he was about to puke and sending the poor guy tottering off down the hall, and locked the door. When he was sure no one was around, he pulled out his satellite phone and dialed Stony Man headquarters.

"Kurtzman here," the gruff voice of Aaron "the Bear" Kurtzman answered. "Good to hear from you, Alpha. You comfortable?"

"Yes, but I don't have much time. The head player here is a guy named Lee Ming, a known pirate in the area. After picking up ten new men, the ship's on the move."

"I know, we've got you in sight the entire way."

"They're going after two cargo ships, but I don't know which ones or why yet. The leader isn't giving his crew a lot of information, but I know it's going to happen sometime in the next forty-eight to seventy-two hours."

"And you have no idea of the target or purpose yet?"

Trent tried not to make his response too sarcastic. "I've been on board for just over nine hours. It might take a bit more time to get them to trust me that much."

"We're aware of that, however, the limited time frame and wide coverage area means that there's a strong chance we might not be able to intercept their operation until it's already begun."

"Understood, and as soon as I know, you'll know."

"I'm sure. Get whatever information you can, and get it to us ASAP."

"Right—" Trent was interrupted by a fist pounding on the door.

"Hurry the fuck up in there!"

"Alpha out." Trent flushed the toilet and shoved his tiny phone in his pocket. He took his time washing his hands, then opened the folding door to see Guong on the other side.

"What took you so long? And who were you talking to in there?"

Trent frowned, staring at the bigger man as if he was crazy. "What the hell are you talking about? I was taking a shit, nothing else. Maybe you been working too hard on greasin' that boy, you need to take a break or something."

Guong lunged at him, intending to pin Trent's throat against the wall, but the *ninjitsu* master grabbed the incoming arm and shoved it out of the way, swiveling at the waist to pull his opponent off balance. The stocky pirate ended up with his own face planted against the wall as Trent twisted his arm up behind his back.

"I think you and I got off on the wrong foot. Now I'm willing to let bygones be bygones, and I hope you're smart enough to do the same, but if you cross me one more time, I'm going to do something more permanent to you. Do we understand each other?"

Trent relaxed his tight grip on the other man's arm just a fraction, waiting for his answer. For a moment, there was only silence, broken by Guong's harsh breathing. Trent ratcheted up his wristlock on the hulking Chinese man a bit farther, eliciting a growl from him, then, finally, "Okay, okay!"

Trent released him and stepped back quickly, just in case the bully wanted to continue the confrontation, which he was more than ready for. Although Guong whirled, he made no hostile move, just rubbed his wrist and glared at Trent.

"I'm glad we had this little talk." Trent turned and headed toward the galley, deliberately showing his back to Guong. He was prepared in case the other man tried something, but was pretty sure he wasn't going to make a move. True enough, Guong let him go, although Trent felt his stare burning into his back as he left.

Navigating his way through the ship, which was now showing signs of life, Trent went to the galley, which was in reasonable shape, all things considered. His growling stomach made him look for something that could be made quickly, so Trent assembled the ingredients for a beef and broccoli stir-fry, glad to see there was plenty of Chinese broccoli available. He'd just finished slicing up a pound of lean meat when he became aware of a presence standing in the doorway. Trent didn't stop his work, however, just finished cutting the meat and tossing it into his marinade of rice wine, soy sauce, water, cornstarch and sugar.

"What the hell you doin' in here?" The boy stared at him out of his one good eye, the other one swollen shut, the skin around it having turned a brilliant range of yellows and greens during the night. He looked like, well, like he had gotten the crap beaten out of him recently, with his lower lip still puffy and bruised, and traces of dried blood around his nostrils. Still, his working eye was bright, and if he hurt anywhere else, he hid it well.

"Making breakfast, since the staff seems to have the day off." Trent washed the broccoli and took it over to the counter, where he sliced it into thin strips, sparing a brief glance at the kid while he did so. The boy was smart, agile and fearless, with a no-nonsense attitude that Trent liked—a lot. Trent got the impression that if the kid saw something that needed to be done, he'd do it, simple as that. Easy now, Trent thought. Don't be getting caught up with the locals—you've got enough heat on you from big and ugly, you don't need to make it any worse.

"You're gonna need a lot more than that."

The boy's derisive tone made Trent pause. "What do you mean by that?"

"No one told you anything, did they?" The boy edged farther into the kitchen, almost as if he was unable to help himself.

Trent watched him approach out of the corner of his eye, knowing something was up, but not quite sure what the deal was. I think he's confused to find me here—in his space, he thought. "Why don't you fill me in?"

"They have this 'tradition' for the new men. The first one who steps into the galley had better make enough food for the entire crew."

"What happens if he doesn't?"

"The last guy who refused to go back and make more got keelhauled—literally. He didn't live too long after that." The boy watched Trent closely, waiting for his reaction.

Trent gave that some thought. The idea of being dragged under the length of the ship, to be torn to ribbons by barnacles and other growth, not to mention the very real possibility of becoming fish food from the propellers, didn't sound very attractive. He walked to the refrigerator and took out five pounds of beef. "Guess we'd better get cooking, then. You know how to make steamed buns?"

The boy sniffed disdainfully. "Better than your grandmother's."

Trent smiled as he located two large woks. "Then put your hands where your mouth is and get to work."

"Don't worry about me. I've been cooking here ever since we took this ship. In fact—" He went to a cabinet and brought out a large ceramic mixing bowl, floured and covered with a dishtowel. Whipping it off, he revealed an overflowing dome of light dough, about to spill over the edges. "This batch is just about ready. I had to hide it from the others. They like to do stuff to the food, even if it means they don't get to eat it."

"So, even though you look like you just got run over by a water buffalo, you came down here, what, three hours ago to prep bun dough?"

"Yeah. I know what to do to get by here."

Trent nodded, impressed by the kid's forethought. He washed the larger pieces of beef and carved them into small pieces with fast, economical slices. "Well, the proof's in the eating, I always say. Still, this is a pretty fancy kitchen. I didn't expect to come out and live in such luxury. Lee must treat you guys well."

"Well enough. This is just one step in the plan. He's got it all figured out. When this is done, we'll all be rich."

Trent tested the heating woks, adding droplets of oil until they sizzled. "Sounds like a great idea. Hey, how'd you hook up with these guys anyway?"

"Who the hell wants to know?" The abrupt change in the boy's tone was unmistakable. Trent half turned to see the kid watching him the way a trapped animal watches the hunter approaching. From his posture, Trent figured he was lucky the kid was making buns; otherwise if he'd had a knife, it might have ended up planted between his shoulder blades.

Shit, moved too fast, you don't have his trust yet, he thought. "No reason. I've been all around the world myself," Trent said, keeping his voice light. "I just like hearing where others come from, that's all. Didn't mean to get you riled."

"Then why don't you tell me where you're from first?" The boy returned his attention to the sticky dough, kneading it hard with his fingers.

"Sure. The earliest time I remember is growing up with my family in Thailand." Trent regaled the kid with stories for the next ten minutes, some of it off the detailed dossier Stony Man had prepared for him, some of it growing up as a mischievous middle-class kid in San Francisco, with those anecdotes spun to give a Southeast Asia feel to them, and other stuff he just made up. "And after my stint in Australia, I drifted north with the current, until I found myself on the docks in Manila, and saw a brave kid about to get a faceful of bruises for his trouble."

"Yeah..." The kid had kept busy while listening to the stories, creating twenty-four individual buns and letting them rise one last time. Meanwhile, Trent had been enlarging his former single serving of beef and broccoli into a much larger portion.

Trent frowned as he surveyed the large stove. "We're going to have to switch off on the cooking, otherwise not all of it will be finished at the same time."

"After hearing how much some of those guys put away last night, they probably won't have much appetite anyway."

"Funny, I didn't see you join the celebration."

The kid pointed to his face. "What can I say. I wasn't in the mood. I certainly heard them, however—the shouting could have woken the dead." A shadow darkened his face for a moment, and Trent considered following up the strange comment, but turned back to the meal being assembled instead. Maybe I can find out what he's hiding later, he thought.

"Regardless of what you think they'll eat, it's always better to make too much than not enough. See if you can find two large pots and get some water boiling in them. We'll do your buns in those, while I double batch the main course. By the way..." Trent held out his hand. "I'm Liang Dai."

"Xiang Po." He took Trent's hand and pumped it twice, then let go. "And, uh, thanks for helping me out on the dock yesterday."

Trent grinned. "Thanks for telling me I had to cook for everyone this morning. Let's get this all finished, okay?"

Soon the water was bubbling and dancing in the pots, matching the sizzling oil in the wok. Trent stir-fried the beef in the wok for two minutes, then poured in the mixture of broccoli, water chestnuts and carrots, stirring them while clouds of fragrant steam rose into the air. "Damn, forgot the rice."

"Don't worry about it." Xiang held up a large bag of instant rice. "It may not be traditional, but it's damn fast." He mixed up a large bowl and set it in the microwave. "We'd never have enough time to boil that and get the buns done, as well. We'll only have a dozen to serve first as it is."

"I like the way you think. Where'd you learn to cook so well?"

Xiang's face darkened, and Trent thought he'd asked the wrong question again. But the kid just shrugged. "Our previous leader liked it. When we hit a decent ship, he'd take the food and make the best meals. I learned from him. When there was nothing, we went hungry."

"That sounds familiar." Trent refrained from asking what had happened to the boy's previous mentor. In this profession, it was survival of the fittest, and it was obvious the leader-cook hadn't made the ultimate cut. He scooped a heaping pile of beef and broccoli into a bowl, and snatched the bowl of rice from the microwave. "Those buns done? Then get this up to wherever the men eat, and get back here so we can get the second round on the way."

Xiang eyed him for a moment, and Trent wondered if he was going to refuse, but he simply nodded, grabbed the large tray and vanished from the kitchen. Trent got the next cluster of buns on the steaming platform and stirred the batch of beef and broccoli, judging it almost done. His stomach rumbled as he tasted and tested, reminding himself that he hadn't eaten in the past sixteen hours.

Xiang was back just as he finished prepping the next tray, panting a bit, his face flushed. He set the empty tray down on the counter and wiped his forehead.

"That was fast."

"Like serving a school of sharks. Whoever got some first is bolting it down, and the others are getting restless."

"All right, take this out, then we'll both serve the last of it." He loaded Xiang down with the second tray, then finished up the last batch of rice, mixing in the rest of the meat and vegetables, and surrounding it with the final bunch of steamed buns. After turning everything off in the galley, he brought the large bowl out himself, meeting Xiang in the hallway.

"Just in time. Get two bowls and two pairs of chopsticks and come with me."

"One more thing. The cook is always supposed to eat last, especially if he's a new guy."

Trent's eyebrows raised in surprise. "Oh, really? Aren't you hungry?"

"Starving."

"Then follow my lead, and whatever you do, *don't* back down."

Trent led the boy down the corridor and into the aft deck, where the men had gathered to dine. Many of them had used plates and utensils from the night before, with some even scooping their breakfast with their fingers out of crystal wineglasses. Everyone was smiling and eating quickly, enjoying the meal. Only Lee Ming sat at the table in the middle of the space, a bowl in one hand and chopsticks in the other.

Setting down the large bowl, Trent shook his head and *tsk-tsked* as he surveyed the scene. "Not sure I care to be cooking for a bunch of barbarians like these guys."

"They're all good men, if a bit rough around the edges." Lee looked at the large bowl of food, then belched and set his empty bowl down. "I've had enough. Anyone else who wants more, come get it."

Trent took a bowl from Xiang and began filling it, conscious of Lee's eyes upon him, along with the rest of the men. He didn't stop, but topped off his bowl, gave it back to Xiang and began filling the second one for himself, hooking a chair with his foot and dragging it out. "Sit down and eat, Xiang."

The boy was so surprised he almost fell over. His eyes flicked to Lee, who barely inclined his head, allowing the break in tradition. The men whispered among themselves, not one willing to approach the table now. A shadow fell over Trent, and he felt hot, sour breath on his ear.

"What, Po didn't tell you that the cook always eats last?" Guong hissed.

"Yeah, he did, but that doesn't make much sense to me. After all, the cook made this delicious food for the rest of you. Without him, you'd all be dining on half-cooked slop, or whatever else you could scrounge around here." Trent pushed out his chair and sat down in front of Lee Ming, staring into his inscrutable black eyes. "I'd say that's worthy of a bit more respect, wouldn't you?" Scooping up a bite of rice and meat, he lifted it to his mouth.

The distinctive click of a pistol action being worked was the next sound that broke the silence, followed by a pressure on Trent's temple and the smell of gun oil wafting across his nostrils.

"Who the hell do you think you are, coming in here and throwing your weight around like *you* run the show?" Guong's voice gritted through his teeth, he was so angry.

Trent didn't do anything at first, just kept staring at Lee Ming, who returned his flat gaze without blinking. To his left, Xiang sat in his chair, as stiff as a mannequin, the expression on his face making it obvious that he expected to be wearing blood and brains in the next few seconds.

Trent ate his bite of food, chewing slowly as he placed his chopsticks on the table and swallowing before speaking. "If you have any influence over your… excitable man, I'd suggest you exert it, and soon."

There it was—a direct challenge to Lee Ming's leadership. If he did nothing, then Trent's accusation that he couldn't control his men would be true. If he stopped his man, then Trent gained a bit of face for calling the leader out and making him do it. Trent waited for the pirate's response, already planning his next move to disarm the burly hijacker next to him.

The seconds ticked, with no one moving a muscle. Then Lee Ming's face broke into a smile, and he nodded and chuckled. Like a switch had been thrown, the rest of the men around them, save for Guong, relaxed.

Lee waved a hand at his underling. "All right, Guong, let it go. You're keeping the cook from his meal." He laughed once more. "You certainly don't lack courage, Liang."

Trent reached for his chopsticks, but caught a shadow flashing over his face as he did so. He threw himself back just as Guong brought the butt of the pistol down where his head had been a second ago. Trent grabbed the other man's wrist with his left hand and pulled it toward him. At the same time, he grabbed the pistol and pushed it away with his right, breaking Guong's hold on it. The larger man wrenched his arm out of Trent's grasp and grabbed his shirt, half pulling him out of his chair. He raised his left hand, now balled in a fist—

"Guong!"

The brute stopped in midswing.

"You've embarrassed yourself and me with this pitiful display. Brawling like a common thug over something so inconsequential. Get out of here. I don't want to see your face for the rest of the day."

Releasing Trent, the man retreated as he had just been beaten. "I want my pistol back."

Lee glanced at Trent. "The choice is yours."

Trent had already safed the gun, and now took a closer look at it. It was a Czech VZ75B, an older piece, but well-maintained. Apparently Guong knows how to do one thing right, he thought, tucking the weapon into his belt. "I'm keeping it for now, to prevent any more… misunderstandings, like what just happened."

Lee nodded. "A wise decision."

Guong seemed about to protest again, but Lee cut him off before he could utter a word. "Why are you still here? Get out, cur!" His words seeming to injure the large man more than blows ever could.

Trent righted his chair, which had tipped over during the short scuffle, sat down again and picked up his bowl, scooping a large bite out and chewing with pleasure. He nodded at Xiang, who grabbed his bowl and ate with remorseless determination, clutching it as if it might be his last meal on earth.

"Slow down. You'll choke if you ain't careful."

Trent's relaxed demeanor caught the attention of the rest of the men, who crowded around the bowl again, good-naturedly scrambling for choice bits of the feast. Trent caught Xiang's eye and tipped him a quick wink, then returned to his breakfast. He looked up only when he was finished to find Lee still watching him as the rest of the pirates drifted away, some with a last bite of food, some licking their fingers and sighing in contentment.

"You know your way around both a kitchen and a pirate group. An interesting combination, Confucius."

The pirate leader's tone was neutral, and Trent took a moment to see which way the proverbial wind was blowing. If Lee saw him as a threat, then he wouldn't hesitate to have him killed. But if he saw a potential ally....

Lee leaned forward. "We should talk more—in private. Come to the bridge in one hour." With that, he got up and strolled away, pausing to glad hand a couple of the men he passed.

Trent looked over at the slack-jawed Xiang. "Close your mouth, unless you're catching flies."

"That was—that was incredible!" Trent could almost feel the hero-worship radiating from the kid's eyes, and had to remind himself that he was only playing a part here.

Trent set his bowl down and leaned over to the boy. "*That's* how you make your way in this world—take the advantage where you find it, and never let go of it once you do." He reclined back in his chair, snatching the last steamed bun from the bowl and munching it. "And follow up on every opportunity that presents itself, like I'm going to do in a little while."

But I'm damn sure going to take that pistol with me, he thought, popping the last bite of bun into his mouth while his eyes drifted to the windows of the bridge above them.

CHAPTER NINETEEN

The morning over Hong Kong dawned bright and clear, and as was his custom, Hu Ji Han rose with the sunrise to greet the new day. After a half hour of fluid tai chi, he enjoyed a light breakfast, then was picked up by his company driver and taken to his office. Anyone looking at him would have seen a man at the top of his game, a captain of industry going in to work to manage his empire.

Indeed, Hu felt that way himself. Once the decision had been made, he had gone home and slept like a child, his rest easy and dreamless. He had awakened filled with the conviction that this was the right thing to do, the just thing to do, not only for him, but for those hundreds of thousands of souls that had never known rest after their deaths. Even the thoughts of his grandmother were more subdued today, as if she was letting him concentrate on doing what had to be done. There was no going back now, he mused, the thought filling him with calm reserve, as if now that his course of action was set, he would be unstoppable.

His driver dropped him off in the underground garage, and Hu took the private elevator up to his office. He entered the spacious suite to find Zheng Rong already there, dressed in a perfect dark blue silken pantsuit. She sat in a chair in front of his desk, engrossed in watching something on her laptop. However, when he came in, she closed it, stood up and bowed.

"Good morning, sir."

"Good morning." Hu crossed to his desk, where his green gunpowder tea was laid out for him to steep when he was ready. "What do you find so involving this early in the day?"

She paused for a moment, the silence making Hu stop making his tea. "It is probably nothing, sir, but when I came in this morning, I got the sense that something wasn't right in the office. That the room's *chi* had been disturbed, and not by you or I."

Hu didn't dismiss her words lightly. Like many Chinese of his generation, he believed strongly in the idea of *chi,* the inner essence of everything on the planet, living or otherwise. He had instilled this belief in Zheng, as well, so when she claimed something was off, he gave her his full attention. "Have you found anything amiss?"

"I've been reviewing the security files from last night, but haven't found anything out of the ordinary. Other than myself coming in to prepare for this morning, there hasn't been anyone else here. Everything was fine..." She trailed off as her brow furrowed in thought, then she nodded at the standalone computer in its alcove. "Did you use the second machine last night?"

Hu reviewed his actions of the previous evening. "No, I had no need to. Why?"

"Because as I was leaving last night, I noticed that the computer itself was on, although the monitor was off."

Hu stared at the computer, then at his desk and the walls around him, suppressing a shudder at the thought of anyone else invading his private sanctum. And if they had accessed what was on *that* particular computer…

He came around the desk. "Is our plan in jeopardy?"

She leaned close to him, her voice low. "I do not believe so, since there is nothing on-site to link us to it. However, it would be wise to speak of it circumspectly in the event that someone may be listening."

"Ah, just a moment, then." Hu snatched a remote from the desk and turned on the flat-screen television on the far wall, tuning to a local financial channel and turning the volume up. "There, that should give us some privacy."

"Yes, sir. If you don't mind, I'm going to keep looking, as well as have this room swept. I'm just not satisfied yet."

"Very well, and see if you can find evidence of anyone having accessed that computer. Even if you don't, it's past time that we moved the data on it to a portable storage option anyway. I should have done so long ago." He shook his head; no use lamenting it now. "What else do you have for me?"

Zheng brought up a chart of the South China Sea on her LCD screen. "The stars have aligned for us at last. We finally have the proper ships moving to the right destinations at the right times." She pressed a button, and the screen split into two different pictures. On the left, two dotted lines left from separate ports, one traveling from Australia to Hong Kong, the other heading from the Philippines east toward Japan. Both routes would take them through an area where they could be intercepted by the waiting pirates. In order to arouse the least amount of suspicion, they had been waiting for the right two ships to come along, already heading toward their intended targets, so the men could take them both and continue on their way without drawing attention to themselves.

The other one showed a picture of the Atlantic Ocean, and two more dotted lines of cargo ships, one heading toward England, and the other crossing the ocean to the United States.

"And their cargoes are acceptable?" Hu leaned forward, feeling his pulse quicken. His grandmother's restless spirit whispered in his ear, demanding the retribution that would be hers.

"All four ships are carrying full loads of ammonium nitrate, at least ten thousand metric tons apiece. The destruction should be tremendous. As long as Lee's men and those mercenaries can pull this off...."

"They will, their greed will ensure that they do. What is this over here?" Hu pointed at a large mass that seemed to be drifting toward the Philippines.

"That is divine providence. A tropical storm front—not a typhoon, but strong winds and rain, and more importantly, heavy cloud cover, to hinder satellite tracking. Lee's men will have a challenge on their hands, but as you say, they should be able to handle it. Shall I give them the coordinates and the instructions to begin?"

Hu straightened, smoothing his crimson tie as he did so. "Immediately."

In his mind's ear, his grandmother's spirit cackled with glee at the impending catastrophe.

CHAPTER TWENTY

Akira Tokaido slumped in his chair, the stress of the past few hours—filled with long periods of inactivity, broken only by hearing how close they'd come to being discovered in China, and then losing all contact with Bolan and the members of Phoenix Force until recently—weighing heavily on him. "That was too close."

"Agreed," Aaron Kurtzman said. "Keep an eye out for that assistant's electronic sweep. We'll have to make the bugs go dormant so they won't be detected." Stony Man's equipment techs were careful to camouflage their eavesdropping devices to match whatever they were placed in or on, so neither man was worried about them being spotted in a physical or visual examination, but it was impossible to hide from electronic sensing devices without powering the bugs down completely, so that was also an option they had developed. There was only one problem with it, however...

"That won't help our information gathering capabilities much, not that we were getting a great deal anyway." Tokaido rubbed his eyes, making the images on the monitors unfocused and fuzzy. "I don't understand why we're having this much trouble uncovering information on this operation, particularly with someone on the inside. There's always a weak link somewhere.

Why haven't we found it and applied the necessary pressure yet?"

Kurtzman shrugged. "Since when have you been so intent on getting results? We've accomplished more in forty-eight hours than any other Beltway agency could have done in two weeks."

"Maybe so, but now our forward momentum's slowed to less than a crawl. You guys have always told me that operations like this always have leaks, loose lips, some kind of trail of purchases, the criminal records of the participants, connections to other people to exploit—something. Yet these people seem to have planned the perfect operation—no tracks, no loose ends. It's almost something to admire. They could give lessons to other small-cell terrorist groups on how to plan and carry out a successful mission while keeping it under wraps."

Kurtzman pursed his lips in disapproval. "Keep in mind that they haven't achieved their main objective yet. If you're truly concerned with learning their plans, maybe we should simply 'borrow' Mr. Hu for an evening. I'm sure David would be able to convince him to tell us everything he knows in short order."

Although Tokaido had done many things for Stony Man, he knew all too well where his real abilities lay, and they weren't in pulling a trigger, or in ordering someone to be kidnapped and interrogated by any means necessary. He knew he was getting frustrated at their situation when he found himself actually giving the idea serious consideration. Despite the abhorrently practical uses for it, he didn't believe in torture or any other coercion methods to wring information out of a subject, no matter what the circumstances.

It was a slippery slope, and the arguments for it were

compelling. After all, weren't those who would kill others for whatever cause they espoused giving up their basic right to humane treatment at the hands of their interrogators? And at what point did the evidence of a mounting terrorist operation justify the use of those means to elicit the needed information?

"Well, we don't have the okay from Hal or Striker for that, right? And David's still watching him?"

"Around the clock."

Tokaido grinned. "He must love that—sitting on his ass in one place for hours and hours. We might as well just keep him there for now unless Striker or Barb says otherwise."

"Don't worry, I'm sure he'll be ready to go the moment he gets the word."

"Right. How're the guys doing in Marrakesh, not to mention what's that enemy force in Morocco up to now?"

Kurtzman wheeled himself over to another computer station. "They've just taken off from the airport and are heading to London to regroup. As for those others, they swept through the arms bazaar with a well-trained whirlwind, leaving the majority of the attendees dead or missing in action, and have pretty much razed the site to the ground."

"Jeez, that's going to put a huge dent in the number of illegal arms dealers around for the next few years. Maybe we should send whoever was behind this a congratulatory note for doing so much of our work for us."

Kurtzman snorted. "I doubt Striker would share that viewpoint. Anyone with the ability to bring that much firepower and force to a single target is a huge red flag for us. No doubt he'll want to know who did it, who paid for it and why. If I were you, that's exactly what I'd be roaming cyberspace for to try to find out."

"Good point. Let's see if we can get something to break, instead of waiting for it to come to us." While he began searching the internet for information on the brutal attack in the African desert, Tokaido brought up the yacht's current location and heading. A few seconds later, a map opened up in his corner of his monitor, zoomed in to show the South China Sea, including the several-thousand-mile area around the Philippines. Ever since they'd located the yacht, Tokaido had plotted its route since the hijacking several days earlier—a seemingly aimless course around the open ocean for two days, then it had approached an isolated section of coastline and berthed, which was when they had put in for supplies and done the hasty hull repainting, including altering the name of the boat, now called *Patriot's Pride.* Afterward, they had headed back to the open sea, and were now sailing due east-northeast, into a landless stretch of the Pacific.

Despite his quest to find out whatever he could about the arms bazaar assault, Tokaido's attention kept returning to the yacht. "Where are you guys headed?" he muttered. "It has to be something bigger than simply piracy. They already have a luxury yacht. What would they want to steal that would be better than it?"

He pondered that question, then brought up the sailing route of every other ship over fifty yards that had set out from a port within the past three days, or was going to within the next twenty-four hours. A few moments later, his once-clean map sprouted hundreds of colored lines from ports of call in China, the Philippines, Australia, Singapore, South Korea and several other places, the tendrils of their journey spreading and crisscrossing and joining and separating, creating a tangled web of ships plying the waterways in the region so thick it made Tokaido's eyes hurt just to look at it.

There's gotta be a way to cut this down, he thought, his fingers flying over his keyboard. Maybe if I remove all pleasure craft from the time frame....

Maybe fifty lines disappeared. He refined his search, removing any vessels that weren't carrying crude oil, or any cargo that could be turned to a terrorist use, like ammonium nitrate. The computer began chugging away, cross-referencing the manifest files of hundreds of vessels.

This is gonna take a while, Tokaido realized.

Come on, he thought as he sifted through hundreds of thousands of texts, cell calls and satellite communications. I know you're out there somewhere....

CHAPTER TWENTY-ONE

Trent reclined in a chair on the aft deck, sipping a glass of chilled mango juice, and tried to figure out when the best time to approach the bridge would be. A piece of advice from his father came to mind: *"When you need them more than they need you, arrive five minutes early. When they need you more than you need them, arrive five minutes late."*

Thanks, Pop, he thought, but you never said how it should go if I need them more, but for reasons they can't possibly know, so I guess I'll settle for being right on time.

After helping Xiang clean up the kitchen, he'd taken a stroll around the large ship to familiarize himself with its layout, locating the bridge, engine room, radio room and any other places he might find useful. He also found several out-of-the-way places that would be perfect for reporting in to the Farm unnoticed—just as soon as he got some useful information.

When the time was right, Trent rose and headed for the stairs to the bridge. On the way up he saw Guong coming down, but the bigger man didn't spare him a second glance, just brushed by him without a word. Trent didn't do anything, either, but he was pretty sure things weren't over between him and the pirate yet.

An armed guard stood outside the door to the bridge.

Trent let him know that Lee had sent for him, and amused himself by coming up with seven ways to take the guy out before he could either draw his sidearm or shout an alarm. The guard radioed in for clearance, then opened the door for him to enter.

Like the rest of the yacht, the bridge was sleek and modern. Several LCD monitors let a crew of two run the entire show, with the clear windows above giving them a more than 200-degree panoramic view of the surrounding ocean. Lee sat in the raised captain's chair, overseeing his two pilots. When he turned to Trent, his face lit up into a smile, and he waved the other man over.

"Liang, come on in!" He waved at the boundless blue expanse around them. "This is thc best view on the boat, bar none. The rest of the men enjoy their booze and the other luxuries below, but for me, this is always the best place to be."

Trent nodded. "Naturally, you'd want to be somewhere so you can direct the action."

Lee's smile turned sly. "Is it always business with you? No matter, after all, that's what we're here to discuss." His expression turned serious. "I like you, Liang. In my line of work, I have to instantly measure a man to see if he's going to be an asset or a burden. Fortunately, based on what I've seen so far, you seem to fit in here quite well."

Trent bowed slightly. "Thank you, it's always a pleasure to work with professionals. There's less chance of things going wrong."

"My sentiments exactly! That is why I've made a few adjustments to my overall plan. I'm going to have you accompany my boarding party." He consulted a paper with a printed map on it, angling it so that Trent couldn't read it. Apparently my likeability only goes so far, he thought while waiting for the pirate leader to speak.

"The operation is simplicity itself. We're going to take over a specific cargo ship and pilot it to its original destination. That's the beauty of it. There's no reason for any one to think they're in trouble. We already have the devices to block the radios for the few minutes we'll need to get aboard, and from there, we simply take it into port."

"So, let me get this straight. We're hijacking a ship to take it into their regular destination? You'll have to excuse me if I fail to see the point."

Lee clapped him on the shoulder. "You don't have to worry about that. All you need to concern yourself with is making sure we control that ship when we go for it. Then you just leave the rest to me, and once we make the harbor, you and the others will be paid your share—one hundred thousand dollars apiece."

"No complaint about that. When do we leave?"

"Soon enough. You'll be staying on the boat for the time being, and I'll let you know when we're going to move. For now, just relax and enjoy the ride."

Easier said than done, Trent thought, but his only outward reply was to smile. "No problem." As he walked out of the room, he heard one more thing from the man at the far console.

"A storm front is approximately two hundred kilometers away, Ming."

"Keep me informed as to its heading and speed, and increase ours to eighteen knots."

Trent slipped out of the room and headed downstairs, deeper into the ship, looking for an unobserved corner.

He passed thought the stateroom floor, heading into the bowels of the vessel, in the aft section of the ship. Pausing twice to see if he was followed, Trent found a small supply closet, squeezed into it and took out his satellite phone.

"Stony Man, this is Alpha." As soon as the connection was made he was connected to Tokaido.

"Akira here."

"They're taking a ship, but I still haven't been able to get any more details yet."

"Got a name?"

"They've been smart enough to keep this yacht off the authorities' radar. They're not going to give the entire plan to the brand-new man," Trent said. "You should be able to narrow it down to ships within the range of this vessel, probably no farther out than five hundred kilometers, and also on the edge of the approaching storm system. If you narrow the search, you should be able to get a range of probable targets in the radius."

"Right. When are you taking the target ship down?"

"I don't have all of the pieces yet, but soon.'"

"Understood. Is there anything else you can tell us?"

"Yes. After taking over the ship, they're going to pilot it to its original port destination, to avoid suspicion from the harbor personnel. I suspect the cargo is either going to be offloaded to different buyers, or else they may be planning some kind of terrorist act against the port itself. Limits the targets a bit, I think."

"Yes, that does help, particularly if your guess about potential terrorist activity is correct. Keep at it, Alpha, and let us know the moment you discover anything else."

"Will do. Signing off now." Trent flipped his phone

closed and paused at the door to the hallway, listening to see if anyone was outside. Hearing nothing but the rhythmic thrum of the twin engines, he stepped out—and came face-to-face with a pirate he didn't remember seeing before.

"That ain't the toilet. Move it, I gotta piss."

Instead of stepping aside, the man just stood there, his hands on his hips. "Who were you talking to in there? In English?"

Trent tried brazening his way out again. "What, is everyone around here hearing things? I don't know what you're talking about. Now get the hell out of my way."

"You're coming with me." He reached for Trent's arm, but Trent moved first, his hand flashing up to grab the man's palm and twist it to one side, making him grimace in pain and drop to one knee. With his other hand, the pirate lashed out at Trent's stomach just as the ninja brought his other hand down in a chop to the back of the thug's neck, dropping him to the floor. The other man's blow thudded into Trent's solar plexus, making him grunt in pain.

Bending to pick the guy up, Trent felt hands grab his throat and squeeze, cutting off his air while his head and neck were wrenched backward. Instead of resisting, he pushed backward, crashing into his attacker and feeling the guy's nose break as the back of Trent's head slammed into his face. The pirate shouted in pain and surprise, but kept his grip on Trent's neck, squeezing harder as they staggered backward down the hallway.

Trent saw bright white stars bursting before his eyes, and knew he was about to pass out if he didn't get some air immediately. Twisting in the man's grip, ignoring the pain as his callused fingers scraped the skin on

Trent's neck raw, he turned enough to get a hand on the man's thumb, and bent it back with all of his remaining strength. The man clenched his teeth to stop from screaming, but before he could release his grip, the digit cracked apart like a chicken bone. The punk shrieked in agony, releasing Trent and driving his uninjured fist into the side of the operative's head, snapping his head back and forcing him to stumble away—right into the body of the other pirate.

Trent fell to the deck but immediately tried to rise, knowing through the haze of pain if he didn't keep fighting, he'd be dead. Lashing out with his legs, he hit something, and heard a cry of pain, then another impact crashed into him, and there was only darkness.

CHAPTER TWENTY-TWO

Only when they were a half hour in the air did Bolan finally relax and turn his attention to the burning questions that plagued him.

Who had the resources to wipe out such a huge concentration of arms dealers at once? Who was willing to risk the wrath of not only any survivors, but criminal organizations around the world, to do that? The men he'd killed had no identifying marks on them; the fatigues were standard digi-camo that could be purchased on a hundred websites around the world, and the weapons were also probably black market ones that couldn't be traced. Hopefully Tokaido can track where these guys were based so they could find them and get some answers, Bolan thought.

Finishing the rest of his glass of ice water, he contacted Stony Man Farm, hoping that Akira had been working on the problem. While he waited for the satellite to connect, he cast a glance toward the rear of the plane, where Uthman and his two bodyguards were sitting, with Phoenix Force in close proximity.

It had been decided to head to London, which was neutral ground for all of the involved parties. Bolan had made sure Kristianna Lofgren was able to contact her employers, and even supplied the portly Arab with a laptop so he could contact his people and put out his own feelers about what had just happened. Of course, the computer was recording every keystroke he made, and tracing every person he talked to, so Bolan could follow up on them later if necessary.

The encrypted satellite connection went through, and chimed to get his attention. Tokaido's face was pale and drawn, with dark half-moons under his eyes. Bolan nodded with satisfaction. The young man had been burning the midnight oil to get what he needed.

"Akira. What have you found out?"

"Whoever's funding that force, they've got some clout, I can tell you that. The entire unit was offloaded from a cargo ship at Agadir, about two hundred klicks north of the site. They convoyed through the desert in small groups and took up a position to the west and south of the main encampment."

"What about the drones I saw in the air?"

"Yeah, well, apparently those were the attacking force's, as well. I hacked some footage of the runs, and they were lobbing Hellfire missiles on fleeing victims. Anyway, the troops and equipment are heading back out to Agadir, presumably to get loaded up on that ship and sail out of Morocco."

"Where exactly are they heading?" As he spoke, Bolan brought up a map of Agadir, noting the airport that could handle the Gulfstream about twenty-two kilometers outside the city.

"The stated destination on their manifest is South Africa, but once they set sail, they could be headed who knows where."

"You got that right. Are any of them at the ship yet?"

"No, but many are on the way. They've also loaded up many of the vehicles used to carry people to the arms sale, and are hauling them back with them, I assume to sell or use themselves."

Bolan contacted Jack Grimaldi on the intercom. "Jack, set a new course for Al Massira airport, outside Agadir."

"You got it, Sarge."

Bolan returned his attention to Tokaido. "Time to pay those guys a visit and find out what the hell's going on. In the meantime, do you have anything new on that pirate situation?"

"Well, given the admittedly sketchy information, combined with the files from our Asian branch, Bear and I are estimating that there's a 67.3 percent chance that there will be a major terrorist incident at a major port in the South China Sea in the next twenty-four to thirty-six hours."

Although already prepared for that possibility, the calm confidence in Tokaido's voice made Bolan pause. "Break that down for me."

The computer hacker continued. "I ran the powered range of the yacht and all of its supporting boats out to their limits, and took into consideration what ships could be reached within that radius. Although there are a fair amount of viable targets around there, this ship caught my interest." With a couple more taps, he enlarged a section of the South China Sea, which had two lines running through it, all named. "The red line is the pirates, and the green line is the ship, a large freighter carrying a full load, ten thousand tons of ammonium nitrate.

"John said they were going to hijack a vessel, but planned to take it into its original destination port, so they don't want a ransom—they want to dock. Well, this ship is headed for a major port, Tokyo Bay."

Tokaido brought up another screen, which was playing one of Hu Ji Han's recorded telephone calls, with a translated transcript of the conversation below. "I'm fairly certain that one of his calls was to a member of Aleph, the Japanese terrorist group formerly known as Aum Shinrikyo. They're still around. Last year a couple of cells were found in the U.S., including one in Los Angeles. They claim to have rebranded themselves as a nonviolent movement after their leader was jailed for that sarin gas attack in the Tokyo subways in the mid-nineties. We're trying to track down the recipient, but apparently these guys know how to stay out of sight."

"So Hu manipulates these groups into claiming responsibility for the attack, while he masterminds the whole thing. To what end?" As soon as he'd asked the question, Bolan answered it. "The massive clean-up that would come in the wake of an event like that—his company would be poised to profit immensely, both now and in the future. Who wouldn't want the company that cleaned up the Tokyo Disaster to work on their project?"

"Sure, but there's an alternative reason for this, as well, and, although not quite as obvious, it does really fit everything together. You see, even though Japan would be a hotbed of business for a company like Hu's, he's never done any business with them—doesn't even have an office there. That seemed very odd to me, so I had a databot give me everything it could find on his background. It's darn good, too. After only twenty minutes I got almost more than I needed. Among it, this little piece of data."

He brought up another screen, and Bolan peered at

what looked like an old Chinese newspaper, with faded columns of characters running down the page in neat rows. Tokaido fiddled with it, and the text translated into English, revealing the headline: Atrocities Committed by Japanese Army at Nanking.

Bolan's brow furrowed as he read it. "The Rape of Nanking? What's that got to do with this?"

"Hu's grandmother was a survivor of the massacre, but she lost almost her entire family, with just one daughter, Ling, surviving. Ling gave birth to Hu, but she and her husband died when he was a child. He was then raised by his grandmother."

"And she groomed him to create this plot to destroy the harbor of their enemy from more than seventy years ago? Doesn't that seem rather far-fetched?"

Tokaido was undeterred. "Maybe, but whatever his reason, which is plausible, we can't afford to take that chance. Anyway, Tokyo is understandable, being the home of the transgressing army and all."

"Well, whatever the underlying motivations, if the incident goes off as planned, what's the casualty potential?"

"Extremely high. I reviewed the worst ammonium nitrate explosion in American history, the 1947 incident at Texas City, where 2,300 tons of it detonated after a ship caught fire, killing 581 and wounding 1,700. This would be much worse, an estimated equivalent of 12 kilotons of TNT. I've worked up the blast radius here, using the estimated 10,000 tons of nitrate in the hold of the ship. It's not pretty."

He hit a key, and a red bloom began in the port waters off Japan, spreading out to encompass both sides of the harbor, reaching a kilometer in diameter. "That's just the initial blast, here's the fallout effects." Another touch, and a yellow ring expanded around the red, reaching out nearly five kilometers. "Preliminary estimates are 5,000 to 15,000 dead and injured, and if the blast occurs during business hours, that would double. Damage in the red and yellow areas is estimated at upwards of five billion dollars, and would probably reach more than ten before it was all over. The intangible business losses would reach fifty billion and counting, as well as cause a ripple effect up and down the entire Asian community, which would naturally spread around the world. Combined with the aftereffects of the 2011 earthquake and tidal wave, it would be, quite simply, the most devastating terrorist act in the history of the free world."

"And all to avenge a travesty that occurred before many of the victims were even born." Bolan shook his head. "Not on my watch. Get ahold of Trent immediately. We have to take them down, now. All he has to do is sabotage the engine, and that should derail their plans enough until someone can take them into custody."

"I can't raise him."

"What do you mean, you can't raise him?" Bolan probed.

"I'm not getting an answer from his sat phone."

"Keep trying. And notify Hal to alert any police or navy boats in the area. Tell them they should board that yacht and subdue those pirates by any means necessary. Try to have them take at least two alive for interrogation. If Hu's behind this, I want to know."

"I'm sending the request now. That one's gonna take some time."

"Suggest that he red-flag it and kick it up the navy

chain of command. That should help. Also, notify Mc-Carter that he may need to snatch Hu in the next twenty-four hours." Bolan grimaced at the idea of Trent in harm's way. "And find another way to contact John. Hopefully he's still all right."

CHAPTER TWENTY-THREE

Xiang stood over the pile of motionless forms, breathing heavily. While coming out of the galley, he'd overheard Guong talking to two men, telling them to go find Liang and see what he was up to. He'd followed them as they searched the boat, locating their quarry deep in the lower levels. When they'd attacked, he had hesitated just long enough to see the second man get the jump on him, then leaped into the fray, bringing the flat side of a meat tenderizer down on the second pirate's head, felling him without a sound right on top on Liang.

Xiang didn't bother to see if he was still breathing, but stuck the tenderizer's handle through his belt and rolled the motionless pirate off the dazed man. While Liang was coming around, Xiang frisked him, coming up with the pistol he'd taken from Guong earlier that day and a small satellite phone, which Xiang slipped into his pocket. Flipping off the safety, he yanked the slide back, then held it steady in both hands and trained it on Liang as he sat against the wall, holding his throat while he tried to speak.

"Xiang…am I glad to see…" The man's hoarse voice trailed off when he saw the pistol in the boy's hands. Instead of blustering or threatening, he remained calm, and Xiang knew this wasn't the first pistol that had been pointed at him. "What are you going to do with that?"

Xiang frowned but kept aiming the gun at him. "I'm going to ask you some questions, and you're going to answer them, but first, we need to clean up here, and by we, I mean you."

Liang actually grinned at that. "You're the boss." Wheezing a bit, he used the wall to lever himself to his feet. "This might go faster if you helped."

"I'm willing to take the chance of being discovered. You, on the other hand, can't really afford to be found like this."

"Good point." Trent dragged first one, then the other pirate into the tiny supply closet, wedging their bodies together, then putting his full weight against the door to shut it, carefully edging away in case it might pop open again under the weight of the unconscious men inside.

"All right." Xiang looked past him down the corridor, then leaned against the far wall, careful to stay out of Liang's reach. "What was he talking about before he jumped you?"

"I don't know. That's the second time someone's come up to me and started talking shit. I'm starting to think everyone on board's going crazy, you know?"

Xiang studied the man while he talked. He was convincing, and his story, half-assed as it was, could have held water, except for one thing. He took the phone out of pocket. "What's a guy like you need something like this for?"

Liang nodded as if expecting the question. "All right, so I'm not *quite* the wandering vagabond I said I was. Truth is, I have family in Singapore, and they worry about me when I travel. Last time I was home, my, uh, mother made me take it. It's on a worldwide calling plan, so if I ever get into any trouble I couldn't handle, I could call home."

"I thought I heard him say you were talking in English."

Liang shrugged. "Like I said, crazy. I mean, I can speak it, but not to my mother. What'd be the point?"

"Really? So they wouldn't mind if you called them right now?" Xiang offered the phone to him. Something about the man's story just didn't sit right, but the boy couldn't figure out exactly what it was. He had tried to learn interrogation skills from Lee, who was professionally suspicious of everyone he met, and had said more than once, "Just because you are paranoid doesn't mean they aren't out to get you."

Liang glanced at thc phone with a dubious expression. "I could, but I just spoke to her a couple of days ago. If I call again so soon, she's liable to worry."

That could be true, for all Xiang knew. Not having ever had a mother, he had no experience to draw on. Still, something just didn't add up. Liang being the hero one moment, then skulking around the ship, as if he was looking for something—or trying to avoid being discovered—the next.

Xiang drew a bead on the man's knee. "One last chance. You either tell me who you are and what you're really doing here, or I'll shoot." Steeling himself to cripple the other man if he had to, Xiang tightened his sweaty grip on the gun handle. It had been one thing to shoot the young man, but that had still been an accident. Now he was threatening to blow apart this man's kneecap. But if Liang was threatening their mission—and their payday—then he was doing the right thing.

Liang held both his hands out in supplication. "Hey,

hey, hey, wait a minute. Look, I'm telling the truth. If I was under suspicion, would your buddy Lee tell me about the ship you're going after?"

That was news to Xiang. "Probably not. So why would Guong tell those two guys to go after you?"

"Are you kidding? I only embarrassed the guy in front of half the crew this morning. Hell, I'm surprised he didn't tell them to just kill me and dump my body overboard. That probably wouldn't have made Lee happy, but it would have been too late to do anything about it by then—at least for me."

In all that excitement, Xiang hadn't considered that. He had seen Guong's face flushed with rage after the standoff over the breakfast table and the rebuke from Lee. Guong certainly would take any chance he could to discredit Liang for his own gain. Xiang decocked the pistol and safed it, then held it out to Liang butt-first. "I think you might need this more than I do."

"You're probably right." Liang grinned as he took the gun and made it disappear under his shirt. "Now that that's over with, let me ask you a question. Is this what you want to do with your life?"

"I..." Xiang's voice failed him as he gaped at Liang. Not only was he not threatening to kill the boy for holding a gun on him and interrogating him about his loyalty, but he was still speaking as if he were an equal, not a cook or slave or whipping boy, but another human being. His brain almost seized up as he tried to comprehend the question. He had always been so concerned about surviving the next week, the next day, sometimes the next hour, that he'd never had time to consider the larger picture of what he wanted out of life. "Why do you want to know that?"

Liang shrugged, as if they were discussing nothing more consequential than what the weather might be like the next. "I've seen and done a lot of things in my life, some good, some bad. And having packed a lot into that time, all I can say is that you don't want to have any regrets. Some of these guys, like that brain-dead hulk Guong, live for the thrill of the kill, but that doesn't last. Eventually he'll come up against someone better than him, and he'll be done."

Liang reached out and tapped Xiang on the forehead. "I think you're smarter than that. I think that if you were given the chance to get out of this, you'd grab it in a second. Am I right?"

Xiang's head spun from the unexpected turn in the conversation. For a moment, his mind whirled with possibilities, then rationality crashed back down on him with numbing force. No one gives anything away free, he thought, drawing himself up with a scowl. "What the hell do you know? You know nothing about me, who I am, what I've done. I'm not going anywhere. I've done things—terrible things. This is where I belong. It's my home."

A bellow from above made both their heads turn. It was Guong, calling for him. "Xiang!"

Xiang's shoulders slumped in defeat. "See? I have to go." He turned toward the companionway at the end of the hall, but was stopped by Liang's hand on his arm.

"I don't believe that, and I know you don't, either. Just think about it. And hey, keep that phone. I think you might need it more than me. If you get into trouble, open it and press the green Send key three times. It will summon help for you."

"Xiang!" The bellow was so loud it seemed to shake

the ship around them. Xiang's face wrinkled in puzzlement, but he tucked the phone away in his shorts and ran down the hall, his footsteps pounding on the floor, his brain still trying to make sense of the conversation he'd just had.

The morning sun was blinding as he came out of the corridor, and Xiang shielded his face just in time to partially block a heavy blow from his tormentor, its force still driving him to the deck.

Guong towered over him. "Dammit, I'm tired of having to call you over and over again! When I call you, you come *now,* got it?"

"Yes."

"And just to make sure..." Guong reached down and fastened something around his neck, cinching it tight. Xiang heard the clink of something metal, and saw Guong straighten again, holding a two-meter long piece of leather, with the other end reaching to him.

He didn't...he couldn't... Incredulously, Xiang reached up to find a thick leather collar around his neck, with an attached ring that was fastened to the leash. The rest of the pirates snickered at Guong's new "pet."

"Maybe this'll keep you in line during our mission. Now come on, dog. We're going for a ride." With a savage jerk, Guong strode toward the aft platform, almost pulling Xiang across the deck until he managed to scramble to his feet and follow, hatred simmering inside, and one thought burning in his mind. Before this was all over, one of them would be dead—and it wasn't going to be him.

CHAPTER TWENTY-FOUR

With the Phoenix Force warriors in tow, Mack Bolan strode through Al Massira airport's large main room, which was split in two, one side handling international flights, the other side handling domestic ones. Although the airport handled more than one-and-a-half million travelers a year, this day the terminal wasn't very crowded, and those heading to and from their destinations instinctively moved out of the way of the five unsmiling, hard-faced men.

Bolan had told Grimaldi to file a continuing flight plan to Gatwick Airport near London, and that the five men planned to return as soon as possible. "We may have one or two new passengers with us," he'd told Grimaldi, who'd simply rolled his eyes, having seen just about everything Bolan could pull out of his hat and then some.

He went to the Europcar desk, where a seven-passenger van with all-wheel drive had been reserved over the web. Five minutes later, the men were zooming down the road toward Agadir proper. Bolan drove, with Manning beside him navigating. James and Encizo were in the middle seats, with Hawkins stretched out in the last one. Traffic was light, and they made the thirteen-mile trip in about ten minutes.

"Not to mess with our good fortune or anything, but

do we have any kind of plan working once we hit the city?" James asked, keeping a watch out on the left-side window. Just because the area around the airport was mostly desert and scrub brush didn't mean threats couldn't be lurking out there.

Bolan didn't take his eyes off the road as he headed into the outskirts of town. "We've gotten as much intel as possible from ancillary sources. Now we're going to pick up some straight from the employees' mouths. Our task is to find the dock these mercs are loading from and capture a couple of them alive. But we have to grab someone higher up in the chain of command—boots-on-the-ground grunts aren't going to cut it. We need to get hold of someone who knows what's going on."

"Right, just sneak in, locate and snatch an officer-level mercenary while he's surrounded by a couple dozen of his buddies. Not to rain on your parade, but just how're we expected to do that?"

Bolan caught Hawkins's puzzled stare in the rear-view mirror. "Don't worry. I've got another six miles to come up with something."

Fifteen minutes later, they were approaching the harbor side of the city. Bolan parked the van in an alley a few blocks from the docks, making sure it was aimed back into the city. A few seconds later, the five men were all surveying the busy area bustling with activity.

Although the city of Agadir seemed to alternate between modern buildings and older crumbling structures that betrayed its true origins and age, the large harbor and dock were as up-to-date as they could be for the region. Cranes were busy loading shipping containers onto a large freighter, while forklifts and tractor-trailers drove around either unloading or loading freight. Men were everywhere, shouting, conferring or simply talking among themselves.

"Okay, there are our targets." Looking through small Zeiss pocket binoculars, Bolan pointed at a group of vehicles painted in desert camo manned by men dressed similarly three docks down. "Looks like they rode hard to get here. Hopefully we can take advantage of that." Lowering the binoculars, Bolan studied the varied activity on the docks for a moment. "All right, here's the plan..."

"MAN, I DON'T MIND POSING as a gang member or even a militiaman to get some intel, but this might just take the cake."

Along with Rafael Encizo, Calvin James was dressed in a stained green jumpsuit that matched every other worker's on the docks. The uniforms weren't the only things that matched, however. Every other man there was either black or Arab, which meant the two Phoenix Force fighters were the only ones who could move among the rest of the workers without attracting undue attention.

"Just relax. You know the secret to successful infiltration, right? Ninety-nine percent of it is simply acting like—"

"You belong there, yeah, yeah." James passed a trio of swarthy dockworkers talking in what might as well have been Greek to him. "Did I mention that my Arabic is not up to this situation, like, at all?"

"You don't have to worry about them. They're our coworkers. They've got their jobs to do, and we have ours." Encizo indicated the man dressed in fatigues directing a group of dusty vehicles onto loading pallets. "That's the man we have to get next to?"

"Sure, and how am I supposed to talk when we approach him?"

"Just follow my lead." With that, Encizo approached the man, who was deep in discussion with another dock worker about several cargo containers.

"Look, I don't care where the fuck you put them, but they're goin' on that ship, you read me? Either someone else's cargo is comin' off, or you get to explain to my commanding officer why we don't have all our gear, got it?"

Shaking his head, the dockworker stomped off, muttering something that from his tone sounded highly derogatory. The fatigue-dressed man was about to turn back to the loading when he noticed Encizo and James, both standing with their heads slightly bowed, as if waiting to be acknowledged.

"Well, what the fuck do you want?"

Encizo did everything but tug on an imaginary forelock as he replied. "My apologies, sir, but we have been looking everywhere for someone who can tell us what to do with the other material left here by your company—"

"What other material?"

"I'm not sure, sir, it is all packed in boxes. But it's definitely from your company and marked as such—"

"Goddammit, why do I always have to clean up after those fuckin' teams? If I get my hands on 'em, they'll be swimmin' home, that's for damn sure." Still muttering under his breath, the short man turned to another a few yards away. "Connerly, take over supervising this mess, will ya? I got another pile of shit to take care of.

And don't take any crap from these people. All our stuff gets on the ship, or they don't get paid!"

While the man was ranting, James exchanged a nod with Encizo—this was definitely the guy they needed.

He turned back to the two Phoenix Force members. "Well, don't just fuckin' well stand there, take me to this pile of yours!"

"Yes, sir, right away." Encizo turned on his heel and began walking down the dock, leading the man away from his compatriots.

"Where are we going?"

"When your other group left, we didn't know what to do with the material, so we had to place it in a storage site that wasn't in the way. There will be, of course, some fees incurred for the storage—"

"Hey, you tell your fuckin' boss he can take any more 'fees' and shove 'em up his arse. You guys've been nickel and dimin' us ever since we got here, and I've had it up to here with it!"

"Yes, sir, I will be certain to tell my superior about your comments."

"Jesus, where the hell'd you put the stuff, Angola?"

They almost had him where they wanted him. Encizo pointed at the alley where the van was. "It is just around this corner, sir."

"Goddamn well better be. We were supposed to be outta here two hours ago—" The man's tirade was cut short when he saw Bolan, Manning and Hawkins all in the alley next to the van. "What the fuck?"

James was right behind him, a silenced Beretta 92S stuck in his back. "Guess what, buddy? You're the cargo we've been talkin' about. Now get moving!" He prodded the man forward with the muzzle of the Beretta.

"Who the fuck are you guys? What is this?"

Bolan pulled the door open. "It's a kidnapping—yours." He grabbed the man's shirt collar and shoved him inside. "Let's go."

The guy hit the floor of the van hard, but popped back up immediately. "Do you know who you're fuckin' with here? They ain't gonna let you just snatch me—"

"Shut up." James duct taped his mouth and snared his hands with a zip tie. He trussed the man's feet, as well, then expertly patted him down. "He's clean."

Bolan was already in the driver's seat and pulling away down the alley. At the mouth, where it would come out into the street, a large truck blocked their way. The Executioner leaned on the horn, but nothing happened.

"Nobody back there should even know he's gone—" Encizo's words were cut off by shouts and the revving of an engine behind them. "Or maybe they do."

Bolan hit the horn again, and the truck began to move again, but slowly.

"They're coming up fast," Encizo warned, MP5K out and ready. "That damn truck out of the way yet?"

"Not yet. We should try to avoid a bloodbath in the streets." The tractor trailer had finally inched forward far enough for Bolan to gun it and slip around the back end, grazing the van's right fender in the process. They pulled out just as gunfire exploded in the alley behind them, starring the rear window and making everyone duck.

Bolan took the winding road out to the Route de Essaouira, where he turned left and tromped on the gas. Their pursuers, at least four men in a Humvee, followed suit, heedless of honking horns and, in one case, the furious driver of a compact car who got sideswiped by the pursuing men's vehicle. On the main road, the van pulled ahead at first, but the Humvee's powerful engine had it catching up far too quickly.

"Where are we going?"

"Someplace we can lose these guys!" Bolan counted cross streets as they drove. Traffic was light on this street, unlike the main thoroughfare, the N1, which paralleled it.

"Incoming!" Encizo yelled as bullets shattered the back windshield. The Phoenix Force warrior popped up and let loose a burst from his own subgun. The bullets ricocheted off the windshield, but the last bullets caught the gunner in the shoulder, making him drop back into the vehicle.

"It's armored, we don't have anything that'll penetrate!"

"That's all right, we're here!" Bolan's memorization of the city map told him this was the intersection they needed, and he cranked the wheel hard right, ignoring the oncoming traffic. Horns blared and tires screeched as cars and trucks got out of the speeding van's way. But instead of getting onto the N1, Bolan kept heading northeast, down a winding road that seemed to head out into the desert. With the way cleared, the Humvee followed, another gunman popping up out of an open window.

"I thought we were planning on losing them!" Manning said, his own MP5K in hand as he watched the Humvee approach again.

"We are. What's the matter, don't you trust me?" Bolan asked as he swung the van around a left curve that brought them to his destination, a crowded neighborhood filled with a maze of buildings piled almost on top of one another, interspersed with narrow roads, dead-end alleys and plenty of vehicle, animal and foot traffic.

"It's not you I don't trust, it's this van surviving the trip!" Manning called back. His reply was punctuated by more bullets whining around them, a burst even coming close enough to tear off the passenger-side mirror.

The main road ran straight along the outskirts of town, but Bolan took a hard left and drove for another quarter mile, then spun the wheel right to head straight into the heart of the neighborhood.

"Just need to find the right alley…there!" Bolan cranked the wheel hard left again, almost missing his target, but shooting the unwieldy van into the gap with less than a foot to spare. The Humvee made the turn more cautiously, pulling to within a few yards of their bumper. Encizo and Manning exchanged bursts of fire with the gunman on the Humvee, neither scoring any significant hits.

"Pull in now!" Bolan ordered, having just spotted the alleyway he needed. Palming the wheel, he cranked it over to the left and turned into the narrow alleyway, the van's sides almost scraping the thick walls. "Come on, come on…"

Caught up in the chase, the Humvee driver took the bait and charged into the alley. His vehicle, however, was at least a foot wider than the European van, and quickly got wedged into the narrow alley, unable to move forward or backward.

"That did it!" Hawkins exclaimed.

"Good, now strip him," Bolan said once he'd gotten them back on the main road leading through the neighborhood. "They were on him far too quickly for it to be chance. There must be a tracking device on him."

James drew his double-edged Gerber dagger. "The things I do to save the world."

THIRTY MINUTES LATER, Bolan stopped the van in the middle of nowhere.

Bleak African desert surrounded them in all directions. Bolan turned the van off and got out. "Bring him."

James and Encizo dragged their victim, now wearing only a pair of boxers, out into the cooling afternoon. His hands and feet had been retied, and his mouth was secured, as well. The two men made sure he was standing upright, then left him on his own. Bolan walked over and ripped the tape from his mouth.

Even unarmed and mostly naked, the mercenary didn't seem the least bit cowed by them. "All right, just what the fuck is this all about?"

Bolan drew his .357 Desert Eagle and crossed his arms. "At the moment, it's all about what you tell us in the next few minutes that determines whether you live or die—and how."

The man eyed all of them up and down. "What, is this a professional hit?" He spit on the ground. "I ain't gonna fetch you shit for ransom, and it's not like I can tell ya all that much, but go ahead, ask away."

"Who hired you to hit the arms bazaar?" Bolan asked.

The man's sandy eyebrows rose. "*You* guys were the ones who escaped that—and you came after *us?* You got brass balls, man."

Bolan leveled the pistol at the man's knee. "You haven't answered my question."

"Hey, hey, hey, just a second now. As one professional to another, I can admire good skills when I see 'em—"

"We aren't even in the same sport, much less the same league," Bolan said, cocking the hammer back. "You have three seconds, or you'll be crawling back to town."

"All right, all right. Look, I'm a company leader. I receive my orders and carry 'em out, all right? Anything I glean about what's going on higher up is purely incidental. However, I got word that we'd been contracted out to some hotshot Chinese billionaire who wanted to pull a job that would draw the world's attention away from the other part of what he was planning—"

This was connected to Hu? Bolan's stony countenance didn't change one bit, but inside he was regrouping after learning this bit of news. "What was his plan?"

"I don't know the particulars, but a couple days ago, two of our smaller teams were sent out into the Atlantic Ocean to capture two targets. Now before you ask me, I have no idea what they were, or what our guys were supposed to do with 'em once they had 'em. My job was makin' sure my boys did their part to reduce that black market bazaar to dust, and that's what I concentrated on." He shrugged. "So you can blow holes in me all day long, but I won't be able to give you anything else."

Bolan eyed him in silence for several very long seconds, then safed and holstered the Desert Eagle. "All right, I believe you." He nodded to the rest of his team. "Bring him back in the van. He's coming with us."

CHAPTER TWENTY-FIVE

Trent gave Guong several minutes to finish whatever he was doing on deck. To pass the time, he checked on the two men in the storeroom, pressing an ear to the door to confirm their continued unconsciousness. With luck, it'd be a couple of hours before they were discovered, and by that time hopefully he'd have found out just what was going on.

He took a circuitous route back to the deck, doubling back at least once on the way. Trent saw other pirates along the way, creating a natural alibi in case he was questioned about the two missing men. At one point, he thought he heard a motorboat power up and head away from the boat, but by the time he got to a porthole to look outside, any trace of it was gone. He kept heading topside, coming out at the ship's bow, which gave him a stunning view of the storm front they were heading straight toward.

The freshening wind ruffled his hair, bringing the sharp scents of ozone and salt spray. Although this ship was one of the largest he'd ever been on, the seemingly solid wall of towering, gray-black clouds ahead looked as if it could swallow the 120-plus meter yacht and devour it without leaving a trace that the boat had ever existed.

Seeing no men up front, he ambled to the aft deck

to see what was going on, and found a few men there, keeping a wary eye on the growing storm clouds. Spotting Trent, one of them nodded at him. "Hey, the captain wants you back on the bridge."

"He say what for?"

"Nope, just to send you up if we saw you." He pointed to the ocean behind them. "It might be something to do with that ship that's been getting closer for the past ten minutes."

Shading his eyes, Trent looked at the large dot on the horizon. The ship was following at a safe distance, but fairly clearly shadowing the pirates' yacht. "Hey, did you guys see one of the other boats take off a few minutes ago?"

Another pirate replied. "Yeah, Guong took a group out a little while ago. I think it was to scout ahead, but I'm not sure. That kid sure looked funny dragging after him, though."

Trent half turned to him. "What d'ya mean?"

"Oh, Guong tied him up to a leash and took him on the boat with the rest of the men."

A cold ball of anger formed in Trent's stomach, but he kept his voice neutral. "Well, guess I'd better go see what the headman wants."

Crap, and he's got my phone, Trent thought. That's not going to sit well with the guys back at Stony Man. He took the stairs two at a time, and when he came to the guard again, the man opened the door without even challenging him. That's more like it, Trent thought as he stepped inside.

"Liang, come over here." Lee gestured him over to the bridge's radio console. "You've got a solid Cantonese accent. Talk to these guys. They say they're having engine trouble, and want our help so they don't get trapped in the storm."

"Why me?"

Lee's jovial face turned grave. "Because I told you to, that's why. Our papers have us coming out of Hong Kong, and I don't want anything to risk breaking our cover, not when we're this close to reaching our target. Get them off our wake, and fast."

Shrugging, Trent took the mike and pressed the transmit button. "This is Captain Liang of the *Patriot's Pride.* What is your situation?"

The voice came back tinny and faint. "*Patriot's Pride,* this is the *Flying Dragon,* out of Singapore. We're having engine trouble and need assistance. We think we can make it to you in the next ten minutes."

Trent exchanged a glance with Lee; he was sure the pirate had used the "engine trouble" ruse himself in the past. "Ah, negative, *Flying Dragon,* I'm afraid we are not equipped to assist at this time. I suggest that you contacting the local maritime patrols in the area."

"No one else is around, *Patriot.* They've all fled the approaching storm. If you don't help us, we'll die out here."

Trent released the mike button and looked at Lee. "We can take them prisoner once they're aboard and stow them in the cabins."

Lee stroked his chin as he considered the idea, then nodded. "I've got a better idea. Have them come alongside." He walked over to one of his pilots and whispered in his ear, making the man to rise from his chair and slip out of the room.

Trent hit the transmit button again. "*Flying Dragon,* this is *Patriot's Pride.* We will assist you. Come up on our port side, at a speed no faster than five knots, acknowledge."

"Acknowledged, *Patriot,* and thank you very much. We'll be alongside in ten minutes."

"We'll see you soon." Trent put down the mike and shrugged at Lee with an "I tried" expression on his face. There was probably a group of overweight, seasick tourists on board the other ship, which the pirates should have no trouble with capturing and keeping them for a couple of days.

Glancing at Lee, Trent noticed the pirate leader had a strange look on his face, as if things were proceeding exactly as he'd planned. "Here come your friends," Lee said, pointing at the approaching boat. Trent stiffened at his words, but realized the pirate was being sarcastic.

He snorted. "Not my friends. They're keeping me from getting started on our job and getting paid."

Lee watched the ship through a pair of Zeiss binoculars. "Good, I was a bit concerned you might've taken a liking to them—but as you said, they're delaying us all." He lowered the glasses and addressed the helmsman. "Cut our speed to four knots and let them draw up on the starboard side, just like the 'captain' here said. What's our ETA to the ship?"

"We're still within our timetable, but we'll need to handle this quickly to stay on schedule."

"Don't worry. Everything is under control."

Lee was calm as could be, but Trent attributed that to him thinking he had the upper hand, and had to keep a smile of his own off his features while he watched the other boat approach. It was smaller than the superyacht, about forty yards long, with only one level above deck, and an open observation deck above that. Two people stood on the open platform, and Trent saw one more on the bridge.

He found himself strangely uneasy, as if anxious for the capture to begin. Casting a surreptitious glance at Lee, he saw the man drumming his fingers on the arm of the captain's chair. Just a few more minutes…

The other yacht was now only about one hundred yards away, and Trent watched it approach, adrenaline drying his mouth and palms. He was so engrossed in watching it approach that he almost didn't hear Lee's single command.

"Now."

A moment later, a loud roar erupted from over Trent's head, and a fiery streak shot from the *Patriot's Pride.* It crashed into the bridge of the other ship and exploded, obliterating the forward structure of the boat and the three people in the resulting fireball. Startled, Trent's eyes widened as a second rocket sped toward the other boat, smashing into the forward bow and blowing a large hole in front of the ship, which shuddered at the impact.

Now the chatter of automatic weapons fire could be heard from below the bridge, rifles hammering large-caliber rounds into the boat's superstructure. Several of them raked it from stem to stern, punching jagged, splintered holes in the watercraft, and most likely anyone left alive inside.

The hole in the waterline was already making the boat list to port, and as Trent watched helplessly, a figure wreathed in flames appeared on the aft deck and fell into the water, arms flailing. An efficient burst of rifle fire chopped the water where he had gone in, followed by something small that splashed into the ocean.

A few seconds later, a geyser of water plumed into the air as the grenade went off, and a blackened, smoldering body floated to the surface.

The yacht settled into the water, the rising waves from the nearby storm lapping at its rear gunwale, but that wasn't quick enough for Lee. "Finish it."

Two more rockets roared into the burning ship, one enlarging the hole in the bow, and the other streaking into the ship's aft section, blowing open a second hole. The yacht listed farther over as thousands of gallons of seawater rushed in, dragging it below the surface. A minute later, all that was left was the stern, then it slid under the waves, leaving only shattered, floating pieces of wood, something that might have been a seat cushion, the dead body and a large oil slick behind.

"Take one of the Zodiacs out, make sure there's no survivors. Let's get moving again, eight knots. Tell them to catch up when they're done." Lee walked up beside Trent. "That went well, I think."

Trent kept his face calm, although inside he was horrified at Lee's brutal solution to their problem. He'd watched the brutal attack and slaughter of the innocent people aboard without any response simply because there was nothing else he could do. Although every muscle in his body ached to grab the pirate next to him and crush the man's head into the instrument panel, his voice was calm and even when he replied, "That's one way to take care of the problem." His stomach roiled at the thought of the men and women on the other boat being blown into hamburger for the sharks to feast on, and he silently vowed to avenge them by taking every pirate on this ship down, however he had to do it.

Lee chuckled. "Glad you approve. With so much on

the line, we couldn't afford to keep prisoners, so it was best to remove them sooner rather than later. You'll see why once the operation begins. Now go back down to the main deck and make sure everything's put away. It's about to get a lot bumpier around here. And hey—you did good, just like I knew you would."

A booming clap of thunder punctuated his words, which already stung like acid in Trent's ears, and he walked out of the bridge on legs of lead, steadying himself against the wall for a moment before straightening and continuing on his way. Walking down to the deck, he reached it just in time to see them set the raft into the water, the men in the search party holding their automatic weapons at the ready, laughing and boasting about their mission. Cold chills shot through Trent as he watched the jesting group, and he whirled on his heel and stalked belowdecks, wanting nothing more than to kill each man there.

As he passed Xiang's stateroom, a flickering shadow caught his attention, and he turned just in time to see a lithe form dressed in black from head to toe grab his arm and yank him into the room, sweeping his leg out from under him to send him crashing to the floor. Trent pushed off to turn himself around with one hand while his other went for the pistol in his waistband.

He flipped himself over on his back—to stare into the unblinking muzzle of a silenced pistol less than three feet from his face. The brown eyes visible in the black face mask were cold and merciless.

"Move and you're dead!"

CHAPTER TWENTY-SIX

"Jesus, what the hell just happened?"

Watching the encounter unfold, Akira Tokaido couldn't help gasping when he saw the first rockets shoot out and hit the other boat. Small orange sparks signaled automatic weapons fire from the pirates' yacht, which chopped the decks of the boat into pieces. The initial ambush was followed by two more rocket attacks, leaving the other ship sinking fast. In less than five minutes, it was gone.

Tokaido's face was pale and drawn. "These guys aren't screwing around. From what I could gather of their transmissions, they let that innocent boat approach, then blew it up with light antitank missiles. The recording of the conversation between the two boats indicates it was John doing the talking on the pirates' end."

"Jesus." Kurtzman shook his head for a second. "Have that file ready for Striker immediately. I'm sure John was just trying to help."

"Goddammit, we need to make contact with him ASAP, but I can't get him on the sat phone. It just rings and rings. How do you want to proceed?"

"There's gotta be a way to talk to him—" Kurtzman's voice was interrupted by the ringing of a phone on the desk, an outside line that only a few select people in the world could call to reach Stony Man Farm.

Tokaido snatched it up. "Computer room."

"DON'T SHOOT, DON'T SHOOT! I'm on your side!" Trent said in English.

"Bullshit! You're just another shitbag pirate who's about to get a bullet through his brain—"

"If that's true, then I wouldn't know that this yacht was taken from Robert Kirkall, who hired you guys to find these pirates and kill them. Am I right?"

The merc's eyes squinted at Trent for a moment. "How the fuck—"

"Listen to me. I'm working on the same goal from another end. You got a sat phone?"

"Yeah…"

"Do me one favor and dial the number I'm about to tell you." Trent recited the direct line to Stony Man's computer room, hoping Tokaido or Kurtzman was on duty.

"Who's this?" the merc snarled into the phone. He listened for a few seconds, his eyes going from controlled anger to puzzlement. He cupped the microphone against his wet suit. "They said if I got this number, one of their operatives gave it to me. What's your name—your real name?"

"John Trent."

The merc repeated it into the sat phone, then nodded and raised his pistol, nodding at Trent to sit up. "Yeah… those fuckers just took out my entire team…you bet your ass I'm gonna stop 'em…all right, we'll play this your way…just as long as every last motherfucker here is at the bottom of the ocean when we're done...right." He held the phone out. "They want to talk to you."

"Thanks." Trent grabbed the phone. "Trent here."

"Why the hell don't you have your sat phone with you?" Kurtzman's voice rasped from several thousand miles away.

"Um, I gave it to someone who needed it more than I did at the moment. He's left the boat for a while—"

"Are you aware that person is now seventy-five kilometers away from you and getting farther away with every second?"

Trent frowned. "Seventy-five... That's too far away for a scouting run. Where the hell are they going?"

"If you have any idea, we'd certainly enjoy being filled in."

"I don't even have a guess at the moment, but I'm sure as hell going to find out. We're going to seize the ship and take the leader for questioning."

"Sounds like a good game plan to us."

"I thought you'd like it. And, Bear?"

"Yeah?"

"I had no idea they were going to blow up the ship. The leader had talked about taking the crew aboard as prisoners, that's all. I was doing everything I could to get them aboard to effect the takeover."

"Understood, but don't dwell on it right now. You two have a ship to capture, and I suggest you get on it."

"Right, Trent out."

KURTZMAN CUT THE CONNECTION and turned to Tokaido. "I want abduction plans for Hu Ji Han in every logical scenario that you have, worked up in two hours at the latest."

"Better yet, why don't I send both you and David the set of plans to take him either at his home or his office, or in transit either way from one to the other?" Tokaido pressed a button as he spoke, and a downloaded file appeared on Kurtzman's screen.

A wry smile flickered on the older man's face. "What took you so long? Just wait for the headman's order for implementation, and don't move before it comes through."

"Don't worry, I'm not going an inch off the rails on this one."

"Good." Kurtzman turned to the folder and opened it. But before he could get very far into it, however, the sat line rang, and he snatched it up. "Kurtzman."

"This is Striker."

"Your timing is perfect, we were just about to call you." Kurtzman quickly filled the Executioner in on what had happened in the South China Sea. "Looks like Kirkall's mercs ran into more than they bargained for."

"Is John all right?"

"Yes, and he's working on stopping the pirates and going after the ones who have already left. The last surviving merc's thrown in with him, and ideally they should be able to get the drop on whoever's left on the yacht. Trent's going to try to capture the leader alive if possible."

"Good. However, our problems have just gotten a lot bigger." Bolan gave him a capsule summary of what they had learned from their captive. "It's not just China and Japan Hu's targeting, it looks like they're going after targets in the West, as well."

"Got any ideas as to where?"

"If they're planning to hit England, London's the

obvious major port. As for the U.S., it could be either New York City or Washington, D.C., take your pick."

"Or maybe both. There's no reason to assume they sent out only two teams," Kurtzman reasoned.

"True. But if what Akira theorized about Hu is true, and he wants to strike at the symbols of the governments that stood by and did nothing while the Rape of Nanking happened, then my bet is that they're going for Washington, the seat of power for the country, not New York."

"Maybe, except..." Kurtzman brought up a map of the Potomac River. "I think it would simply be too difficult to get a large tanker all the way up the river to D.C. It would be headed off, since there wouldn't be any logical reason for a fertilizer ship or oil tanker to come that close to the capital."

He heard silence on the other end for a few moments. "Good point. In terms of feasibility, an attack on New York City's harbor is much more likely. Run the numbers on both, just to be sure. Is Able Team's status still green?"

"Yes, they're on base and ready to go."

"Good, get them on standby until we've identified a viable target. Akira and you both need to start sifting through the Atlantic traffic to figure out which vessels are the most likely targets. Radio traffic about oil supertankers or freighters carrying volatile chemicals are our top priority."

"Got it, we're starting now. What about Hu? I'd just gotten the proposed plans to pick him up."

"Oh, yeah, we definitely need that bastard on ice. Make him disappear—quietly."

"Hmm, with David handling things, well, I'll tell him word came down from you personally to keep it black."

"Don't worry, David will pull him in with a minimum of fuss. He knows what's at stake here. We're en route to London, and will be in position to intercept and stop the ship heading there once it's identified."

"Roger that, we're narrowing our search as fast as we can, and I'll have the targets to you and Able as soon as they're confirmed."

"Good work, Bear. Striker out."

Kurtzman hung up the phone and turned to Tokaido, who was already pounding keys. "I've got programs already running down every ship that qualifies in every single Atlantic shipping lane," he said without looking up. "Should havc a list of probables in the next one to two hours. Then it's gut check time."

"The second you have it narrowed down, holler, and we'll bring Striker back in to confer and make the final decisions." With that, Kurtzman pushed everything else out of his mind and focused on doing everything he could to help stop these thugs before they committed their next act of ruthless violence—one that would affect much more than a half-dozen people.

CHAPTER TWENTY-SEVEN

On a slightly rolling Atlantic Ocean one hundred nautical miles from the American East Coast, Acting Captain Markus Tennacht stood on the bridge of the oil tanker *Esso Argonaut,* fully laden with 105,000 tons of crude oil and traveling at a sedate twelve knots. Only a few hours from landfall, he sipped his sixth cup of strong coffee in twice as many hours, wiped his brow and breathed a sigh of relief that his first transatlantic cruise was about to come to an uneventful end.

Having been at sea for more than half his thirty-eight years, this was the first time he'd ever been in command of a vessel this large. During his more than two decades at sea, he had served at every position on bulk carriers, as well as container and tanker ships, from steward to engineering to deck positions, including rising as high as second officer before landing the position of first officer on the *Argonaut.* And when the captain and a quarter of the crew had taken ill with food poisoning the day before yesterday, Tennacht had assumed command of the tanker and kept it and its reduced crew steady on its course to the harbor of New York City.

Actually, they were heading to New Jersey, where his cargo of crude oil would be unloaded for refinement and distribution along the East Coast. But Tennacht liked the idea of his first command ending at New York

City. It was the culmination of his boyhood dream ever since watching the big ships dock at the port in Oslo, Norway. Ever since he'd laid eyes on the huge container and tanker ships there, young Markus had known he was destined for a life at sea.

And now that life had reached its latest pinnacle, command of a ship in circumstances that could be considered dire, and coming through with flying colors. The fact that he had slept only eight hours out of the past forty-eight was of little consequence to him—only that he had borne up under the responsibility of commanding this vessel safely to its destination, and had acquitted himself with calm, assurance and poise in the face of adversity mattered now. However, a small part of his mind couldn't help wondering what his reward from the fleet company might be for bringing the mission to a successful close. His own command? He banished the thought almost as soon as it had arrived. He shouldn't count his money before it was paid—after all, they weren't in port just yet.

Tennacht took another moment to scan his officers on the bridge. His second officer, a quiet, intelligent, black man from Tobago, was at the helm. He'd also taken double-shifts to ensure that the ship's course was accurate and their route was trouble-free, and Tennacht made a mental note to recommend him for a promotion if possible. He'd also brought up his third mate, normally in charge of the deck crew, to back them both up if necessary. But everything was going perfectly.

Therefore, it was a tremendous shock to him when what sounded like gunshots rang out near the bridge. Tennacht and his second officer exchanged confused looks, and he reached for the radio microphone to find out what was happening on deck. Before he could press the transmit button, the door to the bridge burst open, and three men dressed in black wet suits with full masks over their faces and holding automatic weapons rushed inside.

"Drop that mike or you're dead!" the lead one barked.

Tennacht set the microphone on the console. "What is the meaning of this?"

"All of you are to continue performing your duties as if nothing is wrong. However, you will be sailing this ship into the port of New York City. Any sign of resistance or sabotage from any of you will result in a crew member being killed. You have the responsibility for thirty-five souls on this vessel, plus thousands more on shore. Be smart, do the right thing and no one will have to die today."

Tennacht exchanged a puzzled glance with his other bridge officers, the same thought running through each of their minds. Was this really happening? Were they being hijacked so close to the U.S. coast?

Of course, with such a dangerous cargo, not to mention the lives of the rest of the crew at stake, there was no choice for Tennacht to make at all. "Very well, we are under your command."

"Continue your course as plotted until you reach the harbor entrance, then you will increase speed to twenty knots and change course for the Port of New York. Further instructions will be given at that time."

"Do as he says, Mr. Stannis," Tennacht ordered, a sinking feeling growing in his stomach as he sensed that this trip was going to end in anything but a typical docking.

"WOULD SOMEONE PLEASE turn off that goddamn Klaxon?"

Captain Jason Horner rubbed his white-stubbled face, hoping that when the warning alarm was turned off, the pounding inside his skull would subside, as well. At last the loud noise cut off in midwhoop, leaving silence to rush back over the bridge crew.

"What's the position of the other ship, Mr. Abrams?"

"Passing by portside at a distance of four meters, sir.... Now five meters.... Now six meters."

Well, thank God for small favors, the captain thought as he sank wearily into his chair. "Get us underway again once they've passed, four knots."

"Four knots, aye, sir." The helmsman gave the other ship a few more seconds, then advanced the throttle forward slightly. Horner felt the deck beneath him thrum slightly as the battered ore-bulk-oil carrier began sailing forward toward London.

For both the aging, decrepit ship and its aging, decrepit captain, this was the end of an era. Horner had served in the merchant marine for more than forty years, rising to captain of a Very Large Crude Carrier in the early 1990s. But when his ship had been involved in a collision, and it was learned that the captain had been drinking, he was summarily fired, and began a long, slow sail to the bottom of his formerly distinguished career. Now, this last-chance job, captaining a thirty-year-old OBO freighter on its last cargo trip before it was being sold for scrap, was going to be his last time behind the wheel of a ship, any ship.

For when he handed over command of the *Peligan Dory* to the scrap yard that was going to hack her apart for the steel they could sell wholesale, Jason Horner was going to drive back to his small room in Bournemouth,

Dorset, collect his hunting shotgun, walk out into the pastureland and blow his brains out.

With that plan fixed firmly in his mind, it had come as a great surprise to find that, when confronted with a potential collision with a freighter drifting out of its lane as the *Peligan Dory* passed Samuel's Corner on its way to entering the Thames River and the winding way to London Port, Horner's captain reflexes had sparked to life for a few brief minutes. He'd taken command from the first mate—a good seaman, but who had frozen at the sight of the 120-meter freighter bearing down on them—and ordered the wheel turned hard to starboard, coming within a few meters of running the *Dory* aground, but giving the Pakistani freighter just enough room to correct its course and avoid running into Horner's vessel by the narrowest of margins.

And for a moment, as he sat in the captain's chair, Horner took pride in the knowledge that he'd saved both his ship and the cargo. Never mind that once their cargo, 80,000 tons of ammonium nitrate, was unloaded for distribution to farmers across the island, his ship—and he—would be finished once and for all.

So when the bridge door opened and three masked men burst in, Jason Horner's first thought was that he was hallucinating, mainly on account that the past ten minutes had been the first in several years that he hadn't been thinking about his next drink. Therefore, he had to be hallucinating. But when his first mate came toward them and was savagely chopped down by the butt of the lead man's submachine gun, Horner knew this was no vision.

"Here now, what's this all about?"

The leader walked up to him, pinning him with gray

eyes the color of a North Sea sky before a storm. "Shut your mouth, old man, and you might live to see the morning. We have your crew hostage. All you gotta do is keep this tub on course and dock in London, easy as you please. You do that, and we'll let you all walk outta here, got it? And before you get any ideas about running this ship aground or any bullshit like that, just remember that we'll parade every last crewman out in front of you and kill 'em one at a time, got it?"

Horner only nodded in reply, suddenly not trusting his voice to reply, and turned to issue orders to his third mate. Inside, he shook his head at their chances. He'd seen that sort of look before, in soldiers way back in Borneo—that hard, merciless look that betrayed whatever words came out of the man's mouth.

The look in his eyes that said Jason Horner and his crew were already dead men.

CHAPTER TWENTY-EIGHT

"What's the game plan?" the mercenary asked as he pulled his mask up, revealing an average face with blue eyes, a narrow nose, full lips and the beginning of a double-chin.

"My HQ wants us to take the ship and keep the leader alive for questioning." Trent answered the question on autopilot, as most of his brain was occupied with trying to figure out where the other boat was going. Where the hell was Guong going with Xiang? he wondered. What could be so important that would make Lee split his crew before heading in to take out their prize?

"Trent? Trent! Hey, jackoff!"

With a start, Trent realized the merc had been talking to him. "Sorry, just readjusting my mission parameters."

"Well, get your head back in the goddamn game! I just lost the rest of my team, and I'm not about to become the next casualty because you're not doing your job."

"Right, sorry. Hey, what can I call you? 'Hey, you' isn't going to cut it."

That got a wry smile out of the other man. "You can call me Simon."

"All right, good to meet you. What'd you manage to get off your ship?"

"You mean before I was practically blown out of the water?" Simon held up a compact HK MP5K submachine gun with sound suppressor, and the silenced SIG Sauer SP2022, both in 9 mm. "You're looking at it. I've got two mags for each, along with two flash-bang grenades. What about you?"

Trent drew the CZ75B. "All I've got is this, and I had to stare down a gorilla to get it in the first place."

Simon spun his pistol around so the butt was facing Trent and held it out, along with the two spare magazines. "Here. You'll need this more than me."

Trent took it, tucking the other gun back into his waistband. "Thanks. So, I'm assuming you're the expert in this, how do you propose taking out at least a dozen armed men and gaining control of the bridge?"

"My usual suggestion would be flash-bangs at the front and back of the ship, followed by two-man insertion teams at each end, with a floater coming up the middle and heading for the bridge, sweeping and clearing from both ends and meeting at the command center." Simon grimaced. "Since that's no longer an option, we'll work with what we have."

"As I see it, we have two advantages." Trent held up the same number of fingers. "First, no one knows you're aboard, and second, they still think I'm on their side."

Simon's stern features broke into a grim smile. "That's the first bit of good news I've heard all day. I'm thinking you lead them into an ambush that I'm on the other end of, right?"

"You read my mind. Security here is sloppy as it is, despite the captain's experience. Let's find a place to get you situated, and once you're set, I'll start bringing them in for the kill." He thought of something else. "Do you speak Cantonese?"

The mercenary nodded. "I can get by."

"That will make things easier."

Simon checked the action on his MP5K. "Let's do it."

Trent led him through the huge ship, checking around corners and down passageways before proceeding. With half of the crew gone, the luxury yacht seemed even emptier than usual. While making their way to the stern, Trent only ran into one problem—one of the pirates had apparently been napping, and came out of his stateroom right between Trent and Simon. Even as he opened his mouth to ask what was going on, the merc chopped him down by slamming the butt of his subgun to the back of his neck. Trent barely caught him before he slumped to the floor, his head lolling bonelessly.

"Hold him." Simon searched the body in less than ten seconds, finding nothing of interest. "One less to worry about. Let's get him inside." They wrestled the dead man through the narrow doorway and tossed him on the bunk. "How many others are there?"

"I'd originally counted at least twenty, but some left in another boat about a half hour ago. There must be at least a dozen left, with three on the bridge at all times. This plan'll probably be good for four, maybe six if we're lucky, then we'll likely have to engage them head on."

"Don't worry about me. You just do your job, all right?"

"Count on it. Why don't we set you up in the engine room? I can say I chased you down there, and there's no way out of it. Let's just clear it to see if anyone's home." Trent swapped out his silenced pistol for the CZ75B, and led him to a narrow stairway leading down. "There's plenty of space to hide down there. Just don't shoot me as I lead the targets in, please."

"Stay out of my way, and that won't be an issue." Simon shouldered past him and took the lead, heading down the stairs, with Trent coming up behind. The engine room was large and industrial, with most of the space taken up by the pair of huge engines in the middle, modern sculptures of metal, plastic and rubber, each as tall as Trent. They also made an unholy racket, rendering normal conversation impossible. Simon was already moving down the middle aisle, leaving Trent to take the left one. They reached the end of the thirty-foot room at the same time, then turned and swept up the leftmost corridor, confirming the room was empty except for themselves.

Trent bent to his ear. "This should do nicely. I'll have the first ones here in a few minutes."

Simon's expression turned deadpan, making Trent very glad he wasn't a pirate at the moment. "I'll have a suitable welcome waiting."

"Right, two scumbags, coming up." Leaving him at the bottom of the stairs, Trent trotted up, then walked down the hallway until he found a phone handset that connected to the ship's intercom. He dialed the aft deck and waited for someone to pick up.

"Yeah?"

"This is Liang, on the stateroom level. Hey, I think one of those tourists survived the blast and got on board." Trent panted as he spoke, giving the impression that he'd been running.

"So? Hunt them down and kill 'em."

"I would have, except they found a gun somewhere, and I nearly took a bullet in the head for my trouble."

"What, where? None of us here heard a shot."

"Of course you didn't, it was near the engine room, you can't even hear yourself think in there. Look, I think they might be trying to sabotage the engine or something. Just send a couple guys down here, and we'll flush out whoever's down there, okay?"

"All right, all right, keep your shorts dry. We'll send someone down. Try to make sure they don't do anything stupid, will ya?"

"Right, just get 'em down here fast." Trent hung up the phone and leaned against the wall. Two minutes later, a pair of pirates clad in identical baggy cargo shorts and short-sleeved shirts came down, each carrying a pistol.

"All right, the guy went into the engine room, so let's get down there and search it until we find him."

The one in front, with buzz-cut black hair except for a long, braided rattail that hung over his shoulder, motioned down the stairs with his gun. "Sure, lead the way."

"Uh, okay." Not exactly what he had in mind, but Trent certainly understood his point. Who wanted to go into a room where someone was waiting to pot the first guy that came through the door? "Let's all go down to the steps right before the entrance, then come in." He turned his pistol around so that he was holding it butt first.

"What are you doing?" the second one asked.

"Do you want to be the one to explain to Lee why we couldn't reach the ship because the engines were damaged by your bullets flying around?"

Both men's eager expressions were replaced by dismay. "Oh."

"Damn right, oh. We have to try to take this guy out without shooting."

The first guy piped up again. "Hey, maybe we should get a couple more guys down here, to guard the entrance in case they make a run for it."

Perfect, Trent thought. "Good idea. You call them, and you—" he pointed at the second thug "—and I will head down. Catch up to us once you've explained to the others what's going on."

The first pirate picked up the phone and began talking while Trent and the second pirate headed down the stairs. At the bottom, they paused, with Trent indicating he would go left and the pirate should go right. The slender Chinese man nodded, and Trent held up three fingers, then two, one—

He burst into the noisy engine room, stepping inside and flattening himself against the wall. Although he hoped Simon was a highly trained professional—most private security men came out of the special forces, or at least the military—he also was aware of the possibility of becoming a victim of so-called friendly fire, which was always anything but. With three aisles to go down, the opportunities to take out the pirates in here were excellent, but a moment's carelessness, and he could easily become one of the casualties.

In fact, as Trent glanced over to check his partner, the other man keeled over in the corner of the room, his left eye now a dark, bloody puddle. Well, I know where he is now, he thought. He looked back up the stairs, to see moving shadows at the top. Good, our reinforcements have arrived, he thought, trotting up to greet them.

"Hey, guys, you been filled in on the situation here?" When both men nodded, Trent slapped his first man on the shoulder. "Come on, we got this guy pinned in the back corner, and can rush him with another man. You two stay up here and make sure we're the only ones coming out, got it?"

The two men nodded, and Trent led the way into the killing field again. He peeked around the right corner to see the body had magically vanished, and smiled at Simon's efficiency. He ducked back again and put his lips close to the pirate's ear. "Take the right way down, I'll take the left and meet you at the other end. If you find the guy running around, go for him, and I'll be there right away."

The other guy nodded, and Trent gave him the three count again, switching pistols for the silenced SIG Sauer with his other hand. They entered the room, and Trent took one step to the left, far enough so he wouldn't be seen by the two guys upstairs. He turned to face the back of the other pirate, raising the pistol to line up the sights on the man's head. The pistol coughed once, and the man fell against the wall before sliding down in a lifeless heap.

Simon's head peeked out from behind the massive engine, and Trent could have sworn the peeved expression on his face meant, "No fair, I had him." Shrugging, he pointed up the stairway and held up two fingers. The merc frowned and waved him up, then made a walking motion of two people descending a staircase. Without waiting for a reply, he grabbed the second body and dragged it farther into the engine room.

Yes, sir, I'll bring you more pirates to kill right away, Trent thought as he switched his pistols again and cautiously headed up the stairs—no sense in getting shot by a trigger-happy guard up there.

"Hey, hey, guys, it's me, Liang, don't shoot." As he came up, he held his pistol out with the muzzle pointing toward the ceiling.

"What's going on down there? We can't hear anything over the engine noise."

"Yeah, try being down there for a few minutes. Look, we got the bastard, but my boy took a graze to the head that rang his bell pretty hard, and he's bleedin' like a stuck pig. Why don't you come down and give me a hand, and you keep watch up here. We should be back in a couple of minutes, prisoner in hand."

Trent clapped one of the new guys on the shoulder and ushered him down the stairs to the room's entrance. Once again, he pointed to the left and let the other pirate go in ahead of him. Trent drew his pistol and took careful aim, all too easy.

The pirate's body fell to the floor, Simon tracking it with his subgun all the way down. Sighing with relief, he raised his gun, then started to rise, his eyes widening at something behind Trent.

Ducking and whirling at the same time, Trent saw an orange tongue of flame spurting from the second pirate's pistol as he stood at the end of the hall. The report of the gunshots could be heard amid the engine noise, but they more or less blended in with the mechanical cacophony in the room. He felt the wind from one of the bullets as it passed through where his head had been a second before.

Off balance, Trent snapped off three shots from the SIG, the bullets punching into the wall near the man as he ducked for cover. Looking back, Trent saw Simon sitting on the ground, examining what was obviously a bullet hole in the front panel of his neoprene wet suit. Trent rose to go to him, but the man waved him off, stabbing a finger at the other end of the room. The message was clear: stop him!

Trent leaped around him to get on the other side of the engine, just in time to see a shadow cross in front of the door. Apparently he had the same idea, Trent thought. Now he had a tough choice: keep going down the middle to see if he could come up and ambush the guy from behind, or stay where he was and hope to catch him coming around the far left corner. He hoped Simon was able to keep it together for another minute as he stepped down the middle passage. He crept forward quietly down for a yard or two before realizing how silly he was being; there was no way the guy would hear him over the racket.

Sweat beaded on Trent's forehead as he approached the end of the engine housing, pistol at the ready. Pausing for a moment, he squinted in the dimness, trying to see if the man was just around the corner, or sneaking up on him in the same manner. The shadows in the room were dark enough to conceal him, along with a couple of friends if necessary. Taking a deep breath, Trent rounded the corner and ran smack into the pirate, who was also bringing his pistol to bear.

Instinctively, Trent grabbed the barrel of the hijacker's gun and pushed it to the side while trying to bring his own around. He squeezed the pistol's trigger, a shot chuffing out, but his enemy had grabbed Trent's pistol, too, and didn't seem to be shot. Even worse, he pistoned a foot out and caught his opponent in the stomach, making him double over. The pirate did it again, almost breaking Trent's hold on his pistol.

His ribs aching, Trent did the only thing he could. With both guns still held off to the side, he charged forward, driving the man backward into the wall of the room. Trent kept going, ramming his head into his opponent's stomach and feeling the air whoosh out of him. Before his opponent could recover, Trent lunged up, catching the brute's jaw with the top of his head. The man sagged against the wall, and Trent wrenched his pistol free and aimed it at the pirate's face. Just as he was squeezing the trigger, the man leaped at him, knocking his pistol out of line and bringing his own around at the side of Trent's head.

The slide smacked Trent hard enough to make him see stars, and he stumbled backward, trying to clear his vision. The man staggered past him, heading for the staircase, pistol still clutched in his hand, its primary purpose forgotten. Pushing himself to his feet, Trent ran after the guy, slamming into his back just as he reached the exit. His clumsy tackle carried them both into the other corner of the room, where Trent extricated his gun first, pressed it to the man's head and blew his brains out.

Rolling off the body, Trent wiped the sweat and blood from his face and checked over his shoulder to see if anyone had heard anything. The entryway was empty. Screw this, he thought, scooping up the dead man's pistol, a small frame Beretta 92S, and sticking it in his pants pocket. Grabbing the body, he hoisted its limp arm around his shoulder and hauled the deadweight to its feet, then staggered to the bottom of the stairwell.

"Hey! Give me a hand down here!"

"Holy shit, what happened to him?" one of the door guards asked as he pounded down the stairs.

"Took a bullet to the head, he's bleeding bad. Come on, get him up to the deck before he dies." Trent kept moving while he was talking, making his helper carry the body back up the stairs before he could realize what was going on.

They reached the top and pulled the guy outside onto the deck, where another guard Trent didn't recognize was just as incredulous as the first. "I thought you told me he had everything under control down there! Hey, wait a minute—this guy's already dead!"

"Just like you two." Trent heaved the dead body at the first pirate, tangling him up in the bloody, flailing limbs, and allowing him to put a bullet into the open mouth of the second guard, killing him instantly. As the guy fell, Trent switched his aim to the first man, who'd just managed to throw the body off, presenting a perfect target. Two shots later, Trent was surrounded by lifeless bodies.

"Quicker just tossing them overboard, if I could," he muttered. Instead, he grabbed each limp form and shoved it down the companionway, trying not to get blood on the floor or walls if he could help it. When he was finished, he scuffed at a few drops of blood nearby, then looked up at the blotch of viscera and brain matter that had sprayed out from the second guard's head. *Guess the cat's out of the bag now,* he thought as he headed down to see find out how Simon was doing.

At the bottom of the stairs, he met up with the merc surveying the pile of bodies. He pointed to the top of the companionway and let Trent lead the way.

"Are you all right?" he asked as soon as they were at the top of the stairs.

Simon pulled at the hole in his wet suit to reveal the black nylon weave of a ballistic vest. "Yeah, just a little bruised. You do good work." He spoke a bit more loudly than necessary. Trent let it slide. After all, he was the one who had spent so much time in the engine room. The other man held a rectangular package in his hand, with a digital timer on the end.

"What's that?"

"I think it's Lee's contingency plan, in case things go really wrong." Simon showed him the end of the brick, which was made of a gray, claylike substance that Trent recognized even faster than he had the timer.

"Plastique? He's planning on blowing the ship?"

"Or at least disabling it. I don't know if he planted more throughout the vessel or what. This one's safe, however."

"We'd better take the bridge—I think we've pushed our luck as far as it'll go. The quickest way up is over here." Trent led him to a spiral staircase, stopping at the bottom to exchange the half-empty magazine in his pistol with the full one. "Follow my lead, but if you see anyone and you have a shot, take 'em out. I'll sweep left in each area we come to, you go right."

"Affirmative—hold on." Simon scrubbed at Trent's face with his sleeve. "You had blood all over. This way it won't be quite so noticeable."

"Thanks. Okay, here we go. Oh, yeah, give me one of those flash-bangs, will you?"

The other man handed one to him, and Trent tucked it into his pocket before ascending the stairs. He stopped just as his head was level with the deck, but still concealed by a solid wooden railing. A few yards away, he heard voices and laughter.

"Give me a ten count, then come up," he whispered to Simon. He shot him a thumbs-up and, keeping the SIG hidden behind his left leg, Trent strolled up onto the deck, the rising wind feeling good after the hot, cramped, dark engine room. The boat rolled a bit more in the increased swells, and the gray-black clouds overhead looked as though they were about to split open and release a biblical portion of rain.

Four men were there, two lounging on reclining chairs, the other two passing a bottle back and forth as they sat underneath the awning. Trent noted that all were armed, but no one's hand was near his weapon, and the visible guns in holsters were secured. His eyes flicked up, to see if anything that was about to happen would be noticeable on the bridge. Although there was a bank of windows overlooking the deck, it didn't appear that anyone up there would be able to see the slaughter that was about to happen directly below them.

"Hey, Liang, you look like shit. You handle whoever was in the engine room?" The speaker was one of the guys in the reclining chair, a martini glass of what looked like bourbon next to him.

Trent recognized him as the one who had answered the intercom phone. "Yeah, no thanks to the assholes you sent down. They almost got me killed. I left them to clean up down there while I took care of things up here, too."

As he finished talking, Trent brought up the silenced pistol and shot the guy twice in the chest, then pivoted to double-tap his drinking buddy. He heard the nearby chairs nearby tip over as the two other men reacted to the sudden murder of their partners, but over that came the peculiar metallic chatter of the suppressed MP5K. Trent turned to see both men collapse to the deck, red stains spreading over their brightly colored shirts.

Simon trotted up the stairs to cover the portside hallway entrance while Trent checked the starboard one. All was clear so far. "How many is that?"

"Thirteen, counting two that were disabled before you showed up. Except for someone sleeping in a stateroom, there should only be the guard at the door to the bridge, and Lee and one or two pilots inside. Come on."

He walked up the stairs to the bridge level, seeing the same guard at the door. Trent strode toward him, the guard's eyebrows rising quizzically as he approached. It was the last sight the pirate would ever see, as Trent raised his pistol and fired a single round into the man's right eye, pulping it as the bullet burrowed through his brain to exit the back of his skull. Dead, but his body not quite aware of it yet, the man teetered back and forth on his feet. Trent sprang forward to stop him from thudding to the deck, supporting him until he could ease the body to the floor.

Simon was at his side, covering the stairway and the small platform. He held up his flash-bang grenade. "I assume you'll want to use these."

"Of course." Trent had already picked out the key to the bridge door, and had his own flash-bang grenade in his other hand, which he gave to Simon. "I open, you chuck 'em in, and once they go off, we go in hard."

Simon nodded, and Trent eased the key into the lock, mindful of the increasing pitch and yaw of the boat as the storm drew closer. When he had inserted it all the way, he glanced at his partner to make sure he was ready. Simon had slung his subgun and now held a primed grenade in each hand, with two pins dangling from his smiling mouth.

Trent opened the door just wide enough for him to toss in both grenades, then slammed it shut on a startled voice saying, "What—?" He turned away from the door, with his hands over his ears, his eyes closed and his mouth open to equalize the shock, just in case.

The grenades went off inside the room with twin claps of thunder. Trent hit the door a second after, SIG in hand, leaving it open to dissipate the smoke as he stormed inside. He felt rather than saw Simon enter right behind him.

White smoke filled the room, along with anguished cries of pain from its occupants. Trent moved forward, sweeping with his pistol muzzle from right to left. The two pilots rolled on the floor, hands clapped over their bleeding ears.

"Cover them!" he ordered Simon, while he walked to the other side of the room, looking for Lee. He found the pirate leader huddled in the corner, tears streaming down his face, clutching something to his chest.

"Show me your hands, or I shoot!" Trent ordered.

"Liang? You son of a bitch!" Lee raised his hands, revealing the item he was holding—a cell phone.

"It's over, Lee. Your men are dead, and that ship isn't going to be hijacked by anyone. Now drop it!" Trent pointed his pistol at the other man's heart.

Instead of blustering or begging, Lee smiled that same odd smile he had worn just before he had blown up the other boat—like he knew something no one else did. "Of course, just let me turn it off first."

"No!" Trent aimed at the device, but Lee had already

pressed a button on it. A dull boom echoed from the bowels of the ship, shaking the whole vessel. It was followed by another, and another. The luxury yacht lurched to starboard, metal shrieking far below them.

Lee tossed the phone at Trent's feet. "You've got about five minutes before this boat sinks and takes us with it."

CHAPTER TWENTY-NINE

Thoroughly miserable, Xiang crouched in the bow of the speedboat as it raced across the stormy ocean. Although the collar and chain restricted his movement, he'd been determined to stay as far away from Guong as possible. When it started to rain, the leather had quickly gotten soaked, along with the rest of him, chafing his skin, but he didn't budge from his spot, despite the occasional jerk on the leash.

Guong and the rest of the men were huddled underneath the canvas canopy they'd put up before heading out. Xiang was too tired and battered to care about what happened to him anymore. For all he knew, Guong was taking him out here to kill him—maybe kill all of them, that was, if the weather didn't do them in first.

Even on the edge, the tropical storm they were skirting was any sailor's nightmare. Twenty-foot swells made navigating the turbulent ocean more than a challenge. It was downright suicidal. Guong had three men on bailing duty, as the spray crashing over the sides had quickly covered the floor of the boat in ankle-deep water. That several men had become ill from the ceaseless and often violent rocking of the speedboat hadn't helped any, either.

They'd been powering through the maelstrom for the past hour, looking for only Guong knew what. By now,

Xiang would have almost welcomed death, to sink into the raging ocean, expel his last breath, to suck in the warm salt water as the consciousness left his body. He tried to curl into a tight ball, but a savage jerk on the leash pulled him off his feet to splash in the salty water on the boat deck. Choking and gasping, he crawled to the cockpit to find Guong at the wheel, one hand on the throttle, working the engine and rudder to keep them all alive in the swirling tempest.

"Nice day for a ride, eh?" He shouted to be heard over the howling wind and waves. "We're getting close to our target, and since you been sulking all this time, you'll be going up the rope first."

"What are you talking about?" Xiang shouted back at him.

"That, fool!" Guong pointed ahead of them, and Xiang followed his finger to see a ship about a mile distant, rising and falling as it plowed through the waves. It was a freighter, much larger than the speedboat, and Xiang turned back to see the look of manic glee on Guong's face, lit from below by the green speedboat dials.

"You're insane!" Xiang had half a mind to tear the leash out of the man's grasp and hurl himself overboard.

Guong unhooked him from the leash. "No, this is the job! And you're going to do it, or I'll go back and explain to Lee why you didn't get the job done. Better yet, you can tell him yourself. And your buddy won't have anyone to protect him from me. If we don't pull this off, I'm going to hurt him real bad, and then I'm going to hurt you even worse."

The rest of the men busied themselves preparing for the assault; some prepping ropes and grappling hooks to catch the railing of the other ship, the rest checking small backpacks they'd apparently be wearing on the mission.

"This is crazy! We're all going to die out here!" Xiang shouted.

"Everyone has to die sometime!" Guong smacked him on the shoulder. "Get ready, we'll be alongside in about five minutes!"

Xiang looked at the freighter, which was growing larger by the second. Its railing looked to be twenty-odd feet above the water, which was an easy enough climb in calm weather, but a death sentence right now. The speedboat bucked and plunged wildly, and one wrong move would find him either crushed between the two ships, or fallen into the churning, angry ocean to drown.

The boy looked around for something, anything to help him, but the speedboat was short of luxuries like climbing gear or gloves. Besides the tarp, there were a couple of flares in a small compartment, several maritime maps, a small container of waterproof matches and, underneath the passenger's seat, a small bucket labeled "Jamaica" that contained pristine, white sand.

Better than nothing, he thought, grabbing the flares and the bucket and taking them up to the front. It would hurt like holding fire, but it might give him the edge to make it up to the deck in one piece.

"Two minutes!" Guong yelled above the pounding waves. He kicked a coiled rope over to Xiang's feet and waved at him, indicating he should pick it up. Xiang did so, feeling the sodden line weigh him down.

"What am I supposed to do with this?"

"You're taking it with you. When you get aboard, you'll tie off the first line, then tie off that one and throw it over for us. And don't fall in. I'd hate to have to go get the rope back!"

The insult brought coarse laughter from the rest of the pirates. Shivering in the driving rain, Xiang slung the thick coil over his shoulder and chest, feeling the rough rope rub against his skin. It was a difficult enough task before this, but now he could hardly raise his left arm before it banged against the thick coil. This is gonna get me killed, he thought, taking it off and tossing it on the deck. He found an end and tied it around his waist, then made sure the rest of the coil was loose enough to unwind as he climbed. He didn't bother glancing at Guong as he worked, figuring their insane leader would protest if he didn't like what he saw.

"Thirty seconds—get those hooks tied off!" Guong gunned the engine, driving the boat up on the crest of a long swell to hang, half in the water, and half out, for a moment before the bow dipped, and the entire craft plummeted twenty feet down the other side into the trough, its bow plunging into the water before slowly coming back up.

"And just in time, too!" The dark hull of the freighter loomed next to the speedboat, dwarfing the tiny craft. "Get ready! Xiang!"

He looked up just in time to catch a small pistol flying at him. Guong held up three fingers. "You got only three shots, so make them count!"

Jamming the pistol into his pocket, Xiang popped the top of the bucket and plunged his wet hands into the sand, coating them with the granules until his palm and fingers were completely covered. He crouched by the pilot's station on the boat, huddling over his hands to try to keep them out of the weather as much as possible.

Guong made one final adjustment to the wheel and the throttle, bringing the boat alongside the huge cargo ship. For a breathless second, the two ships were moving on a parallel course. "Now!"

Four neoprene-covered grappling hooks arced out from the speedboat to the larger craft. Two missed completely, underthrown, to splash into the water. The third hit the rail but failed to catch and slid back down into the ocean. The last one, however, sailed through the railing and latched onto the steel bars.

"Go! Go! Go!" Guong howled as he tried to keep the boat at a steady distance from the ship. This was the trickiest part of the entire operation. The men holding on to the line would have to play out enough slack when the boats separated so they didn't get pulled into the ocean, but would also need to haul in the line without tangling it if the boats came together, to avoid fouling their propellers, and dooming them to a sure death on the furious water.

For his part, Xiang just wanted off this boat by whatever means necessary. He rose and headed for the taut line, now held by three men straining with every bit of strength they possessed. Making sure his own line was clear, he grabbed the slick rope and hauled himself up hand-over-hand, his dangling foot accidentally catching one of the men in the face, making him curse and spit blood.

"Sheng, you let go of that line and I'll throw you to the sharks myself!" Guong bellowed from the helm.

The boy didn't waste time apologizing, his hands were already more than full just trying to keep moving forward. The rope was like a living creature, writhing and bucking in his fingers. The sand helped for the first few seconds, then it was wiped away by the constant spray pelting every inch of his body. He didn't look down, but kept his eyes on the only goal in his universe at the moment, the rising, falling, swaying deck, still at least fifteen feet away.

As he climbed, Xiang did his best to keep himself facing the side of the freighter; if he slammed into it before he had a chance to protect himself, he wouldn't be able to maintain his hold, with a very terminal result. One handhold at a time, Xiang pulled himself toward the railing. His hands soon ached with the effort of gripping the slick rope. The freighter wallowed in a huge trough, the railing tilting over to hang above his head. Gritting his teeth and clenching his fingers on the rope so hard they ached, Xiang tried to tuck his legs up in front of him, knowing the ship was about to right itself, and fearing a dreadful collision with the side.

The ship yawed back over, and the slippery, steel hull rushed at him. Wrapping a coil of the loose rope around his wrist for a brief illusion of safety, Ziang managed to get one leg out in front of him to take some of the impact, but he still hit with breath-stealing force. Somehow, he retained his grip on the rope, but his head swam with pain and his vision blurred for a moment. Disoriented, he looked down for a moment as the pressure increased on his trapped hand.

Below was the churning sea, a long way down, and a bit farther out was the boat and the men, all looking anxiously up at him except for Guong, who glared at him with a ferocious expression on his face. As he stared, the pirate motioned for him to continue with a quick jerk of his head. Shaking off his stupor, Xiang looked up to see the railing only a few feet away. Locking his numb fingers around the rope, he disentangled his other hand and forced it to reach up and grab the wet line, then repeated the process. One agonizing handhold at a time, he inched closer to the railing.

At last he reached the deck and pulled himself aboard, collapsing on his back with a sob of relief. His hands had been reduced to curled claws, the skin on his palms and fingers abraded and bleeding, but he rolled over, untied the rope around his waist, secured it to the railing, then did the same with the grappling hook rope.

The pirates wasted no time abandoning their boat, which was quickly swept away by the towering waves. They swarmed up the lines and headed for the deck, but as the first one swung his leg over, a stream of water jetted from the forward deck to slam into him like a liquid sledgehammer. Already off balance, he toppled over the railing to fall with a wailing scream into the black ocean, vanishing as if he had never been there in the first place.

"Xiang! Xiang!"

The voice shook the boy out of his lethargy, and he rolled over to see Guong swinging back and forth on one of the ropes, wind and rain lashing his face. "They got…a fire hose…to keep us off! Stop them…before we're all blown away!"

Xiang fell back on the deck. And just how'm I supposed to do that? he thought. Patting his pockets, his hand found one of the flares he had taken off the speedboat, and a crazy idea came to him. He stuck his head back over the side and shouted, "When you see the flare, climb up!"

Moving more by instinct than anything else, he got on his hands and knees and began crawling forward, sticking close to the side of the main bridge deck until he reached the corner. Peeking his head around, he saw three men behind an upside-down lifeboat, manning a canvas fire hose that snaked back to the wall on the other side of the corner Xiang was lying next to. Another blast shot by, but they didn't appear to have noticed him yet, their attention drawn to the invaders coming over the rail.

Xiang drew the small pistol and checked its load, making sure it was cocked and ready. He held the flare in his other hand, the end held near the deck to strike and ignite it. Raising the pistol, he triggered three quick shots just as one of the sailors on deck poked his head out to take a look. The bullets whizzed by his head, one of them punching a hole in the boat hull, making him duck back under cover. Xiang slammed the flare on the deck once, then again, until it burst into brilliant, incandescent life.

Scrambling to his feet, he darted around the corner and cranked on the wheel, controlling the water pressure until it spun tight, cutting off the flow. Then he jammed the flare into the hose, the molten magnesium eating through the tough canvas in seconds, unaffected by the jet of water that spurted from the hole. Xiang held the flare to the hose until it was severed, tossing the useless tube to the deck.

With the hose disabled, Xiang stumbled back to the railing and threw the burning flare over the side. Moments later, six men clambered aboard, the last one Guong, who clapped Xiang on the shoulder as he went by.

"Good work, now get up off your ass and follow me, we've got to the secure the rest of the ship!"

CHAPTER THIRTY

"Jesus Christ, what did you do?" Grabbing the pirate leader by his shirt collar, Trent yanked him to his feet. He spun the man and patted him down with one hand while keeping the muzzle of his pistol jammed into his neck. "The engine room wasn't the only booby trap, was it?"

Although his eyes were red-rimmed and teary, and his nose dripped from the flash-bang grenades, Lee's voice was perfectly clear. "When Cortez came to the New World, he burned his ships to motivate his men. That was my plan, before you foiled it. Now I only hope I can take you down with me."

"Like hell." Trent headed for the door, hauling the unresisting man behind him. "Simon, get these two up and out the door. Get to the life rafts on the aft deck. We're getting out of here."

The yacht was already listing heavily to port, and Trent estimated it would be going down in as little as four minutes, faster if a large wave hit. He elbowed the door to the bridge open and cruised through, towing Lee with him. Behind, he heard Simon herding the two pilots along, as well. They trooped down the stairway to the aft deck, where the wind had kicked up even more, howling around them, and sending sheets of spray over the tilted deck.

Opening a storage compartment underneath a deck seat, Trent pulled out a bright yellow package with a red pull-tab. He was about to yank it when he noticed covert glances exchanged between Lee and his two henchmen.

Tucking the bundle under his arm, Trent walked over to the nearest man, raised his pistol and put a bullet right between his eyes. As the body fell over, Trent raked the other two with a cold gaze. "I only need Lee alive, so if you want to try anything, I'll leave you for the sharks with a bullet through each knee and elbow. If you'd rather live through this, however, don't make a fucking move!"

The remaining pilot raised his hands in abject surrender. Regarding Trent with a cool stare, Lee inclined his head in what might have been a nod of respect.

"Watch them while I get this thing into the water." Simon gripped his subgun firmly as Trent stepped to the edge of the boat—just above the waves crashing against the side of the deck—set down the package and pulled the cord. With a loud pop, the round life raft inflated into a large doughnut capable of holding all of them comfortably, with a canopy that would keep most of the wind and rain off them, as well.

"All right, let's go. Simon first, then Lee, then the pilot, and I'll bring up the rear. Lee and the other guy, if you know what's good for you, you'll grab a paddle and start pushing water when you get down there."

The survivors filed aboard, and Trent took a collapsible paddle, locked it into one piece and used it to push them off into the ocean. He propelled them away with powerful strokes, not wanting to be caught in the suction caused when the yacht finally sank. He spared a quick glance over his shoulder at the vessel, seeing the once-majestic superyacht now lying almost completely on its port side, being smacked by the high waves. As he watched, the bow dipped beneath the surface, raising the stern until it lifted completely out of the water, hanging vertically for a moment before it settled beneath the waves in a froth of churning bubbles.

Turning back to the rest of the group, Trent settled against the back of the raft, keeping his pistol trained on their two prisoners. "Well, at least that's the only ship going down because of you today, Lee."

Again the pirate leader smiled his inscrutable smile. "That's what you think, Mr.— What are you exactly, Chinese navy? Hong Kong police? Singapore customs?"

Trent exchanged a tight smile with Simon. "We're people you do not want to cross, Lee."

"Ah, so you are both working together."

"That's irrelevant. What'd you mean when you said, 'That's what you think'?"

"Just that the target vessel I was going after was not the only one I was planning to hijack today."

"There's another ship being taken over?"

"If my other team has done its job, they should be on the bridge right about now."

Trent's mind raced as he absorbed the implications of this, and he cursed inwardly for not putting the pieces together earlier. And Xiang was on that other boat, too, he thought. "What's its name? Where's it headed?"

Lee sat back and folded his arms, looking like he was the one holding a gun instead of staring into its muzzle. "I'm afraid that information will not come so easily—at least, not until I have a signed document guaranteeing me immunity from prosecution for my testimony about that particular ship and where it's headed."

Trent rocked to his knees right in front of Lee, pressing the muzzle of his gun into the man's forehead. "Or you can tell me the name of that ship right now before I splatter your brains all over this raft. Or maybe we'll just throw you overboard until the helicopter gets here—it'll be at least two hours, and that's a long time to swim."

Lee's cold, brown eyes met Trent's glare without flinching. "Nice try, Mr. Government Agent or whoever you are, but if I get shot or drown, then you don't know which ship is the target, or what it's supposed to do once it reaches its destination."

"Punch in that number I gave you for my base," Trent snapped to Simon.

"I'm already trying, but there's some interference from the storm—communication is going to be difficult at best."

Trent showed his teeth in a death's head grin. "Just get that line open—I'm sure they'll want to hear what our good buddy here has to say."

"WHAT'S GOING ON OVER there? First they sink another boat, then the pirates' boat sinks thirty minutes later? It's as though they're trying to cast themselves adrift out there with a tropical storm about to smack 'em all upside the head."

Tokaido stared at the latest satellite feed, using thermal imaging to track the yacht by its engine signature, a bright red-orange dot amid the swirling gray and white of the storm in the area. However, in the last few minutes each shot had shown the yacht's engine signature lessening, and the one normal picture they had gotten—a one-in-a-thousand shot caught by a passing satellite—

showed the yacht on its side and low in the water, as if it had suffered engine trouble, or was being swamped by the high seas, they weren't sure which. He couldn't get good enough resolution to see who was still on board or what they were doing.

Hell, at the moment Tokaido didn't even know if Trent was dead or alive. Unfortunately, the sinking ship was all he had at the moment, despite his best efforts to open a channel to that sat phone.

"Come on, come on!" Tokaido knew he shouldn't have been that worried. If the boat sank at its current position—about seventy-five miles away from the ship they thought was its target, then there was nothing to worry about. Hijackers stopped, mission accomplished. But if that was true, why was he still concerned that he was missing something?

He ran though the still-scant data one more time: Hu Ji Han, his secretary, the pirates, the strange phone calls to Japan and the Uighur—the two phone calls. But the Uighur separatists had nothing to do with Japan. They wanted autonomy for their own region, he thought. Meaning they'd rise up against China itself.

And where better to launch a massive terrorist demonstration of their might than Hong Kong?

Add to that Hu's desire to avenge the injustices visited upon his grandmother. What if that had been warped over the years into a desire to punish not only the invaders, but the government that had done nothing while Nanking had suffered? It was not uncommon to transfer those feelings of hatred not only to the perpetrators, but also to those who might have helped but didn't.

The realization of what that meant made the hacker's jaw drop. For a moment, everything faded into the background as Tokaido saw a conflagration that would dwarf anything created by man in the past one hundred years explode in his mind's eye. And that ship might be on the way now, for all they knew.... Tokaido's fingers flew over his keyboard, running a search for any ship in the area that would fit Hu's twisted plan and that was already heading for Hong Kong.

He was brought back to reality by Kurtzman's insistent voice. "Akira? I've got John on line. It's a tenuous connection, so talk quickly."

Tokaido touched his earpiece. "Put me through."

Trent's voice sounded as if he was sitting in a wind tunnel. "Sto—an, this is Alp— Ship sank, captur— lead— Two ships targ— Repea— Two ships—targeted—"

"Yes, Alpha, we'd reached that conclusion here, as well. We believe the target is Hong Kong, and that it will occur in the next six hours."

"Listen—the kid who has—phone—on—sec—ship. Use—to triangul—current—posit— Repeat, use—phone to triangulate current position."

"Of course!" Tokaido brought up a sat phone triangulation program on a separate monitor. "Damn it! The storm's throwing up too much interference. We need to call him. The signal will be stronger if the phone is actually broadcasting. I repeat, Alpha, call your phone directly. That'll open up the channel we need to get a fix on its position."

"Affirmati—"

Kurtzman spoke up. "We're sending a rescue helicopter from the Philippine navy to assist you." Tokaido nodded, who got on his computer and began typing. "You'll have to mount an assault from the helicopter in order to stop the ship. Once we have its location, you will board it and neutralize the pirates, I repeat, board it and neutralize the pirates."

"Affirmat—Alpha out." The connection broke up in a squeal of static, then a dead line.

"McCarter." The autodialer brought up his number and put Kurtzman in contact with him immediately.

"Yeah?"

"It's time we had a little chat with Hu Ji Han. Bring him in as quietly as possible, all right?"

"About bloody time. I'm on it—gonna have to call in a few favors from some friends in the area. I'll be in touch once he's secure."

"All right, then." Kurtzman broke the connection and leaned back in his chair, hoping they were right about everything.

CHAPTER THIRTY-ONE

Clad in a silk robe and soft paper slippers and bearing a small, covered tray, Hu Ji Han walked into a small room and slid the door closed behind him. It was completely silent in there, and he felt the tension and stress of the outside world recede with each step he took.

The space was mostly bare, with only woven bamboo mats on the floor. The walls were painted a soft, calming yellow, the color of heaven, where Hu sincerely hoped his grandmother had gone after her death, to find the peace that had been denied her during her life. But just in case her soul still wandered this plane of existence…

Against the far wall was a small table and on it was a vertical stone tablet inscribed with Chinese calligraphy that was the symbol of the Chinese god of Thunder, Lei Gong. Han's grandmother had worshipped the deity through her life, praying for the time when he would smite her enemies, and she could at last take her revenge on those who had abused and betrayed her. The stone slab was known as a spirit tablet, placed in the home to venerate previous generations. Hu didn't have one for his parents, only for his grandmother.

Setting the tray on the floor, Hu knelt before the altar and lit two small red candles, placing one on either side of the stone. There was also a place to set *joss,* or sticks of burning incense, and he lit one of sandalwood—his grandmother's favorite scent—and placed it in front of the stone, its smoke wafting up in front of him. Next, he uncovered the tray, revealing an assortment of fresh fruits and small pastries. An orange for good fortune, a melon for family unity and an apple for peace; again, in hopes that she would finally find the serenity she had sought all her life. Serenity that he was now in a position to give her. Along with the fruit, Hu placed her favorite pastries on the altar, a delicate almond cookie and an egg tart. Finally, he poured a small cup of steaming green tea and placed it on the altar with everything else, filling every inch of the available space with his offerings.

He sat back on his heels, satisfied with his arrangement, then bowed his head to the floor in complete obeisance. "Most honored Grandmother, your unworthy grandson is, at long last, going to strike the blow that you have waited for so long to pass. My only regret is that you are not in your earthly body to see this, but it is my fervent hope that your spirit will see the fireball that will soon visit not only the land of the invaders across the ocean, but also of the nation that did nothing to help you while you suffered at their hands."

He closed his eyes, and for a moment it was as if he was sitting at her knee again in the small garden of her home outside of Hong Kong, listening to her as she detailed what he would do: "You must punish *both* nations, the Japanese for the atrocities they committed against us, and the Chinese for doing nothing while it happened. Also, you must punish the round-eyes of Great Britain and the United States, both of whom idly stood by and would not help us in our time of need. Only then will the souls of the dead find the peace they deserve."

"It is my deepest wish that this come to pass, honored one, and that you find the peace in the next world that was denied you in this one."

He stayed there for a long time, his head pressed to the ground, trying to put into words the feelings roiling deep in the pit of his soul. The shame he felt because he hadn't had the courage to strike while she was alive, so that she could see her revenge with her own eyes. His unworthiness that she had sacrificed so much to raise him, and he hadn't been able to do the one thing she had asked of him while she had lived. He didn't speak a word of any of this, but the twin trails of tears on his cheeks stood as mute testament to his sorrow.

His reverie was broken by a faint knock at the door. "Mr. Hu?"

It was Zheng. Hu rose from the floor and composed himself before answering "Yes?"

"Please come here. There is trouble."

That got Hu moving quickly, crossing the room to the door and sliding it open. "What do you mean?"

If she noticed his distress, she gave no sign, but instead took his elbow. "I apologize for my rudeness, but there is no time. We must go, now. There will be time to dress later."

Hu tried to extricate himself from her grip, but the woman's fingers were like steel as she shepherded him toward the front door. "What is this? What is going on?"

"I was finishing up at the office and was about to come here when the front desk let me know that two men wanted to come up. On the security cameras, they looked to be from the government. I told them I would be down to see them immediately and took the elevator to the garage, got the Range Rover and came here to collect you. We'll need to stay at one of the other buildings, but away from the waterfront—"

"Surely this is a misunderstanding. I will talk to them, straighten this all out."

"Mr. Hu, it is too late for that now! There is only one reason that these kind of men would be coming to see you, and that is to arrest you. I will not let that happen."

They were at the front door of Hu's home now, and Zheng didn't hesitate, propelling him through the opening and to the rear passenger door of the Range Rover. Over his protests, she helped him inside, slamming the door behind him and getting in the driver's seat.

When he had moved to the hills above the city, Hu had spent thousands of yuan to landscape his driveway into a circle, with the center shaped into a beautiful garden built into the hill, with a small waterfall and koi pond that was the pride of his grounds. Now, Hu looked out at it, wondering if he would ever come back to see it.

Zheng had just started the engine when two cars appeared on both curves of the driveway, one in front, one in back, cutting off their escape. Hu's bodyguard didn't hesitate, but cranked the wheel to the right and gunned the powerful engine, the thick tires spitting gravel as the SUV shot forward—straight toward the raised garden.

"What are you doing?" Hu cried as the four-wheel-drive vehicle tore its way through the immaculate landscape, leaving it in rutted ruins. He bounced around in the backseat as the Range Rover shook and rocked over the terrain. At one point, he heard the undercarriage scrape on stone, and thought they were done for, but Zheng mashed the gas pedal to the floor, and the SUV powered itself free with a shriek of tortured steel.

They made the exit just as one of the cars came around the turn, aiming straight for them. Zheng jerked the wheel to the left, nudging the nose and front rack of the Rover into the car's fender, the heavier off-roader sending the sedan careening into the carefully sculpted bushes.

Peering over the top of the driver's seat, Hu saw the entrance to the street at the bottom of the hill—and something else. Across the driveway was what looked like a long rectangular bright-yellow box a few centimeters high, small enough for them to pass over without incident. Zheng, however, apparently felt differently, for the moment she saw it, she slammed on the brakes, a potent curse spitting from her lips.

"What? What is it?" he asked just as the second car smashed into the back of the Rover, propelling them across the long yellow rectangle. As soon as they passed over, the tires of the Range Rover burst in four loud explosions, and Zheng wrestled with the wheel, trying to haul it over enough to turn onto the street. She managed to guide the four-wheel-drive vehicle in the right direction, but slammed on the brakes as soon as she did.

In front of them was a large panel truck blocking the entire road, too big to drive over, too wide to drive around. A man with blond hair and sunglasses was in the cab, and two more were on either side of the vehicle. All carried compact submachine guns that could devastate the SUV if fired upon from that distance.

The car that had been behind them stuck to their tail, slewing around in a bootlegger's turn to plant its side right next to their rear bumper. Two more men got out, each armed, as well. The man in the truck cab got out, walked up to the window of the Rover, and tapped on it with the barrel of his machine pistol.

"Mr. Hu? There are some people who would like to speak with you. If you and your assistant would come with us, please."

Hu met Zheng's eyes in the mirror, and he knew that if he gave the word, she would fight until her very last breath. He shook his head.

"No, my dear, it is over. We will go with them. Besides, they cannot stop what we have put into motion now, no matter what they do."

Her hands tensed on the steering wheel, and for a moment he thought she was going to disobey him, but at last her shoulders slumped, and she put the SUV into Park and turned off the ignition.

"Very good." Pulling his robe around himself, Hu opened the door and got out. "I am Hu Ji Han, and I demand to know the meaning of this illegal intrusion."

"There'll be plenty of time to discuss that later, Mr. Hu. And I assure you, no laws have been broken here, because this never happened."

The sunglasses-wearing man brought up a small aerosol sprayer and hit Zheng in the face with a blast, then turned it on Hu. His vision immediately turned gray, and his thoughts slowed and grew muddled. He felt the overwhelming desire to sleep, and before he succumbed to it, he felt strong, gentle hands ease him to the ground.

His last thought before the darkness swallowed him was a confident one.

They cannot stop what I have done....

No one can now....

CHAPTER THIRTY-TWO

Xiang lay curled in a ball in the corner of the freighter's bridge. The ship was named the *Divine Pearl,* but divine rust bucket was more like it. If it had ever seen better days, those had been at least twenty years ago, and its age showed with every wallow in the violent seas. But although it creaked and groaned in protest, the orange-streaked ship kept battling against the storm, unwilling to stop doing what it had been built to do so long ago.

Guong was at the wheel, steering a course only he knew, but at least he seemed to be taking them out of the bad weather. Once they'd overpowered the sailors on the deck, taking the bridge had been easy. Guong had simply swaggered up, hammered on the door with the butt of his pistol and informed the captain that he would kill one crew member for every minute the bridge crew didn't surrender. Forty-five seconds later, the door had opened and the captain relinquished command of his vessel.

The big man had immediately set up there, keeping the captain bound in his chair to answer the radio, and dispatched the rest of the men, all of whom were now carrying the loaded backpacks. Some he sent into the hold to see if there were any other crew members on board, the others to do something else Xiang didn't quite catch. He wasn't even paying much attention—he was too busy warming up on the comfortable bridge.

In fact, he was so comfortable, and so exhausted, after the effort of getting on the ship, that he found it hard to keep his eyes open. Huddled in the corner, he concentrated on making himself as small as possible, so as not to attract attention. Therefore, no one was more surprised than him when his pocket started to vibrate.

Xiang came awake in an instant, one hand stealing down to cover the quivering part of his clothing. He looked around, but neither the captain nor Guong had seemed to notice, their attention focused on the lashing rain and howling wind outside the bridge windows.

Slowly, carefully, his fingers crept into his pocket to withdraw the phone. His eyes flicked up to Guong again, but the large man was staring into the storm-tossed night, completely intent on holding his course.

He wriggled it free of his shorts and, cupping it in one hand, levered open the top. The tiny screen flashed to life before automatically dimming, and Xiang hid it in his sopping wet shirt again, turning to the corner of the room before daring to look at it again.

A face on the small screen broke into a wide grin. "Hey, buddy," Liang whispered. "What's happening?"

Glancing over his shoulder, Xiang ducked his head and whispered back, "We've taken the ship. I'm on the bridge. Guong is piloting, but I don't know where we're going. The rest of the men are in other places on the ship, but I don't know what they're doing, either."

"How many pirates are on board?"

"Seven, counting Guong and myself. You want me to find out what's going on?"

"That's all right, don't worry about it, just keep yourself in one piece. Do you think you can get me a look around the bridge with the camera in the phone?"

"I can try." Xiang snuck another look at the pirate leader before extending the phone over his shoulder and panning it around the room. Before he could bring it back in, a big, hard hand clamped down on his shoulder, and the boy was jerked off the floor to his feet. He tried to conceal the phone again, but Guong's other hand grabbed his wrist and bent it back until he howled in pain, his hand popping open to let the phone clatter to the floor.

"What the hell are you doing?" Guong scooped up the phone and hurled it into the wall, where it hit with a crack that most likely signaled the end of its working life. He turned back to Xiang, leading with a sweeping backhand that rattled the boy's teeth and sent him spinning into the wall.

"Who were you talking to?"

Xiang rose to his feet, swaying unsteadily, and spit a mouthful of blood into the face of the man looming over him. "Nobody. I found the phone on the other ship, and was playing with it, that's all."

"Bullshit, I saw the reflection of the screen in the window. You were sending a picture somewhere, weren't you?"

"I don't know. I couldn't read the buttons. They were in English."

Guong reared back, and Xiang expected another blow to fall, but he didn't flinch or cower. Instead, Guong dragged the boy to the bridge chair and produced the leash again. "Don't fucking move." Clipping one end to the metal ring on the collar around Xiang's neck, he looped the other end to an arm of the chair, tying the strip of leather into a complicated knot. When he was done, Xiang had a few feet of slack in the leash, enough to stand or sit, but he couldn't take one step away from the chair without cutting off his air. The captain, bound right next to him, gave the boy a sympathetic look.

"That will keep my dog heeled until I'm ready to retrieve him." Guong grabbed the boy's jaw and brought his face, with the blood still dripping from it, right up to Xiang's. "And you're going to pay for this mess—oh, yes, you most certainly are." Without wiping his face, Guong took the wheel from the other pirate and resumed piloting the freighter toward its destination.

"SHIT!" TRENT CUT THE connection on Simon's phone.

"What happened?"

"I think he got busted. The picture blurred, then I heard shouting, then a loud noise, like the phone had hit something."

"Do you think they got enough of a signal from it?"

"We'll know soon enough, I guess." Trent stared at the phone as if he could will it to ring, but the device remained stubbornly silent.

"Problem with your connection?" Lee taunted from the other side of the raft. Although Trent and Simon had made their exchange in English, Lee must have known enough to be able to catch the main gist of the conversation. As soon as Lee spoke, Trent checked on the second man, making sure he wasn't about to try anything. It would have been hard for either pirate to make a move, especially since Simon had bound their hands with the plastic zip ties he'd produced from a zippered pocket in his combat vest. Combined with the fact that he was still covering both of them with an MP5K made an uprising very unlikely.

Trent didn't know what was worse—the satisfied smirk on Lee's face as he sat in the buffeted raft, or his own increasingly distressed stomach. Although he was at home on the sea, having sailed and surfed it for years, he also knew when to come in out of the storm. The constant swaying and heaving to and fro was having an effect on all of the passengers except Lee, it seemed, who rode the rising and falling raft with calm indifference. Conversation was nonexistent, with Trent just wanting the call to come in that would allow him to wipe that smug smile off the pirate's face.

Simon's phone buzzed in Trent's hand, and he flipped it open. "This is Alpha… You got it… Yes… Excellent." He nudged Simon and nodded at the flap. "The helicopter's approaching? We'll send a flare for them to mark our position."

Simon was already at the small supply box, locating the brand-new LED flare and switching it, choosing the bright white setting. He sat near the opening and held it pointed at the sky, keeping his eyes—and the pistol in his free hand—on their two prisoners, and his ear on the rest of the one-sided conversation.

"Yes, I understand. We'll proceed there directly upon pickup. Affirmative—stop the vessel at all costs. Alpha out." He snapped the phone shut with a triumphant click and turned to Simon. "They got a bearing on the second ship. Once the chopper picks us up, we'll be heading for it directly. Looks like it's on the way to Hong Kong."

Trent had been watching Lee while he talked, and he savored the look of shock that appeared on the pirate's face. Trent spoke in Cantonese so Lee wouldn't miss any of his meaning. "Too bad you didn't give up that information when you had the chance, Lee. Now it seems you're just as expendable as your buddy there."

"Maybe not, Liang. You know who's in control of that ship—Guong. Remember how fond he is of you? I'm sure he'd like nothing better than to paint that ship with your blood, and that of anyone who tries to stop him. But if I were to step out of the helicopter with you, he'd think I was coming aboard because of a change in the plan. You could take the entire ship without firing a shot, and in return, all I'd ask for is whatever leniency the organization you work for can provide."

Above the declining storm, Trent could hear the steady chop of helicopter blades beating through the wind and rain toward them. He exchanged a glance with Simon, and the merc leaned forward.

"I think I caught all of that. You don't actually trust him to keep his word, do you?"

"I'd trust a shark more, but it's worth trying. All we have to do is figure out when he's going to try to ambush us," Trent stated.

"Great. My enemy is my friend until he becomes my enemy again."

"Something like that." Trent turned back to Lee. "All right, Lee. You agree to try to help us take the ship, *and* provide whatever testimony we need to nail the people behind this—don't look so surprised, we knew you weren't pulling the strings here, you're just a pirate-for-hire—and I'll see what we can do."

Lee's expression tightened at hearing Trent's description, but after a few seconds he realized that was as good as he was going to get, and he nodded. Trent poked his head outside the flap to see the helicopter—a large, transport model he didn't recognize—hovering about twenty yards above the churning ocean, the downdraft from its rotors kicking up a large cloud of fine mist all around them.

A minute later, a six-foot-long wire mesh basket dropped from the sky, swinging wildly in the wind. Trent sat on the edge of the raft, making sure that Lee and the other pirate weren't about to try anything funny, and waited for the basket to come to him. Eventually the spinning mass of wire and metal came close enough for him to grab, and Trent managed to get one hand on it and pull it closer.

He waved the second pirate over. "All right, you first."

"What about my hands?" the man wailed.

"Grab the bottom and hope the wind doesn't flip you over." Trent shoved him into the wire basket, uncaring that his head smacked into the side. "Hold tight!" He flashed a thumbs-up sign at the man on the winch, and the pale-faced pirate rose into the air, the wind plucking at his clothing with invisible fingers. Spinning and swaying, the basket reached the open side door of the helicopter, and the prisoner was lifted inside.

When the basket arrived again, Trent motioned to Simon. "You're next."

He slung his HK and grabbed the line before glancing back. "You sure?"

Trent never took his eyes off Lee. "Yeah."

He slid into the basket and flashed the thumbs-up sign to the guys above. "See you up there." The basket was pulled back to the helicopter, and Simon got out.

Lee smiled. "Last chance to join me as a pirate, you

know. See the world, meet interesting people and steal from them."

"The two days I was aboard your boat was enough, thanks. Get over here, you're going up next."

Lee got onto his knees and awkwardly waddled over to the opening. "What makes you think I just won't pitch myself into the ocean, make your job that much harder?"

Trent shrugged. "Simple—you want to live too much. You're no martyr, sacrificing yourself for a cause. You're only in this for the money."

"One of my more regrettable flaws, I'm afraid. What else have you learned about me so far?"

"That you plan things carefully, but you can also think on your feet. And you always think you can come out on top in any situation. You may have in the past, but not this time."

Lee smiled again, an affable grin so easy that it could have fooled Trent into thinking it was real if he hadn't known the guy. "As long as one is alive, there is always an opportunity to survive, and perhaps even come out ahead. We'll see what happens, won't we?"

"Now who's the philosopher?" Trent kept the pistol trained on Lee's midsection while he waited for the basket to swing over. Once he had it, he pulled it inside. "Get in."

Lee turned around so that his back was to the cage, then sat himself inside, wriggling up to fit more comfortably. "Better than a coffin."

"Don't try to screw me, and I'll make sure you don't end up in one." Trent gave the chopper the thumbs-up, and Lee was lifted into the air. Trent waited until he was almost at the door before tucking his pistol away and readying himself to leave. At the last moment, he grabbed the small LED flare and tucked it into his pocket.

The basket returned, and Trent grabbed it with both hands, swinging himself aboard and kicking the raft away. He gave the winch operator the thumbs-up and was hoisted into the air, each second taking him farther away from the churning sea. A few seconds later, and he was helped aboard the helicopter by the winch operator, who quickly stowed the basket and pointed Trent to a seat. Lee and his pilot were sitting on the same bench seat, covered by Simon.

Trent sank into his own seat and accepted a pair of headphones. "Did he fill you in on where we're going?"

"Yes, sir, and we are under orders to provide whatever aid we can. We're making all due speed possible. Our ETA is eighteen minutes, so stay sharp, because we'll be there in no time."

"Right." After the events of the past day, all Trent really wanted to do was sleep, but his senses were already in overdrive, and all he could do was sit back in his seat and stare at Lee, trying to figure out what was going on behind that expressionless face.

CHAPTER THIRTY-THREE

"We've got Hu Ji Han," Tokaido announced.

Kurtzman nodded. "Good, and our improvised strike team's on the way to intercept the ship. How far away is it from Hong Kong?"

Tokaido checked the ship's heading. "Current distance is less than fifty nautical miles."

Kurtzman's brow furrowed slightly. "Should we send David from the mainland to join them? If the airborne team doesn't make it or accomplish their goal, there'd be nothing to stop that ship from running right into the harbor."

"Before you make that call, Bear, you might want to look at this." Tokaido waved the wheelchair-bound genius over to his monitor.

"Okay, what am I seeing?"

"This projection of the ship detonating anywhere within ten miles of Hong Kong, and what might happen if the resulting tidal wave hits the shoreline." Tokaido tapped a few keys, and a map of the sprawling city appeared, with a small red dot below it representing the ship. One more tap, and the dot disappeared, replaced by yet another circular blast wave that radiated out to the coast line, flowing over the islands and into the mainland beyond.

"The initial calculations present a tidal wave at least

fifteen feet tall, possibly as high as twenty-five feet, which could cause not only severe damage to Hong Kong, but might impact the Philippines and surrounding islands, as well. Although damage to the city itself wouldn't be as extensive, that would be offset by damage to other surrounding nations."

Tokaido watched the simulation unfold with a thoughtful expression. "I thought large explosions didn't cause tidal waves. After all, the nuclear tests in the South Pacific never produced any."

Kurtzman answered with a shake of his head. "That was because the temperatures produced by the atomic and nuclear bombs were high enough to vaporize a large quantity of water, leaving, in essence, a hole in the ocean. The surrounding water rushed in to fill it, and that was that. But this, which is in effect a huge conventional bomb, doesn't reach those kinds of super temperatures. If the explosion goes off, it'll send out a shock wave that will displace the water around the blast site, creating exactly what we don't want—a tidal wave. So, other than stopping the pirates before they blow the thing, how do we make sure this scenario doesn't happen?"

Tokaido enlarged a portion of the map near the seaside city. "The best way to protect Hong Kong is by aiming the ship toward this island." He highlighted a long, narrow island about three miles south of the city. "In the event of a detonation, it would break the wave enough to reduce its force, and send the energy off to the east and west sides. The southern areas, however, would not be so fortunate, but the damage estimates to the city itself fall to about ten percent of what they would be if the wave hit at its full strength."

"We'd better get on the phone and let them know that under no circumstances should that ship get any closer to Hong Kong. And plot a course for the ship to head to that island…" Kurtzman trailed off as a thought struck him. "Also, find out if there are any people on that island, because heaven help them if there are."

"And we'd better ready David to launch from Hong Kong anyway—if he has to, he'll fly right down that ship's throat to stop it."

Tokaido's computer chimed, and he turned back to see what it had come up with. "Bear, I've got the two most likely targets for those other teams near London and the U.S.—an ammonium nitrate freighter called the *Peligan Dory* heading to London, and a big-ass oil tanker called the *Esso Argonaut,* out of Oslo, that's heading for Jersey Harbor right now."

"How sure is the computer?"

"Seventy-eight-point-six on the *Dory* and eighty-three-point-four on the *Argonaut.* The secondary choices on both are in the low to mid twenty-percent range."

"Good enough for me. Get that intel to Striker and Able Team ASAP. Both should be close enough to stop those ships before it's too late."

"Shouldn't we alert the Port Authorities about the possibilities of bomb ships heading toward their harbors?"

Kurtzman stroked his beard. "Normally I don't like to punt these, but I'm calling Hal and getting his take on this. Most likely DHS will send out an Elevated Threat Alert about this, but Hal can probably contact the folks who really need to know." The computer genius put his headset on and speed-dialed a number. "Hal… Yeah, it's

Bear… You know that South China Sea incident you'd asked Striker to look into?… Well, it turns our that it's a hell of a lot worse than we expected….”

CHAPTER THIRTY-FOUR

Trent had just finished prepping for the insertion onto the ship, with his pistol reloaded and snugged into the small of his back, where his shirt would cover it from casual inspection, when the winch officer tapped him on the shoulder.

"Incoming call from your HQ."

"Go ahead." Trent adjusted his headset and waited for the connection.

Kurtzman was back on line. "We've run some simulations, and I've got an additional objective for you. The ship must not be allowed to detonate at all costs. Collateral damage from an explosion, even at sea, could be dangerous."

"Affirmative. That was understood from the start."

"However, if there is no other choice, we're downloading a course for you to sail the ship aground at an island 10.6 miles south of Hong Kong. Just get those coordinates into the navigation computer on the freighter, and it should pilot itself to shore."

"Got it, I'll inform Simon of the backup plan. Of course, you know we're not going to let that ship blow up if we can help it."

"I'm sure you won't, but you also know we can't take any chances. Good luck. Stony Man out."

Trent motioned Simon to him, and quickly explained

the change in the scenario. He nodded and checked his phone, indicating that he'd received the nav data file.

The pilot's voice clicked on in Trent's headset. "We have a visual on the ship. ETA three minutes."

Trent signaled the winch officer. "What do you have in the way of personal weapons on board?"

The officer unlocked a cabinet mounted on the wall, revealing a selection of Heckler & Koch submachine guns and pistols, along with magazines of ammunition. Trent selected another MP5KA4 along with a short suppressor, which he threaded onto the barrel, and three magazines, tucking them into the side pockets of his cargo shorts. "All right, hail them."

Lee whistled loudly. "It might be best if you let me talk to Guong, otherwise he might just try to blow us out of the sky."

Trent scowled. "With what? Did you send portable rockets with him, as well?"

"Let's just say he would be able to bring down a helicopter like this with little difficulty."

"All right, but I'll be listening, and the first attempt to signal him in any way earns you a bullet in the brain."

"It wouldn't be very prudent of me to blow up the helicopter I'm sitting in, now would it?"

Trent drew his pistol and placed it on Lee's chest, making sure no one would be in the path of the bullet when it exited the pirate's body. "No, but giving him a signal to kill anyone except you could be done very easily."

Despite his position, Lee actually laughed at that. "You give me too much credit, Liang. I would not have foreseen this situation occurring in a hundred years.

Now, open a channel to the ship, and let's get this over with."

A moment later, Trent heard a clicking in his headset, and the winch officer nodded. "You're on."

"*Divine Pearl, Divine Pearl,* this is Helicopter Delta One-Three approaching on your port side, please acknowledge."

"An unfamiliar voice crackled in the headphones. "Delta One-Three, this is Captain Bai Aiguo of the *Divine Pearl,* is there something we can do for you?"

"Captain, I know your ship has been taken over by pirates, since I'm the man who told them to do it. Put their leader on the mike right now."

There was a rustle as the microphone was passed over, then Guong's voice sounded in Trent's ears. "Lee, what the hell are you doing here? What's going on?"

"Calm down, there's been a change in plans. I only found out about it a half hour ago myself—"

"What about the other ship? Where's the yacht?"

"I left two men on board to guard it, don't worry. Look, this helicopter is from our employer. I'm coming aboard, so don't try anything funny, all right?"

There was a long pause before Guong answered. "Okay, but the moment you get here, get up to the bridge and fill me in on what's going on."

"Don't worry, soon you'll know everything that's happened. We'll be setting down on the aft section. Liang is with me, and we'll be heading there right away."

"What's that bastard doing here?"

Lee shrugged apologetically at Trent, who waved the insult off. He'd been called much worse in his day anyway.

"Didn't really have much choice in the matter. Besides, he's all right. We'll see you in a couple of minutes."

Guong's snort was audible though the earphones. "Just get your ass up here."

Trent signaled for the pilot to cut the connection. "Take us down on the aft section, and watch the rear boom. We're going to need a ride home still."

"My orders are to drop you off, then circle at a safe distance until the ship is secured. You can radio from the bridge when you're ready to be picked up again."

"That works. We should be in touch soon." Trent scanned the freighter as they came over it. It looked like any one of the thousands in the area, roughly five hundred feet long, able to carry at least 20,000 tons of whatever cargo needed transporting. Trent repressed a shudder as he thought of what kind of damage that could do to Hong Kong and the surrounding areas. The ship certainly looked as if it had seen better days, its hull heavily splotched with rust under shabby upper and bridge decks, their once-white paint now peeling everywhere, with bare metal showing in many places. The pilot brought them in from the rear, passing over the stern and the furiously churning propellers.

"Hey, what about my hands? It would look a bit suspicious if you take me aboard tied-up."

Trent grimaced, but he couldn't fault the guy's logic. If Guong was watching, that would be a definite red flag that something was up. He nodded to Simon. "Cut him loose."

Simon produced a matte-black folding knife and thumbed it open. "You sure?"

"Like he said, we don't have much choice. Don't

worry, I'll keep him real close. You pop out on the other side and start taking out the others. See if you can free the crew. We'll need to get them off the boat anyway. Once you get that done, meet me at the bridge. If anything goes wrong, evac immediately."

Simon cut the zip-tie off Lee's wrists, and the pirate massaged life back into his hands as they lined up for their final approach. The weather had calmed to a steady rain, and the ship easily rode through the smaller waves. The pilot brought the helicopter down on the deck, matching the roll of the deck with what looked like practiced ease. The moment the wheels touched down, the winch officer slid the door open, and Trent prodded Lee out on to the slippery deck, instinctively ducking to avoid the rotors, even though they were several yards overhead.

As the helicopter took off again, Trent kept his hand on Lee's arm, and snugged the barrel of the pistol into his side. "Just remember, this is pointing at your stomach at all times. I've heard it's a nasty way to die."

"Believe me, I don't plan on experiencing it just yet. Look, there's Guong." Lee waved to him, his index and middle fingers held up in a V, and the stocky pirate waved back from an open platform next to the bridge deck—then raised a stubby submachine pistol and aimed it at both men.

"Shit!" Trent tried to duck behind Lee, but the other man brought his arm down in a half-assed but effective chop, shoving the silenced pistol out of the way.

Trent grabbed for the pirate leader, but Lee twisted away, shouting, "Kill him!" as he ran for cover.

Trent snapped off three shots at the gunman above him, hoping to make him duck back into the wheelhouse. Guong apparently had more guts than brains, because he stayed right where he was, his subgun spitting fire and lead at Trent, who was forced to dive for the cover of a hold hatch, bullets pinging off the metal all around him.

Shoving his pistol into its holster, Trent grabbed his subgun, aimed at the platform and squeezed the trigger, sending two 3-round bursts toward the pirate. That got his attention as the slugs whizzed past him, and he disappeared into the wheelhouse. Trent used the break to rush forward to the back of the upper deck. That didn't go as planned, he thought. Lee would try to finish the job, so he'd want to make sure the bombs were placed in the hold to set off the fertilizer, then escape in a lifeboat. They were close enough to the coast that he could make land in a couple of hours.

Trent headed toward the nearest hatch cover, looking for a way down into the ship's interior. There was a smaller hatch nearby, and he unlocked it, revealing a maintenance ladder leading into the hold. Trent got out the LED flare, which, as he suspected, also had a flashlight setting. He activated it, then slung the HK, drew his pistol and, after clearing the immediate area below the ladder, descended into the bowels of the ship.

Trent reached the bottom of the hold and shone his light around. Everywhere the beam hit revealed huge shipping containers, all filled with ammonium nitrate. He tried to ignore the fact that he was standing in the middle of what could be transformed into a massive floating bomb, and set out to find Lee. Searching the hold, he found no one, although he did locate an opened container with a brick of C-4 plastic explosive attached to the side of a pallet loaded with bags of nitrate and wrapped in plastic. While he wasn't sure the charge would be enough to set off the industrial fertilizer—his knowledge of it indicated that it was a very stable chemical compound—Trent wasn't taking any chances. A quick examination of the bomb showed the detonator to be directly connected to the explosive, with no alternate triggering devices or traps. He easily removed the timer detonator and turned it off.

At the end of the hold he found a door marked To Hold No. 4 and gently raised the lever to open it. Leading with the pistol in one hand and his light in the other, Trent eased through the door, pushing with his shoulder. A loud clank nearby made him freeze, but the noise continued, and he covered his light with his shirt, leaving him in near total darkness, and slipped the rest of the way through the entryway.

This hold was just as large and just as filled as the previous one. Trent edged forward, covering his light so that only a thin ray emanated from one side, giving him just enough to see. He was only a few yards away, and crept forward with slow, careful patience. Close enough to hear voices, he caught the familiar tones of Lee, exhorting one of the other men to work faster.

"We just have to set this charge, and we can get the hell out of here. Once we get off this tub, we'll get paid and get out of the area for good. Make that connection there…and there. All right, now let's—"

Trent stepped around the corner and leveled his pistol, holding his light in his left hand and bracing it against his right. "Hold it right there, Lee!"

Lee didn't even pause in his actions, but shoved the other hapless pirate at Trent as he took off around the corner. The other man barreled forward, and Trent took one step to the side and chopped down on the man's neck with the butt of his pistol, sending him crashing to the floor, unmoving. Trent didn't waste time checking his vitals, but paused only to disarm the new bomb before trotting to the corner and peeking around it—and almost getting his face shot off for his trouble.

Gunshots echoed through the cavernous interior, and a bullet ricocheted off the side of the freight container in front of Trent, making him duck back behind it. Sticking his pistol barrel around the side, he triggered two more rounds in the direction the bullets had come from, then took off across the aisle to the next row of stacked containers. Hopefully, I'm on the same side as he is, Trent thought, walking to the far end of the row and poking his head out quickly before jerking it back under cover. The cross-aisle looked empty, but he couldn't take the chance that Lee was waiting in ambush somewhere.

Holstering his pistol and slinging his subgun, he stuck his light in his mouth, then placed his foot on a hinge of the nearest container and began climbing. The sides of the huge cargo haulers were smooth, with little to hold on to except for the hinges and the narrow space between the top of one container and the bottom of another. Trent made it a point not to look down, and also not to think about what might happen if the stack suddenly shifted and crushed his fingers or toes. With one more heave, he reached the top and rolled onto his back. Getting to his feet, he began cross-checking the aisles, moving in the general direction the bullets had come from. He would flash the light over the side and check, then jump to the next row, pausing for a moment to listen for any noise from the floor. He had just hit the end when he heard a series of high-pitched metallic beeps—as if someone was programming a timer.

Hiding the LED light against his shirt, Trent crawled to the far edge and listened intently, moving along the lip of the container until he figured he was right above the pirate leader. Slowly he drew his pistol and extended it down over the side so that it would be pointing at the pirate's head, then he placed the flare with the beam pointing down on the top of the case, so when he moved it off the metal, the beam would shine right down on his target. Trent took a deep breath, released it and held the flare out over the side, sticking his head over at the same time.

The halo illuminated a startled Lee with his face turned up, mouth agape, eyes squinting into the white light. His right hand rose, and Trent sighted down his own pistol barrel and squeezed the trigger three times. With a surprised grunt, Lee fell over.

"Don't move, Lee, I'm coming down."

The pirate laughed, the sound trailing off into a choked cough. "I wouldn't do that, unless you want to go up in a big bang."

Shit, he's already primed the bomb, Trent thought. "Don't do anything foolish. It doesn't have to end this way." He had just thrown a leg over when a fusillade of bullets cracked out from below, and a sharp pain seared his thigh. Trent threw himself back over the top just as a huge explosion tore through the hold, knocking the stack of containers off balance and making them crash against the next set like huge building blocks knocked over by a careless giant.

Although shielded from the brunt of the blast, Trent had still suffered from the shock wave. He couldn't hear anything but a loud ringing in his ears, his vision was blurred and teary, and his head felt as though it had been split open with a claw hammer. He'd lost his LED light, but that didn't matter anymore, because he saw light coming in through the large hole that had been blasted in the hull. As he got his bearings, Trent realized that, as he had guessed, the ammonium nitrate hadn't detonated—obviously, since he was still alive. Above the dust and debris kicked up by the explosion, he also smelled something else—the sharp tang of seawater. Dragging himself to the side of the askew container, Trent looked down to see the ocean pouring into the broken hold. It was time to go.

He took a second to examine the wound on his leg, and was relieved to find it was little more than a flesh wound, with the bullet carving a furrow through the fleshy part of his thigh. It stung like hell, but he could walk without too much difficulty. Trent leaped off the listing containers to the next solid row, biting back a scream as he landed on his injured leg. Okay, maybe a bit more difficult than I realized, he thought. From there he traversed the row until he came to the end of the hold, where he saw a ladder leading up to a hatch in the ceiling. The distance to it, however, was about ten feet away.

Gritting his teeth, Trent backed up a few steps, then hobbled as fast as he could toward the edge of the container, leaping off at the last second. He hit the metal ladder with breath-stealing force, and felt a sharp pain in his right ribs, but managed to grab it long enough to get his feet on a rung. Clinging to the patterned metal, Trent began climbing to the top of the hold, his bruised, battered body protesting every movement.

CHAPTER THIRTY-FIVE

"Just a little farther. Come on, you can do it."

With the *Divine Pearl's* captain's words exhorting him on, Xiang stretched his body to the breaking point, the already tight leather collar choking off his air as he tried to snag the phone in the corner of the room with his foot.

As soon as Guong had left the bridge, Xiang had gone after the device, hoping against hope that it still might work. His breath came in shallow gasps, which was all the collar would let him take in, and his vision was turning gray at the edges. His ribs, which still ached from the beating he had taken in Manila, and which had been hurt again when he had slammed into the ship, positively screamed with the effort of flexing to give him even half an inch more reach toward the phone. But throughout it all, the small piece of plastic remained stubbornly, maddeningly just out of reach.

"I…can't…can't…get it." After one more strain that nearly caused him to pass out, Xiang collapsed against the chair, wheezing for breath.

"That's all right, you tried your best." The captain regarded the closed bridge door with a mixture of fear and suspicion. "I wish I knew what was going on out there."

"I don't know. Other than the leader of the pirates coming on board from that helicopter, along with the guy who I know is some kind of government agent, I'm not sure what's happening."

The answer came a moment later as both he and Xiang heard a short burst of automatic weapon fire, followed by return fire from somewhere else on the ship. Guong burst through the door and slammed it shut, locking it and stalking into the middle of the room to check their course with a satisfied nod. "It won't be too long now. We'll deliver our special payload, and then take off to get our payment." He leered at Xiang. "And you're coming with me. That's my bonus from this job."

Xiang pulled uselessly at the shrunken leather strap that bound him to the captain's chair. "I'll kill myself first."

"Oh, you'll wish you were dead before I'm through with you, I guarantee it." Guong grinned as he shoved the throttle forward, coaxing a bit more speed out of the engines. "Ten more minutes, and we'll be close enough to blow this floating hulk out of the water, and then it'll be time for some well-earned rest and relaxation—at least for me."

Xiang was only listening to him with one ear, his attention drawn to the bridge door, and its lock, which was slowly turning as if being unlocked from the outside. Needing to keep the big brute distracted, Xiang spit at him. "Fuck you, you inbred, monkey-screwing goat herder! I'll bite my tongue off and bleed to death before going anywhere else with you!"

Guong whirled on him with frightening speed, his hand blurring out to smack Xiang across the face again, loosening a tooth and making him jerk up tight against the strap, which creaked under the strain.

"You'll be more compliant after I snap those chicken

bones you call arms and leave you in a room with no food or water. A few days of that, and you'll be begging to do anything I say."

The door lock turned another centimeter, and Xiang kept up the distraction, lashing out at the pirate with his foot, trying to connect with the man's genitals, but hitting his thigh instead. Cocking his own large leg back, Guong smashed his foot into the boy's leg, impacting squarely on the muscle, and making his vision go red for a moment as blinding pain overwhelmed his body, making him collapse to the deck and nearly hang himself by the collar.

"Leave the boy alone!" the captain said.

"Shut up!" The meaty thud of a fist striking flesh told Xiang that Guong was out taking his frustration on the helpless man. As his eyesight returned, the boy saw the door slowly open, and a black-shoed foot ease inside. Unfortunately, the door creaked as the intruder tried to open it farther, alerting Guong.

Xiang looked up to see the big Chinese man bring his submachine gun around and put a burst through the door, hurling the person outside backward with a surprised grunt. Xiang clawed at the pirate, who swatted him off like an elephant removing a fly, and stalked over to the doorway, where a black-clad figure was trying to draw in a breath while raising a pistol. Guong stepped on the person's wrist hard enough to crack bone, causing a scream of pain. Although the person kicked at his legs with all the force they could, he ignored the blows as he pointed the gun at their face and pulled the trigger. The form stiffened, then relaxed in death.

"No!" Xiang slumped against the chair, all hope lost. "Liang…"

"That wasn't Liang, you stupid bastard. More's the pity. Some asshole dressed in stealth gear—not stealthy enough, I think." Guong threw his head back to laugh just as a massive explosion rocked the bridge and the rest of the ship, throwing him into the instrument panel and giving the freighter a pronounced list to starboard.

Guong hauled himself back up to the wheel and grimly held on to it. "The charge must have gone off prematurely. Just a few more minutes, and we'll set the entire South China Sea ablaze."

I can't let that happen, Xiang thought as he pulled helplessly at the tether binding him to the chair. But I don't know how I can stop it, either....

TRENT DRAGGED HIMSELF out of the hold hatch and lay on the deck, trying to catch his breath. The rain had subsided to a light drizzle now, which felt good on his face.

The ship listed even more to starboard now, and he forced himself to rise to his feet and stagger to the stairway that would take him to the bridge deck. At the foot of it, he met another of the pirates who was also going up.

"Hey, Liang, what's—" was all the man got out before Trent raised his pistol and shot him point-blank in the chest. The unfinished question died along with its asker. Trent hauled himself up to the boat deck, where several men were working to swing a lifeboat out on its davits in preparation to launch it. When they saw him, the group raised their hands, except for two, who started for him, heedless of the smoking gun in his hand.

Trent raised the pistol so that the muzzle pointed into the air. "Hold up, guys, I'm on your side."

"Why are you shouting?" one of the sailors asked.

"I was in the hold when the explosion went off. Can't hear much of anything. Where's your captain?"

The two men exchanged glances, then the first one answered, speaking slowly so Trent might have a chance to understand him better. "Still on the bridge, held by that crazy man. The other man who freed us headed up there to see what he could do."

A burst of gunfire from the bridge made everyone except Trent flinch and look up. It was followed by a scream that was cut off by a second, shorter burst. Off their expressions, Trent asked, "What happened?"

The sailor shook his head. "I think that man just got killed. Do you need any help up there?"

"No, get this boat launched and try to stick near the freighter if you can. If it looks like it's going down, and you don't see us, get away. Someone will pick you guys up—if not the helicopter, then they'll radio for assistance."

The sailor clapped him on the shoulder, making Trent stagger a bit. "All right. Are you sure?"

"Just go." Trent turned and began climbing the final staircase, leading with his pistol again as he cleared each step. When his head drew level with the platform near the door, the first thing he saw was Simon's lifeless body, his face mangled and burnt by several bullets fired into it at close range. A small knot of anger flared in his belly, and he pushed on, climbing the last few steps and creeping to the edge of the open door, which swung back and forth. Trent listened for any sign of life inside, but couldn't hear anything over the dying ship and the patter of the rain.

Taking a deep breath, he booted the door open and covered the small room with his pistol. A bound and gagged man sat in the captain's chair, his eyes wide. Behind him was Xiang, his mouth open to shout.

The door violently rebounded on Trent, slamming into his arms hard enough to knock the pistol from his grasp. Before he could recover, Guong popped out from his hiding place on the other side, grabbed Trent and whipped him into the room. Hurtling through the air, he smacked his wounded leg against the chair, which stopped his forward momentum and sent him crashing to the floor.

Trent couldn't think, couldn't breathe. Every limb, every nerve in his body shrieked in agony. He hawked up a glob of phlegm and blood and spit it out on the deck before Guong's hands lifted him off the ground. Trent retained enough awareness to bring his hands down on the bigger man's eardrums, popping one. Guong screamed in pain and slammed his adversary against the side of the chair, fracturing one of his ribs with a sickening crack. "I'm going to enjoy smashing you to a pulp."

The American brought his open palm up, intending to drive his heel into Guong's nose, but the other man saw it coming and turned his head, the powerful blow landing on his cheek, snapping the bone. In answer, the bigger man reared his head back and drove his forehead into Trent's face, breaking his nose and rocking his head back with a guttural grunt of pain. Guong liked that reaction so much he did it again, breaking his opponent's right cheekbone this time. Trent lolled in the pirate's grip, semiconscious, his right eye already starting to swell shut from the injuries. Guong pounded on his already weakened rib cage, and Trent's face came to rest on Xiang, who was crouched by the side of the chair.

"Sorry…kid…" The last blow delivered by Guong

cracked something else in Trent's chest, making him cry out in agony. Even through the haze of pain and shattered bones, even with his ears still ringing from the blast, somehow he heard Xiang's voice.

"No, Liang, you *did* save me."

As Guong wound up for another strike, Trent looked down to see his HK MP5K in Xiang's hands, the muzzle of the sound suppressor pointed at Guong.

The burly pirate looked at the kid in shock. "What the hell—"

Xiang squeezed the trigger, and the twenty or so rounds left in the magazine pulped Guong's chest, tearing through skin, smashing his ribs to splinters and pulverizing his lungs and heart into jelly. The large man staggered backward, his expression turning to disbelief, then blank as his brain shut down and he fell on his face to the floor.

Trent lay half on, half off the chair, struggling to draw a breath. All he wanted to do was to rest for a bit, but there was this annoying voice in his ear that wouldn't let him.

"Liang, Liang, wake up! The ship's going to sink, and we're going down with it if you don't free us!"

"Sir, please wake up, you need to find a knife or something to cut us free." The captain's voice also cut through Trent's haze to galvanize him into action.

"Okay, okay, just give me a minute." Trent cast about for a blade, remembering something about Simon… he had a knife on him. He rolled off the chair and fell to his hands and knees, screaming in pain when he hit the deck.

"Liang, please hurry. The water is almost up to the bridge deck!"

Trent crawled forward until he came to Simon's legs, then fumbled at his combat vest until he found the pocket with the knife in it. "Here—catch!" He tossed it through the air, and Xiang strained up to grab the lockblade, snagging it with the tips of his fingers. He flipped the blade open and slashed the leash apart, then cut the captain free.

"Xiang, get my phone from the corner." Trent gasped, fading in and out of consciousness.

"Come on, sir, we have to get you out of here." The captain navigated the inclined deck to make it past Trent to the platform outside. Xiang was right behind him, having scrambled down to retrieve the sat phone, then used the chair to help him reach the outer door. Along with the captain, they helped Trent move toward the stairs, ignoring his hissing breath that came out with each tug.

"Son of a bitch, that hurts!" Trent smiled as he stared into Xiang's eyes. "You're risking your life to save mine…you know that, right?"

"You did the exact same thing for me, remember?" They'd reached the door, and the captain propped it open and pulled on Trent's shirt while Xiang pushed him out onto the bridge landing. "Now I get to return the favor!"

The ship's deck was awash now. It was going to be afloat for maybe a few more seconds. Trent pointed overhead, where the helicopter was hovering, the basket coming down toward them. "Captain, I want you…to take the boy off…the ship. If there's time, come back for me."

"No! No! No! I'm not leaving you, Liang!" Xiang said. The captain reached for the boy, but backed off at the pistol held in his hands. "You get in, then have them send the basket back down. Liang and I will come up next. Go!"

"I will make sure they drop the basket again." The captain climbed in, holding on to the sides tightly. Xiang gave them the thumbs-up, and the basket rose into the air.

"Come on, Liang, stay awake! You can make it!" Xiang kept Trent sitting up as the ocean waves began lapping their way up the stairs to the bridge. Before they got that far, the rear of the ship began rising into the air, taking the bridge, Trent and Xiang with it. Trent blinked away drops of seawater and stared up at the helicopter, which had recovered the basket and offloaded the captain. The ship shuddered underneath them and began to sink into the ocean.

"Xiang…I want you to get into that basket."

"Not without you. You go, I go!"

"Don't be a fool!"

The basket came back down, blowing around in the downdraft from the chopper's blades. Xiang leaned out over the vertical railing and grabbed for it, missed, then waited for it to come back to them. The second time he snagged it with his fingertips and brought it close.

"Get in, damn it!" He pulled the basket as close as he could. Trent gathered everything inside him and pulled himself up just long enough to fall into the basket, the hard wire mesh making every inch of his body flare with pain. It got even worse when a weight piled on top of his chest, forcing nearly all the air out of his lungs, and they were rising into the air.

Trent ended up on his stomach, his face pressed into the wire of the basket, and he watched as the ocean sucked the ship down, closing over the bridge and stern and making the ship vanish completely, as if it had never existed in the first place.

Then there was nothing but wind and air around them, and the last thing Trent remembered was the masked face of the helicopter crewman as he pulled them in and wrapped them both in a blanket. Trent felt a prick in his arm, then there was nothing but darkness.

CHAPTER THIRTY-SIX

Eighteen thousand feet above the Atlantic Ocean, Carl "Ironman" Lyons gripped the edges of the open door of the C-130, waited for the green light, then dived out into the night sky when he got the signal.

Although he'd had minimal training in skydiving, Lyons took to it like a hawk to the air, letting himself free-fall for several seconds before pulling the ripcord and feeling the jerk in his shoulders and thighs as the ram-air parafoil inflated above his head. Activating his night-vision goggles, Lyons saw the other two chutes, representing the other two members of Able Team, Rosario "Pol" Blancanales, and Hermann "Gadgets" Schwartz, falling toward the calm ocean—and the oil tanker far below them. Off to their right, the lights of New York City blazed in the night sky.

Pulling on the cords of his steerable chute, Lyons came up behind the oil tanker, aiming for the aft section of the ship, the most dangerous part to land on, simply because it was so small. However, all three of the men had decided that it would be their best shot at getting aboard the ship undetected. Adjusting his airfoil to slow his speed, Lyons was only about a hundred yards above the fantail of the tanker when a sudden gust of wind lifted him another twenty yards into the air. He quickly bled air from underneath his canopy to try to hit his landing target, but saw he wasn't going to make it. However, a secondary landing area was within his reach—the roof of the bridge itself. The only problem with that was the tangle of antennas sprouting from all over the damned roof, not to mention the huge smokestack mounted right behind the bridge, which Lyons was coming up on very fast.

He pulled on his right cord, making him slip to starboard, narrowly missing the stack. Unfortunately, he was heading straight into an antenna array. Before Lyons could avoid it, his ram-air chute tangled in it, whipping him around to slam into the metal frame with breath-stealing force. Lyons's tactical vest absorbed most of the impact, but it still took the breath from his lungs for a few seconds.

The only upside of this was that his chute had caught on the antenna, suspending him at least twenty feet above the bridge roof. Grabbing his lines, Lyons carefully twisted himself until he could grab the antenna frame, then hit the release on his harness, leaving the chute snagged on the antenna. He climbed down to the roof and scanned the aft section of the ship for Blancanales and Schwarz. Not seeing them, he hit his throat mike. "Pol, Gadgets, report."

"Hey, Ironman, Pol here. We're both aboard, although I rolled my ankle when I landed. You all right?"

"Yeah, nothing I can't handle up here. Can you still handle freeing the crew?"

"Yeah, I'll just have to cover the rear, and let Gadgets clear the way. How about you? Are you gonna need help handling the bridge?"

"No, it's all under control. I'll report in when it's secure. Ironman out." Readying his silenced MP5K,

Lyons headed to the side of the roof and peeked over, spotting a guard standing outside the door. He drew a bead on the man's head and fired, opening the top of his skull with three rounds. Instead of falling forward, as Lyons had expected, the body thumped against the bridge door.

"Shit!" Before he could get down there, the door opened. "What are you—" was all the person inside could say before Lyons had pulled two flash-bang grenades off his vest, armed them and tossed them inside the bridge with a silent apology to the civilians about to get caught in the blast radius.

Sure enough, the M84 grenades detonated with their 170-decibel reports going off in the closed space, along with the 100,000-candlepower flashes from the ignited magnesium. Having taken cover on the roof, his mouth open and ears covered, Lyons rolled off and landed on the platform outside the bridge, just missing the dead man outside. The doorman was half in, half out of the doorway, his hands clamped ineffectually over his ears, his eyes screwed shut. Lyons made sure he was a terrorist before putting three bullets into his chest.

Without stopping, he charged inside, his night-vision goggles protecting him from the nonlethal smoke the flash-bangs had filled the space with. A figure charged out of the haze at him, gun waving wildly, and Lyons put the man down with a burst to his abdomen, then moved to sweep and clear the rest of the room. Finding a third terrorist huddled in the corner, blood leaking from his burst eardrums, Lyons disarmed and zip-tied him, then radioed to the rest of Able Team.

"Bridge is secure."

"Yeah, we heard it all the way down here. Great distraction, though, it enabled us to kill the last hardguys."

"Good." Lyons turned to the captain, who had already powered down the engines, and turned to the masked, black-suited figure.

"Thank you!" he shouted.

Lyons nodded. "You're welcome. Sorry about the ears!" he shouted back, pointing to his own to make sure the man understood.

The captain smiled broadly. "Rather be deaf and alive than hearing and dead!"

"Amen to that," Lyons replied. "By the way, I left my parachute up on your antenna. We should probably get it down before we reach the port."

IN THE STILL WATERS of the Thames, Mack Bolan swam on an intercept course towards his target, a rust-bucket oil tanker called the *Peligan Dory*.

After they'd gotten confirmation of the terrorists' target, Bolan and the members of Phoenix Force had hit the ground running the moment Grimaldi had touched down at London City Airport after a heated conversation with the air traffic controller. Bolan had arranged for car rental on the fly, and the five men had taken duffel bags loaded with the gear they'd thought they would need to get on the ship.

Unfortunately, the inner city traffic had been worse than expected, and Bolan's first plan of attack—rappelling down onto the boat from the Queen Elizabeth II Bridge on Canterbury Way—had been scrapped when the ship had passed the bridge before they could get there. Undeterred, Bolan had initiated their backup, driving like a bat out of hell to get ahead of the freighter again and entering the cool waters of the Thames to intercept the ship.

All five were dressed in wet suits and buoyancy control vests with pony tanks; they weren't planning on going underwater as it was a moonless night and the sentries didn't seem to be using night vision. Bolan and the rest of his team were all strapped with NVG, and they also had odd, heavy gloves on, and a strange contraption that looked like leg braces strapped to their lower legs, ending in an unusual boot with a large bar of metal attached to the inner side.

Stony Man was always trying to come up with better ways to allow access to all vehicles, and when Tokaido had seen a small company on the web marketing its metal wall-climbing gear, complete with gloves and foot braces, he was positive that the engineers at the farm could improve on the idea. Bolan and the men of Phoenix Force were going to try out these magnetic gloves and boots this night, intending to scale the side of the ship near the rear, where the engine noise should drown out any sounds of their ascent. The engineers had even created a detachable flipper, enabling the men to swim out to the ship with ease, then detach the flippers and stow them prior to beginning their climb.

Now, the men bobbed in the river as the tanker glided closer to them, its rusty bow still cutting a proud line through the water. Bolan gave it a fifteen count, until the noise from the propellers was almost deafening, then he reached out and planted a hand on the side of the ship, the powerful magnet sticking with a clank that was all but lost in the churning water of the tanker's wake. Bolan quickly brought his other hand up, then slapped a knee onto the hull, as well. With the ease of long practice, he scaled the thirty-foot-high hull with ease, only slowing when he got closer to the deck, not wanting to alert any of the mercenaries on board. Below him, the four members of Phoenix Force were following him up, clearing the vertical wall in less than ten seconds.

Five feet below the deckline, Bolan shrugged off his right-hand glove and drew his silenced Beretta 93R. When he was ready, he waved Gary Manning up beside him. Manning took out a fiber-optic scope and infrared lens and extended it up to take a look around the deck. Immediately he pointed toward the forward part of the ship and held up two fingers. Right afterward, Bolan heard the thump of combat boots treading the deck. Quickly shrugging off the left glove, he leaned back, his weight fully supported by the magnets on his legs, and motioned for Manning to hit the side of the boat with his hand. Manning did so, making a loud clank.

The boots stopped, then headed toward the two men. A second later, two heads looked over the railing, illuminated as clear as day in Bolan's night vision. At less than ten feet, he couldn't miss. Two silenced shots later, both men crumpled to the deck without making a sound.

Manning did one last sweep and pronounced the area clear. Bolan and the rest of Phoenix Force climbed onto deck and hit the quick-release straps on their braces to remove them. Encizo, James and Hawkins split off to locate and rescue the crew, while Bolan and Manning prepared to retake the bridge.

The duo ran through their plan one last time, then Manning carefully began climbing the superstructure of the bridge, his black wet suit blending into the shadows draped over the ship. Meanwhile, Bolan started around to the staircase leading to the bridge, on the port side of the tanker.

He was just rounding the corner when he came face-to-face with another one of the terrorists, who clawed for the submachine gun at his side while opening his mouth to shout a warning. Bolan was far quicker, however, and put a 9 mm subsonic bullet through the soft palate of the rear of the man's mouth, blowing out the back of his head. The dead man fell backward, but not before Bolan caught his web gear and eased him to the ground.

Locating the metal stairway, he quickly ascended the steps, and was soon standing outside the bridge door. He was still within the mission timeline, and after swapping his Beretta for a suppressed HK MP5K, simply waited a few seconds until Manning made his distraction.

Moments later, he heard the crack of shattering glass as Manning shot the side window out with his silenced submachine gun. With everyone's attention suitably focused on the noise, Bolan opened the door and stepped in, his NVG automatically compensating with flare dampeners so he wouldn't be blinded by the console lights.

Everything had almost gone according to plan. Of the three terrorists on the bridge, two were firing out the starboard window. The third one, however, was watching their six on the far side of the captain's chair, and had leveled a stubby submachine gun at Bolan.

Before the Executioner could fire, the grizzled captain launched himself at the third hijacker, grabbing at him with rough, swollen fingers. The terrorist fired a burst straight into the man's chest, but the old captain pitched forward, barreling into the other man and taking him to the floor.

Bolan sighted on the other two and took them out with precise 3-round bursts into the upper chest. He then stepped around the captain's chair and drew a bead on the third terrorist, who had just freed himself of the dead captain and was raising his subgun when Bolan blew his head off with one more 3-round burst.

"Bridge is secure," he said into his throat mike as he went to check the vitals of the old captain. When he turned the man over, he saw that he was dead, but on his face was an odd expression—a contented smile.

"Crew is secure, no injuries," Encizo's voice reported in his ear.

The first mate had gotten up from the floor, and stared at Bolan's black-clad form in amazement. "Who the fuck are you?"

Bolan shook his head. "No one you've ever heard of. Do you have things under control here?" At the man's stunned nod, he headed back out the bridge door. "Phoenix Force, evac now."

In less than five minutes, the Stony Man team was back on shore, and beginning the mile-long walk back to the van.

EPILOGUE

Hu Ji Han sat at a bare metal-and-plastic table, on a metal-and-plastic chair that was bolted to the floor, in an otherwise empty, windowless room with light pink walls. Although he attempted to carry himself with the same dignity he had once possessed, it was obvious that captivity was wearing on him. His slumped shoulders, the dark circles under his eyes, his unkempt hair and dull expression attested to that. He was dressed in shapeless, gray cotton pants, a short-sleeved shirt and cloth slippers. There was nothing on him or in the room that could be used as a weapon.

The lone door to the room opened, and a smartly dressed young woman entered, her shoulder-length blond hair drawn back in a simple twist. She wore a white lab coat over her camel-colored turtleneck, dark brown slacks and brown pumps. She carried a clipboard and two pens in her pocket. "Good morning, sir. How are you today?"

As defeated as he looked, something gentlemanly responded in the old Chinese man, and he straightened and looked the woman directly in the eye. "I am fine, thank you. How are you?"

"I'm well, too, thank you. We have some more tests we would like to run today."

Hu deflated at that, shrinking back into his chair.

"Always with tests, more tests, every day. When will I be allowed to leave this place? My company needs attending to. And when do I get to see my lawyer?"

In the beginning, his demands for an attorney had been more frequent and vocal, but now he asked the question by rote, as if it was simply part of his daily routine, and as if he knew there was little hope of receiving a positive answer.

The young woman replied the same way she always did. "I've passed on your request to my superiors, and they are looking into it. Your cooperation is appreciated, and I'm sure they'll be in touch soon regarding your status. Now, let's begin, shall we?"

In spite of himself, Hu leaned forward, pathetically eager for the contact with another human being. He would perform as well as he could on the tests, simply because they were the only thing to do in the room, the woman his only contact with the world outside.

"NOT SO MUCH THE MASTER of the universe now, is he?" Akira Tokaido mused as Mack Bolan, Aaron Kurtzman, and he, along with Barbara Price and Hal Brognola, watched through the one-way glass at Stony Man as the interview began.

"Not even close," Price said, opening a manila folder. "Unfortunately, he's quite insane, although at a high-functioning level. Obsessive personality, transference, et cetera. From the psych evaluations, it's been growing worse over the past year or so, beginning around the time of his grandmother's death, which might hold the key to why this was all put in motion. He's been very reticent to discuss that aspect of his life so far, but I think Ms. Smith is slowly making progress in regards to it. Perhaps, eventually, we might know exactly what tipped him over the edge, or whether it was a longer, slower process."

Bolan's eyebrow arched. "How long are you planning to keep him out of sight?"

"Barbara and I were just discussing that," Brognola said. "There's certainly a limit to how long we can keep him here, not to mention the tensions that are already rising due to unsubstantiated reports of American agents operating in China—pure nonsense, of course."

"Of course. Besides, David's British." Tokaido grinned.

"Fortunately, with the witnesses Able and you and Phoenix captured, I'm sure the State Department will have no problem extraditing him to a neutral country for a handover to the Chinese government. With the evidence we're assembling, the last thing they'll want is this story spilling around the world."

"Of course not." Bolan stared at the hunched-over Chinese man as he replied to the psychologist's questions. "I want to talk to him when she's through."

Price's eyebrows arched in surprise. "You do?"

"I want to look into the eyes of a man who would commit these acts against a populace who had nothing to do with the event he wants revenge for."

"I'm not sure that's a good idea, Mack. His psyche is very fragile right now. If you tell him all his planning has been for nothing, it could send him over the edge."

"Don't worry. I'll be gentle. I only need five minutes."

Price exchanged a glance with Brognola, who nodded. "All right, five minutes."

BOLAN WALKED INTO THE featureless room, pulled out the empty chair across from Hu Ji Han and sat down.

For nearly a minute, the two men simply stared at each other.

"Who are you?" Hu finally asked.

"My name isn't important," Bolan replied. "On one hand, I suppose I could almost owe you my thanks, since the attack you organized on the Sale in the Sands probably set back the global black-market arms network by a decade at least."

Hu's expression remained impassive. "I have no idea what you are talking about. I wish to see my lawyer—"

"Save it, Hu. You didn't get anywhere with Ms. Smith, and you're not going to get anywhere with me." Bolan leaned back in his chair. "It's too bad, really. You and I might have been on the same side once. But then I found out that you'd killed all those people as a diversion so your *real* operation—making undeclared war on innocent men, women and children—could get underway. Not on my watch. Not during my lifetime."

He leaned forward. "Those four ships were stopped before they could reach their targets." The older man deflated as Bolan continued. "The Japanese navy intercepted the ship heading for Tokyo, The Chinese-bound ship sank before it could reach Hong Kong and my people stopped the vessels bound for New York and London. No explosions, no fires, no citywide destruction…no innocents harmed. Your plans for global terror have failed."

Tears streamed down the old man's face as he rocked back and forth, mumbling a phrase over and over.

Rising, Bolan walked out of the room, leaving the old man there, begging forgiveness from his ancestors that would never come.

Only Brognola remained when Bolan came back out. The two men regarded each other for a long moment, then Bolan broke the silence. "I'm going to head over to the hospital. John Trent's getting out today, and I want to be there."

"He's going to be all right?"

"Yeah. He got banged up pretty hard, but he's as tough as they come. I also wanted to update him on Xiang's progress on becoming an American citizen and adoption. Thanks for fast-tracking the paperwork on that, by the way."

"After all he did, it was the least I could do in return. Tell him he has the thanks of four grateful nations, as well as the Kirkall family, for his part in uncovering and stopping this plot."

"I will." Bolan turned for the door.

"And, Striker…?"

"Yeah?"

"Thank you for everything," Brognola said.

Bolan turned to look at his old friend. "You're welcome, Hal, but I would have done it anyway. And I'll get up tomorrow and do it again, as long as there are animals like these—" he waved at the man in the bare room "—who think they can get away with it."

With that, he turned and walked out of the room.

* * * * *